THE ENCHANTED
VILLIA FLATBOTTOM

And The Island of the Blue Moon

THE ENCHANTED VILLIA FLATBOTTOM

And The Island of the Blue Moon

SUNNY ALEXANDER

Cover design by Jeanine Henning
www.jeaninehenning.com

Book design by Maureen Cutajar
www.gopublished.com

Print ISBN: 978-0-9982029-2-1
E-book ISBN: 978-0-9982029-3-8
LCCN: 2020902827

CASTLE OF RHIANNON

THE LAKE OF DREAMS

THE LAKE OF WISDOM

THE LAKE OF SORROW

DESERT LAND

N
W   E
S

PALOS VERDES

A WHILE AGO

Palos Verdes, once part of the Mexican land grant Rancho de los Palos Verdes, was booming with new construction, showing every indication of becoming another upscale California suburban development.

The developer, Dawley King IV, gobbled up blocks of prime ocean view property for what would be, in his hyperbolic words: "An unparalleled architectural development paying homage to our Spanish heritage with integrity and élan."

Known for his exaggerations bordering on lies, he chose to ignore the fact California had once been part of Mexico. He simply erased that part of history and created a new reality.

Dawley IV was a burly man with hands the size of baseball mitts. Every morning after eating his Paul Bunyan breakfast consisting of three eggs, four slices of toast, six pancakes slathered with maple syrup, a rasher of bacon, and four sausages he complimented himself on the fact that he always took his toast dry.

He never failed to stand in front of his full-length mirror murmuring, "Mirror, mirror, on the wall, who's the greatest of them all?"

And while the mirror remained silent, he was quite certain he knew the answer.

Dawley King IV considered himself the world's unsurpassed deal closer and was ready to begin construction. Only one thing stood in his way: the last stubborn holdouts, Villia Flatbottom and her husband Oran.

The Flatbottoms refused to sell their property, and not just because it had been in the family for generations. There was another reason, one so unusual that some might say it bordered on delusional: a secret so deep it was known only to those who carried the Flatbottom name.

Villia Flatbottom's ancestors had purchased 160 acres in 1851 as part of a Mexican land grant sell-off. Over the years, parcels of the original acreage had been sold until all that remained was five acres that included Villia and Oran's home, the original adobe house built in the 1840s, and a natural harbor with direct access to the Pacific Ocean.

Dawley King IV was not one to lose graciously. With the development's advertising campaign ready to be launched, all that was lacking was the Flatbottoms' property. Dawley operated on the premise that everyone has a price, and he would find theirs.

∞

The phone calls from Dawley King IV started off friendly enough.

"Hell, we're almost cousins," he chortled. "Both of our families helped settle this area."

Dawley King IV made his best pitch, promising he would honor early California history in the homes' design, and even threw in the Flatbottoms' pick of a new house as a bonus. When they wouldn't budge his smile disappeared and he turned to what he did best: scheming.

Calls to the city and greasing politicians' palms brought a deluge of inspectors to their home, resulting in a long list of housing code violations and, eventually, condemnation proceedings. Dawley IV was a man who always got his way.

The case was brought before Judge Nancy Sinker. Photos of the Flatbottoms' home and testimonies by experts as to its poor condition failed to sway the judge.

In rendering her decision, Judge Sinker remarked: "After reviewing the documentation and listening to the testimonies from the plaintiff and the defendants, I find the evidence justifying cause for condemnation lacking, with one exception." Judge Sinker addressed the defendants.

"Mr. and Mrs. Flatbottom, I agree with one issue, and that is the repair to your foundation. Take care of that and this case will be closed."

Judge Sinker, who understood the weight of carrying an unusual name, smiled inwardly as she banged her gavel on the sound block.

∞

The houses were built with a touch of Spanish influence, exactly as Dawley King IV had promised. The entry door and shutters looked like wood but were made of fiberglass. To make the door more appealing a speakeasy grill was offered as an option. Who could resist? After all, one could never be too careful, even in a development as safe as Casa Palos Verde.

The contractor in charge of the roofing material suggested clay tile and provided Dawley King IV with photos and samples. "True to history and guaranteed for fifty years," he declared excitably. Dawley IV, glowering at him through narrowed eyes, told him he was fired. He hired someone who found a cheap look-alike with a three-year guarantee.

To demonstrate his commitment to the community he had his son's family ensconced in the largest home in the development. Dawley King V tried to follow in his father's steps. He was ruthless but lacked smarts and cunning, and remained a small piece of turd stuck to a dog's backside.

As far as his father was concerned, the only thing Dawley V had accomplished was fathering Dawley VI, who, at the age of five, showed every outward sign of being a true King. Like his grandfather, he was a petulant, tantrum-throwing brat and didn't give up until he got what he wanted. Dawley IV had great plans to continue the lineage by molding him in his image.

Dawley IV sat back and viewed the world he had created. It would be perfect except, he could not let go of his anger towards the Flatbottoms. He may have lost the court battle but he wasn't finished just yet.

The Kings spread vicious rumors about the crazy old woman who lived in the tumbledown house. Over time the stories grew until only the bravest neighborhood kids dared to knock on the Flatbottoms' door on Halloween. The trick-or-treaters were certain Villia was a witch who murdered cats during the nights of the full moon.

To complete Dawley IV's plan for revenge, he received permission from the city to surround his development with a spectacular eight-foot wall made of beige slump stone. It also completely walled in the Flatbottoms' property except for the driveway that led to their harbor and the main road.

What he didn't count on was the Flatbottoms' desire for privacy. Oran and Villia considered the wall a bonus.

Villia could see glimpses of the development from her property. With a heavy heart she knew that beneath the facade of red-tiled roofs, shuttered windows, and Mission-style stucco lay slab floors, cheapjack drywall, and shoddy workmanship.

No matter how one changes the exterior, it's the interior that tells the true story.

CHAPTER 1
2006

The Flatbottoms' house stood on rickety stilts, leaning ever so slightly toward the bluff and the Pacific Ocean below. Repairs to shore up the foundation after the court proceedings were initially successful, until one night the house shuddered and the next morning the floor, level the night before, appeared askew.

Oran Flatbottom placed a marble on the kitchen floor and watched as it rolled an inch or two, then stopped.

"Oran, we can't lose this house," said Villia, lips trembling, "and we can't afford to fix it again."

"It's just a slight bit of settling," Oran reassured his wife.

But Oran's words did not soothe her. Every Monday morning, before coffee and the arrival of the *Palos Verdes Times*, Villia Flatbottom placed a marble on the kitchen floor and watched as it inched slowly toward the sea. She took out a sample size can of white paint from beneath the kitchen sink and dribbled a dot, barely discernable against the aged linoleum, where the marble had stopped.

No one could predict when or if the house, believed by Villia to be a living entity, would finally settle where it needed to be, or if, as had happened to other nearby homes, it would finally be given to the sea. Villia tried to accept that the outcome was up to the whims of the gods and goddesses. Yet, she couldn't help but worry. Not about her fate, but about her commitment to the Island of the Blue Moon.

One Monday morning, a little over a month ago, Oran watched as Villia placed a marble on the floor. It rolled and stopped at the previous dot of paint. Oran spoke with the wisdom of one who had lived most of his adult life at sea as a Merchant Marine and had developed a respect for the power of nature.

"You see, no more movement!" he proclaimed. "I think the house had a bit of an itch and needed to scratch." His hand sympathetically strayed to his stubbly beard.

Villia smiled, touching his face. "I know you won't shave while you're away. Two months! I hope I recognize you when you return."

"It's a tradition we have on our ship. I'm not sure how it started, but not shaving has become a good luck omen."

"For the women too?" she teased.

He chuckled. "So they say, but I only have eyes for you. Another tradition is a dance before I leave."

Oran walked toward the cradle used by past generations of Flatbottom babies. Built more than 150 years ago by Dylan, the first Flatbottom immigrant, it had survived fires and floods, times of joy and times of grief. Now it was used to store their collection of phonographic records, themselves reminders of a more recent period in history. The records came in various RPMs (revolutions per minute): the shellac (and easily breakable) 78, the vinyl 33 1/3 LP, and the 7-inch single, also vinyl, affectionately called a 45. The single he wanted was in its usual place at the front of their collection. He placed the 45 on the portable player's spindle and turned to Villia.

"May I have this dance?" he said, holding out his hands.

She smiled, her worries forgotten at the vision of her beloved. He placed his arms around her waist, and they began swaying to "Once Upon a Dream" from Walt Disney's *Sleeping Beauty*.

He asked, "Remember when we met and had our first dance?"

"How could I forget? It was at your sister's wedding. They played this song and you swept me off my feet."

"It was a warm summer night. Afterwards we walked outside and looked up at the stars." He paused and added shyly, "I kissed you."

"And I told you my secret."

"I didn't believe you about the island, not at first."

"I had never told anyone; I just blurted it out. Oh my, the look on your face! I could tell you didn't believe me. I was sure you thought I was crazy."

"I didn't care if you were. Do you remember when I proposed and you told me I would have to take the Flatbottom name?"

"I explained it was a family tradition but didn't tell you the full reason. I was convinced I had lost you at that point."

"Not a chance! I thought, Oran Davis, don't let this girl get away. I must admit I struggled when you told me you wanted to spend our honeymoon on an invisible island filled with mythical animals."

"Struggled? You clucked your tongue in disbelief!"

"Did I? Yeah, I guess I did."

"But you came around soon enough."

Oran sighed, basking in the memories. "Our honeymoon was in the most romantic tropical setting, a bamboo hut on the banks of the Lake of Dreams. And the animals! In my wildest dreams I never would have believed I would be petting the head of a unicorn. And then, when Hairy Ella-Phante came to welcome us, I shook and so did the earth! The way she lumbered down the path to our hut I thought we were having a 9.0 earthquake!"

"It's not often that the Wooly Mammoths leave their valley. You didn't seem to mind when she offered you a ride."

"There was no way I was going to miss that! I felt I was on top of the world and in a way, I was."

A shy smile played across Villia's face. "I sometimes worry that you may have regrets. I know it's not always easy being married to the Keeper of the Island of the Blue Moon."

"I have never regretted one second of our time together. Villia, have you noticed that when we dance the floor is as smooth as the Lake of Dreams on a warm summer night?" To illustrate the point, Oran expertly dipped his bride.

"Ah, true, but only when the island inhabitants aren't splashing around in the water."

"Seriously, you're sure you'll be okay sailing to the island on your own?"

"Hmm...I think I can manage. Oran, you'll be extra careful on this voyage? It's your last one."

"When I return we'll celebrate my retirement. Plus, then I'll be able to share more of the load with you. There's also a few updates I'd like to make to the boathouse, just to make it more secure."

"Why, has anything happened?" asked Villia.

"Remember a few weeks ago when we took the flatbottom boat out for a test run?"

"Yes. We got a lot of attention from other ships."

"More attention than we needed. A couple of boats followed us near to home. One was the Kings' boat. You know their kid, don't you?"

Villia glowered. "You mean the latest one, Dawley VII?"

"Yep, he's the one.

"His father, Dawley VI, was the bully who attacked Bruce. Rotten apples the whole bunch of them, and they sure as shit—pardon my French—don't fall far from the tree. He stared right at me, and gave me the bird. You know the kind I mean?"

Villia nodded. "He walks around with his BB gun, shooting at birds and animals. The Dawley kids have been nothing but trouble for years now. One generation after another."

"When I get back, I'll set up an alarm system and put bars on the windows."

"It's a heavy weight to carry," said Villia sorrowfully. "When we're gone, who will look after the boat and the island? Both of our children refuse to believe in the old ways. Bruce is in Europe most of the time, and Ebrill—"

"You mean April. She always hated the name we gave her."

"After all these years," Villia said in a faraway voice, "I still think of her as Ebrill, and sometimes I forget to call her April. I feel I failed them in so many ways. I was distracted and couldn't fully give them what they wanted—or needed."

Oran pulled Villia tighter to his chest. "As the Keeper of the Island you were chosen to safeguard all who live there. It's both a blessing and a curse. Who else in this world but you could tell the story of a time long ago when gods and goddesses roamed the earth and humans and animals shared a common language? Who else could explain how man's greed took that away? Maybe someday, the world will be ready to hear your story."

Villia replied by grasping Oran's hand as if he alone could keep her and the house upright.

The music stopped.

Oran said, "I've got to leave. I've checked the sailboat and it's in tip-top shape."

"And the flatbottom boat?"

"Amazing condition, considering her age. There's something about the wood. Oak for sure, but it has a different feel. Oh, I guess others might think I'm losing all my brain cells, but I'd say there's something spiritual about it. You know, like when you walk into a holy place. Hard to handle, though; it takes *two* people when we take her out to sea."

Villia crossed her arms defiantly. "I'm a better sailor than you, and you know it."

"I do know it. But I'd feel a whole lot better about all this if you promise me you'll take the sailboat."

She nodded. "Deal. But only if you promise me you won't take any crazy risks, what with pirates back on the high seas and all."

Oran chuckled. "Taking a cargo ship from Los Angeles to Hawaii is as safe as floating in a warm tub of water in my own bathroom. My last trip, love. I'll see you in two months."

CHAPTER 2

Villia Flatbottom sat on a kitchen chair, her feet not quite touching the floor. She scrolled through the growing stack of emails from Oran. One a day for a month, just as he had promised. Always telling her he loved her and was safe.

They opened with, "Not a pirate in sight." The middle part was chitchat. What they had seen, what they had eaten for dinner, a funny story, and always asking about her day.

The most recent email had included a photo of the crew. She had to squint to find Oran in the haze of beards. It was the twinkle in his eyes and the way his smile lifted the corners of his mouth that made her say out loud, "That's my Oran." She kissed her fingers and touched the photo.

Oran closed each email with: "You are my love, my heart. I'll see you soon."

Pooch, her dog of many breeds, placed his chin on top of her bare feet. "Flattery will get you breakfast," she said, rising from her chair. Pooch reacted by licking her big toe and waiting patiently while Villia filled his bowl. She rubbed his head, always delighted at the way the black curls covering Pooch's eyes expressed his Portuguese Water Dog DNA. Pooch responded with his finest doggie grin before turning to his food. He sniffed, knowing that Villia had hidden a treat somewhere in the middle. He poked around until he found a Newman's Own peanut butter dog biscuit. He wagged his tail and gobbled down the treat.

"That was supposed to be a surprise," Villia scolded.

"You know my motto: dessert first," said Pooch between gulps.

"What might you have been in your past lives?" Villia mused softly. "A butcher, a baker, a candlestick maker?" She paused, thinking of Pooch's relentless habit of chasing female dogs. "Or perhaps Don Juan?"

Pooch lifted his head for a moment. "Spot on, milady. And I've paid the price in this life for my past indiscretions. I remember waking up at the vet and looking down. Yep, they finally took my manhood. Oh, well, this gig isn't so bad after all. At least I get to hop in the sack with a woman. A bit on the ripe side, but she does like to cuddle in the middle of the night. I guess I haven't lost all my charm."

Villia cocked an eyebrow. "Ripe side, eh? See if I give you any more treats."

"Aw, you know you love me."

"Almost as much as you love yourself. Now, onto Edgar and Anabelle." Villia's stomach grumbled. "Then it will be my turn." She removed apple slices and hardboiled eggs from the refrigerator and placed them on two of her best paper plates purchased from the Under-A-Buck store. She scattered an assortment of dried fruits and nuts between the apples and eggs. Pleased with the arrangement, she ambled outside to the glass-enclosed deck.

"Good morning," she said to the two crows resting on their perches.

"Is that before or after coffee?" Edgar asked.

Villia rolled her eyes.

"Bit of a grump, are we?" said Annabelle in her well-practiced British accent. "Before coffee, no doubt. One of your least desirable human qualities. However, I do fully empathize."

Edgar surveyed the food. "Any meat? We're allowed when we're off the island. Road kill will do."

"Haven't you heard about gratitude, you insolent fowl?" Villia snapped.

Edgar cawed loudly and flapped his wings. "Heck, I'm just foolin' with you."

"Sorry. Just my hunger talking."

"I thought as much. How's this for gratitude? Many thanks for the vittles. Can't say that I enjoy being locked up though."

"It's for your own good. Remember the last time you visited?"

"Remember? I'll never forget getting shot at by that kid with a BB gun. Ole whatshisname."

"Dawley VII." Villia sighed. "I have had the misfortune of meeting four generations of Dawleys."

"As in d-o-l-l-y?"

"No, as in D-a-w-l-e-y."

"Well, no wonder he's so messed up."

"It's a family name."

"Like Flatbottom?"

"Something akin."

"Last time we were here," Annabelle chimed in, "we taught Dawley VII a lesson. When we left we dropped a load right on his head. Splat! You should have seen that kid doing the razzle-dazzle jazz dance."

Edgar cawed raucously in recollection. "That was a highlight, my love, but for now tick-tock—it's nearing time for us to leave. Villia, you remember the fourteen-day rule, of course?"

"It's tattooed in my brain. It is written in The Book of Truths that if you are off the island for more than fourteen days, you shall turn into run-of-the-mill crows, subject to the laws of man, and with no one to serve you the delicious, hand-selected feasts that I provide."

"Cawww, don't remind me!" cried Edgar. "Foraging for one's own grub is such a pain in the tookus. Well, Villia, my love, we hate to leave you, but our job here is done. We were sent to deliver a message and a package from Rhiannon, the Ancient One, and methinks we may have overstayed our welcome. Don't forget, the Resetting of the Calendar Ceremony is two weeks away. Of course, you and yours are always welcome to come earlier. We do keep the human hut in A-1 condition. In fact, we just reroofed her. You should have seen the elephants and chimps in action."

"I just might take you up on the offer. I could use a vacation," Villia said morosely.

"The Ancient One and I had a heart-to-heart. You know, we all worry about you. Pooch was my idea." Annabelle puffed out her breast proudly.

"Your idea?"

Edgar snarled, "Annabelle, haven't you heard about good deeds are only good if you don't brag?"

"I'll ignore *that* comment, Edgar."

"I'd like to hear more," said Villia.

"We were having a friendly chit-chat while basking in the Lake of Dreams, when the Ancient One asked my advice about your upcoming birthday. You do know how she loves to get the perfect gifts for you.

"I said, 'Villia needs someone to share her most inner thoughts, especially when Oran's away on the high seas.' I went into a deep, contemplative place, then added: 'What about a dog?' Well, I thought the Ancient One was going sink to the bottom of the lake. In fact, she did do a dive. When she came up, she said, 'A dog that can speak aloud and communicate telepathically. Perfect!'"

"And that's how Pooch came to be Villia's boon companion."

"I do love that dog, although he's a bit high on the narcissistic chart."

Edgar said, "No one is perfect. Except for my Annabelle, of course."

Annabelle took a beak full of nuts and fruit. "I've got the munchies and your *mélange de fruits* are perfect. You're a fabulous hostess, Villia. Back home on the island, you're known as the hostess with the mostess."

"Easy on the grub, Anabelle," Edgar cautioned. "You don't want to ruin your figure."

"Too late, lover boy. I'm eating for three or four or six!"

"Again?" asked Villia.

Edgar winked. "Can't stop a stud like me!"

"Humph! Don't think I haven't considered a chastity belt," said Annabelle, ruffling her tail feathers.

"You wouldn't!" protested Edgar, flapping his wings.

"Oh, but wouldn't I."

Edgar turned to Villia. "Any last-minute messages for the Ancient One?"

"No message, but do you think Rhiannon has accepted the fact that I may be the last Keeper of the Island?"

"She's aware that we are all in peril, but accepted it? None of us have."

Annabelle bobbed her head sadly. "Truth be known, Rhiannon has aged a thousand years. You'd think a goddess would be above it all, but I've seen her pacing up and down, awash in unease."

"You know I hate gossip," Edgar chimed in, "but before we came here I saw her soaking in the Lake of Wisdom for over an hour. She's been worried for all of us and fears for the well-being of the Island. If there's no Flatbottom to attend the annual Resetting of the Calendar Ceremony, the island and all of its inhabitants will disappear forever."

The three spoke in unison: "So it is written and so it shall be."

Villia said, "My mother explained to me that when the gods and goddesses created the island, they were in constant disagreement about the flora and fauna it should contain. They finally came to an agreement but kept arguing about its name. One faction wanted the island to be named The Island of Lamentations, while others wanted to call it The Island of the Blue Moon."

"Lamentations sounds so, so distressful," said Annabelle.

"That name was meant to be a reminder that while the island's inhabitants live in harmony, paradise is fragile and can be easily lost. Remember, the island came into being during a time of peril and disaster."

"How did they ever resolve it?" said Annabelle, taking another bite of fruit.

Villia laughed. "They finally threw up their hands up and said, 'Let the inhabitants of the forest decide on the name for their new home.' And so, it was put to a vote."

"The owls handled that one, didn't they?" Edgar prompted, while cracking a nut.

"So I was told. It was a tie vote and Rhiannon had to make the final decision."

Annabelle asked, "She liked the Island of the Blue Moon better?"

"Yes. I think it resonated with her for a personal reason, but to keep the peace, she suggested they name the valley where the prehistoric animals live The Valley of Lamentations."

Edgar lifted one foot and scratched his beak. "Brilliant move on the Ancient One's part. Except for the few who live there now, they were all wiped out. But what about the annual ceremony? Whose bright idea was that?"

"Not mine," Villia said, laughing. "We can blame the gods and goddesses again. My mother said they needed to know that there could be one human they could trust to act as a go-between. My family has had this honor for over 150 years, and so long as there is a Flatbottom willing to be the Keeper, the island will continue to exist. Once a year, a Flatbottom must return and repledge their commitment to the island. Otherwise, the island and all who live there will vanish."

Annabelle let out a mournful cry. "I don't want to disappear."

Villia pulled a hanky from her pajama pocket and dabbed the tears from Annabelle's eyes. "I didn't know that crows could cry," she said softly.

Annabelle sniffled. "It's the island that changed us. Run-of-the-mill crows can't, and they don't know what they are missing. It's so cathartic!"

Edgar let out a mocking caw. "What a drama queen." He cocked his blue-black head at Villia. "You're not going to let us down, are ya?"

Villia smiled. "So long as there is breath in this ripe old body, as Pooch would say, the Flatbottom tradition will endure. Tell Rhiannon I will be there for the ceremony."

"Thank you, Villia," said Annabelle. "I'll name one of the kids after you."

Edgar pecked a kiss on his wife's face. "Okay, sweet bird, ready for our takeoff?"

"Just one last thing," said Annabelle. "Villia, have you taken care of the blue velvet pouch we brought you from Rhiannon?"

"Not yet."

"The Ancient One said, and I quote: 'Do not tarry lest the Elixir begins to lose its potency. The contents must be placed in a clear glass jar and kept away from direct sunlight.'"

Villia nodded. "Will do."

Annabelle flapped her wings. "Oh, dear, I do hope I can fly; I ate too much!"

Edgar tested his wings. "Working better than ever. I told you to do your Pilates every morning. However, I have a solution. Look down at the beach—isn't that the Dawley kid? It looks like he's toting his BB gun. Just took a shot at a rabbit. Missed. Good! Which generation is he, again?"

"The seventh."

"Well, that kid is trouble with a capital T." Edgar laughed. "And that's right out of *The Music Man*. I would sing it but I'm not sure I could improve on Robert Preston. Close, maybe...."

Edgar turned to Annabelle. "To the rescue, mother of my children?"

"You aren't going to...?" asked Villia.

"Just watch! They don't call me the black tornado for nothing. Ready, Annabelle?"

"Missiles loaded, lover."

"Here we go with our famous maneuver, The Double D: diving and dropping bombs."

They took off. Thirty seconds later, with Villia looking on, Dawley VII ran screaming along the beach with the crows, cawing riotously, in hot pursuit. The kid dropped his BB gun and then tripped on it, plunging headlong into the sand. He rolled over on his back just in time to receive Edgar and Annabelle's twin volleys. One plastered his right eye, the other found his gaping mouth.

"Better than an Alfred Hitchcock movie," chuckled Villia.

Villia had to admit she enjoyed Edgar and Annabelle's company. How many people could say they conversed with crows—and not your run-of-the-mill crows, but ones with musical talent and an attitude?

That didn't mean that she wouldn't enjoy the solitude that followed their departure. She supposed she could...*should* clean, but it clearly wasn't her strong suit. Oran didn't seem to mind the dust bunnies on the floor or the fact that their bed wasn't always made.

"Not as long as you're in it," he had said more than once.

Villia stood on her tippy-toes to reach the box of Cream of Wheat cereal. Her mother had always kept it on the second shelf and that's where it remained, even though at an even five feet tall, it was a stretch for her. She had complained about being the shortest in her family, to which her mother had replied, "Good things come in small packages."

She turned the box to read the directions in spite of having cooked it every morning for more than forty years. She waited impatiently for the water to bubble before sprinkling the cereal in as fine a circular pattern as she could manage. It was not only a habit but also a reminder of breakfast with her mother. Her mother's cereal always had lumps in it, something she despised as a child, but now missed. No matter how negligently she stirred, hers always came out as smooth as a baby's backside.

If only I could find some lumps, she told herself, *everything would be okay.*

She was, as her brothers and sister constantly reminded her, the baby. With book bags slung over their shoulders before leaving for school, they turned as a well-rehearsed group and taunted:

"Baby, baby, baby!"

Hoping to time it right, and avoid any reprisals from Mam, they belted out the Cream of Wheat radio jingle:

> *Cream of Wheat is so good to eat and we have it every day*
> *We sing this song, it will make us strong, and it makes us shout*
> *"Hooray!"*
> *It's good for growing babies and grown-ups, too, to eat*
> *For all the family's breakfast,*
> *You can't beat Cream of Wheat!*

They followed the song with hysterical laughter while Villia held her hands over her ears. She didn't want to cry; after all, she was almost six and enrolled in afternoon kindergarten class.

As the kids turned to leave for school, they were confronted by Mam holding her famous and well-worn wooden spoon. Mam was the Marine sergeant barking out orders to her recruits, all the while tapping her open hand with the spoon. Chills ran down the spines of the unholy three.

"John, come home after school. You'll be working in the garden."

"But Mam, I have football practice."

With a mighty whack, John got the spoon on his backside.

Mam growled, "Anyone else care to argue?"

The kids stood with their heads hanging down, barely breathing, frozen in time.

"Angharad, you will be cleaning out the chicken coop."

Angharad wanted to say, "Please call me Angie," but thought that would be like facing a dragon with a feather.

"Harry, you will write out the words of the Cream of Wheat song twenty-five times. All verses and on proper lined paper. Now, scoot! And if you're late for school don't expect me to write an excuse."

Villia had never seen her older siblings move so fast unless they heard the Good Humor ice cream truck coming down the street.

Once they were out of sight, Mam threw up her hands and said quite dramatically, "Thanks to the gods and goddesses, that wild bunch is out of the house."

Villia, scrunching up her heart-shaped face, asked somberly: "Mam, why do they hate me so?"

"They don't hate you, lamb, but I do think they're jealous."

"But why?"

"Perhaps it's because you're the youngest in the family." Mam let out a great sigh. "Or perhaps it's because you are next in line to be the Keeper of the Island of the Blue Moon. Now, Villia, enough of this feeling sad about what we can't change." Mam lowered her voice to a whisper. "We will have our breakfast, and I'll tell you a story about the Flatbottoms."

Villia loved storytelling more than anything, even though Mam had told her that stories were also lessons, just like in school.

School wasn't as much fun. Her kindergarten teacher, Mrs. Cheatem, had been showing her pupils the alphabet and teaching them words out of the *Dick and Jane* readers. Why would she want to hear about the insufferably dull Dick and Jane and their dog Spot, when she could hear about rainbow fairies and dragons who used their fiery breath to melt marshmallows? Besides, she already knew how to read.

Mam scooped the cereal into two crazed bowls discovered at the Goodwill store, and with an impressive swirl threw a tablecloth, embroidered with a forest scene, over the kitchen table, creating a tent of imaginative proportions. When they scooted underneath, the world changed from ordinary to otherworldly.

Between spoonfuls of cereal, Mam delighted Villia with stories about the time when gods and goddesses ruled the world, and fantastical animals, now only found in books on mythology, were commonplace.

Mam spoke in hushed tones. "We've talked about the many stories of how the world began. One that you have heard is from a book called the Old Testament. In that story Eve was blamed for eating an apple from the forbidden tree of knowledge, and as the biblical story is told, Adam and Eve were punished by God and sent away from Eden. Today I'd like to tell you a different story, one you've never heard before."

Villia let her spoon drop into the bowl. A new story. One she has never heard before!

"Take another bite of cereal, Villia."

Villia did as her mam requested but made her "I hate lumps" face. Mam, oblivious, continued. "In the beginning humans and beasts shared the world in harmony. They even spoke the same language. One day, a farmer came across a wild ox. She was crying in pain, both physically and emotionally, for her baby had died. The man felt sorry for the ox and asked her how he could help.

"The ox said, 'I know you can't bring my baby back, but my body aches to be milked.' The man leaned over and began to milk the ox. Being curious, he tasted the milk and thought it was good. Now, food wasn't always easy to come by, and the farmer thought he could feed his children from the ox's milk.

"'Why don't you come home with me?' he asked in a seductive

voice. 'I can care for you, and my children will be like your children and taste the sustenance you so readily give.'

"The ox followed him home. He opened the gate to a corral and ushered her in. When he left he fastened the gate with a thick piece of rope. The ox looked at the locked gate in bewilderment.

"'Why do you tie the gate shut?' she asked. The man said, 'It will give you privacy during your time of mourning.' He smiled and gave her the sweetest hay she had ever tasted.

"Every morning, the farmer relieved the ox of her milk and left a bushel of hay. The ox, certain she had fallen into ox heaven, thought, 'This human must not be too bright. Here I am, not having to forage and having all my needs met, and all he gets is a bit of milk.'

"The time came when the ox was no longer in distress. She thanked the man and said she was ready to return to her family and friends. But the man, having become accustomed to her milk, did not let her go. He began to think of how animals could be used for his own good.

"The man's neighbors, seeing that his children were plumper than theirs and stayed healthier, also began to think about how they might use animals for their own benefit. They lost sight of the harmony they had once shared, and the feeling of unity was replaced by greed."

Mam paused. "Take another bite of your cereal," she ordered, seeing her breakfast was largely untouched.

Villia scooped as small an amount of cereal as she could get away with, and put it to her lips. Her mouth puckered.

"Mam, my cereal's cold."

"You're sure it isn't the lumps you're avoiding?"

Villia hung her head, but couldn't fully hide the smile that now played across her face. Mam reached into the pocket of her apron and pulled out an apple.

"Can't say I blame you a bit, my love," she said, placing the apple in the little girl's palm. "Have you had enough storytelling for one day?"

"Please, more!" she said, opening her mouth as wide as it would go and taking a ginormous bite with her newly acquired permanent front teeth.

Mam continued. "Do you remember what I told you about the goddess Rhiannon?"

Villia nodded, remembering Mam's rule not to talk with her mouth full.

Mam said, "Do you want to play the Finish The Sentence game?"

"It's my favorite!" She put the apple down and drank her milk in a single gulp. "Okay, I'm ready!"

"Once upon a time, a Great Goddess of Wales was born from a dragon's..."

"Tears."

"Yes! Her name was Rhiannon, and when she opened her eyes and looked at the land she cried because..."

"It was sooooo beautiful."

Mam smiled. "Very good! For the beauty of the world moved her heart. However, one day, she looked out and saw it was not as beautiful as before. Some of the animals had been put into cages and were not treated kindly. They had become so frightened that they had lost their ability to speak. Trees were cut down, and the streams had become filled with trash. Rhiannon cried again but now they were tears of..."

"Sadness."

"Yes." Mam lowered her voice. "Rhiannon closed her..."

"Eyes."

Her mam nodded. "And with a sweep of her hands she made the most beautiful forest with trees from around the world, an abundance of food, and the clearest of streams and lakes. But Rhiannon was not without anger and the lust for revenge. She and all the gods and goddesses put a curse upon mankind, that those who dared to walk into the forest would never be seen again.

"She then sang as only a goddess can, and her song spread throughout all the lands. Hearing this enchanted melody, the animals traveled from near and far to seek the safety of the forest. And that forest, so many years ago, was right here on this land."

"All the animals came, Mam?"

"Sadly, no. Some were imprisoned and others chose to stay with humans."

Villia teared up. "I feel sad for all the animals."

"I would expect no less."

Mother and daughter sat quietly for a while, each filled with their own sadness, sitting inside a make-believe tent but with all-too-real feelings.

"What happened to the forest?" Villia asked at length.

Her mam smiled, a small, secretive smile that said little but knew much. "When you become older you shall be able to read the story in your ancestor Branwyn Rees' journal. You have much to learn, but for now, I think we should bake chocolate chip cookies."

"Walnuts too, Mam?"

"Yes, my love. Walnuts too."

Villia smelled the scorched Cream of Wheat. *Damn these trips to the past!* When would she learn not to fall into a trancelike state? She scooped the cereal into her bowl and sighed with relief to discover that only a thin layer of blackened residue clung to the bottom of the pot.

She grabbed two framed photos from the kitchen counter and ducked under the table. Filled with a sense of peacefulness and magical memories of her mother, she picked up the first photo, one of her family taken when she was ten. Mam and Tad stood behind their four children seated on a redwood bench.

Gazing upon her siblings' youthful faces, Villia reflected on their life trajectories.

Harry, who had to write the lyrics to the Cream of Wheat song twenty-five times, became an author of scary children's books.

John never quite forgave his mother for missing football practice. He was dropped from the team not because of that missed session, but because there were others better than him. Yet he blamed it on his mam and the missed practice. Blaming others became his life's theme.

Angharad/Angie cut most of her family ties and found solace in a fundamentalist church. The last time Villia saw Angie was at their father's funeral. Angie had remained dry-eyed and made excuses about not attending the reception. Before leaving, she stood across from Villia and held her hands.

"I'm sorry for the way we treated you," she said, genuinely contrite. "We were all unhappy and took it out on you." Then she paused and squeezed Villia's hands. "How can you bear it? To believe in an invisible island, animals that talk, and gods and goddesses. It's blasphemy!"

Her body shook; her voice was a ferocious whisper. "Your children will suffer as we have all suffered."

Villia tried to hug her sister, but Angie moved away, creating more distance between them.

"We may have our differences, Angie, but we are still sisters. Can't we at least stay in touch?"

Angie shook her head and left.

How could she ever explain to Angie or the others about the magic she found on the island? The sense of being surrounded by everything that was pure and innocent? The clarity of the river waters that flowed from pristine mountains into the all-knowing and all-giving lakes? The trees and plants that held remedies for mankind's self-inflicted illnesses? Each time she set foot upon the dark green moss that covered the island, she felt energized and her hope for the future was renewed.

Villia studied the second photo, a family grouping taken when she married Owen. They had an intimate wedding, with only immediate family and a few close friends in attendance. Oran was dashing in his Merchant Marine uniform and she resplendent in a celery green silk shantung suit. *Was I ever that young...or thin?*

Before meeting Oran, she wasn't sure if she would ever marry. What self-respecting man would entertain the preposterous notion of a magical island filled with creatures that talked? And, on top of that, be willing to change his name to Flatbottom? But Oran, a true man in a million, didn't mind. He said, "Davis or Flatbottom...hmm...Davis or Flatbottom. You know, Flatbottom does have a certain ring to it. Besides, I'm looking forward to spending time on the island."

"Really? Because I thought it would be perfect for our honeymoon."

"I can't wait," he replied, without a moment of hesitation.

Her mam had died years ago but she still wondered where she was now. Was she in a sacred place or had she returned to the earth to rise again in another form? Villia wished her mam was here to hold her and share her wisdom. She longed to hear her say just one more time, "Everything will be fine. You'll see."

All those hours spent under the table with Mam and here she was, a grandmother still eating breakfast under the same table covered with the same forest tablecloth. How her mother loved this table, even though its legs had been gnawed by generations of teething puppies and babies.

Mam never got angry at the scars. "They tell a story, can't you see?"

"What kind of story, Mam?"

"Of life and love."

She remembered when the dining room set first became an integral part of their home. Mam rejected most material things; a curbside castoff was good enough for her. But then the Sears Christmas catalog, which everyone in Villia's generation called the Wish Book, arrived. One particular page of the catalog, Villia recalled, had the corner turned down—a subtle indication of Mam's rare material desire. And there it was, Mam's dream set, a hard rock maple dining room set consisting of a table with two leaves and six chairs.

How many years ago? *Let me see,* she mused. The parade of years she once could have easily calculated plodded through her brain, now a complex arithmetic problem. She counted on her fingers, a holdover from her childhood.

Villia blew a fierce breath upward to stir the hairs that hung over her eyes like a wispy white curtain. She realized it must be fifty years ago, give or take a few years.

Her father had also seen that look on her mother's face and had purchased the set on layaway. The item sat somewhere in a warehouse waiting for the balance to be paid in dribs and drabs. *Did stores still have layaway?* Villia doubted it.

Every Friday after payday her father drove to Sears, took the escalator to the second floor, and stood in line at Customer Service. Some weeks he paid $5.00, some weeks a bit more, and some weeks he didn't go at all. Then the big day arrived. A knock on the door and two delivery men arrived with the table and six chairs—room enough for all! Mam had wiped her tears of joy away with her apron.

Villia hadn't thought about Mam's apron for years. "Bury me in this apron," her mother had demanded. "I don't know where it ends and I begin."

Her apron, even then worn and threadbare, was from a bygone era. As a child Villia was certain the apron, yellow with red cherries, possessed magical powers. Two large pockets could hold a surprise—a box of Crackerjacks or Atomic Fireballs, maybe ... a dime store yo-yo or a set of jacks—or a hanky for tears. When Villia was sad, Mam would lift the apron up and she could hide inside its folds and feel the comfort of her body until the sadness faded away.

The children hadn't buried Mam in the apron. But when no one was looking Villia had tucked the beloved relic in the casket underneath her head. As much as Villia cherished the apron, it belonged with Mam; it was indeed part of her.

So many lingering memories from those long-ago years. Now the table had lost its luster. *Not unlike myself,* she thought, as she wiped with her pajama sleeve a trickle of tears falling slowly down her round cheeks. *No hanky in an apron pocket to wipe your tears, no hidden treasures.*

She had let her children down, of that she was certain. Bruce and Ebrill, the loves of her life, had suffered the most. A crazy mother who told them stories about an invisible island filled with talking animals was a heavy cross to bear.

She had always known that Bruce had a bent for the law. *My, but how he could argue.* She chuckled at the memory of her three-year-old son, trying to convince her that they should have ice cream for dinner and broccoli for dessert. Her "legal eagle" she had called him from that day on. He laughed at the name but became a prosecuting attorney of some renown.

Bruce had followed his passion, but remained emotionally distant. What did his last email say?

"Hi Mam, Hi Tad, I'm presenting at a conference in DC. Will try to make it home to see you." How long had it been since Bruce had found his way home? Six months? A year?

And Ebrill, who was everything she wasn't. Tall and slender like her father with green eyes that changed color to match her moods.

Villia could feel Ebrill's rage oozing out when they spoke or saw each other, unable or unwilling to understand or forgive.

What price had they all paid for her being the Keeper?

She shivered, despite the ancient furnace sputtering to life with a train-like chugging noise and spewing forth warm air that fought for dominance with the cold air wafting through drafty, weather-beaten windows.

The phone rang but she chose not to answer it. After five rings it would go to the answering machine. She knew it would take at least ten rings for her to wiggle over Pooch's slumbering heap and clamber from under the table.

That cursed machine had been another bone of contention between her and Ebrill, who carped, "For God's sake, Mother, it's 2006. At least enter the 1970s!" She might not have answered the phone, but there was no getting away from listening to the message.

"Mother, it's April...Ebrill. I know you're having breakfast under the table. Call me as soon as you can. Mother? Are you listening?"

April's voice took on a frustrated staccato rhythm: "Damn it, I wish you'd give in and let me get you a cell phone! Maybe one of those Jitterbug flip phones—so easy even *you* could master it..." Her voice trailed off.

Villia knew that April/Ebrill was off and running on another project.

"Call. It's urgent!" she demanded.

"Everything's always urgent with that girl," Villia muttered underneath her breath. She spitefully decided to take her time before returning the call.

She counted herself blessed that her relationship with her own mam had been so idyllic, for the most part. Her mind drifted back to the eve of her twelfth birthday when Mam told her it was time for her to visit the island.

She had finished her homework and Mam was brushing her hair— one hundred strokes, no more, no less, every night without fail.

"Soon, you won't want your mam brushing your hair," Mam said softly.

"Mam, I'll always want you to brush my hair. Unless," Villia added with a sudden burst of rebellion, "I decide to cut it super short."

Mam smiled. "There comes a time when girls pull away from their mothers. They grow, they change. They become women."

"Oh, that. Well, Mam, you know that already happened and I still want you to brush my hair."

Mam counted: "Ninety-eight, ninety-nine, one hundred!" She set the brush on the nightstand and kissed the top of her daughter's head, the traditional finale of their nightly ritual. "Villia, there's something I need to tell you," she said.

"What is it, Mam? You look sad."

"Sometimes parents have to hold onto information until their child is of an age to understand."

"I'm ready," she managed to squeak out, wondering if she was going to find out she was adopted, as her siblings had told her on numerous occasions.

"Come, let's sit on your bed."

"Is that in case I faint?"

"No, it's in case I do."

Mam pushed away the dirty laundry and wrinkled clothes. Usually, she would have chastised Villia on what she called her slobbery, but on this night, she was silent.

"When you were two months old Tad and I took you on a trip to the island. There, Rhiannon the Ancient One spoke your name. Your eyes grew wide and you held out your hand for her to take. She whispered to me, 'Villia will be the next Keeper of the Island.'"

Villia's eyes widened. "There's a real Keeper?"

"Yes, with each generation there is one Flatbottom who is selected to protect and care for the island and all who live there. I am the present Keeper. The vacations your tad and I took... they were always to the island."

"Are you telling me that all those stories you told me at breakfast time were true?"

"It was the best way for you to know the island without actually seeing it. You were being prepared."

"But why me and not one of the other kids? They're older and smarter."

Mam couldn't help but laugh. "Older, yes, but smarter? Of that I'm not so sure. We brought all the babies to the island, just as we did with you. And each time, the Ancient One would speak their name and wait for them to reach out to her, in some way. But none did. And she knew they would not be the Keeper. Mind you, it didn't mean they were inferior or unqualified, but only that their destiny lay in a different direction.

"Infants can't decide if they are willing to make the lifelong sacrifice that is required by the Keeper. It is written in the Book of Truths that a future Keeper cannot make their final decision until they are twelve. Therefore, Villia, it is time for you to visit the island and either consent to or decline the position of Keeper."

Villia had been listening intently. "I already know the answer. I want to care for everything that grows and lives there. But how do I know if I can do this?"

"You must trust the Ancient One and yourself. She will meet you and guide you through the island's three lakes. Each lake will reveal a part of who you are and who you are destined to be."

Mam's voice fell to a spellbinding whisper. "There is no wonderment in the world as great as what you will see and feel. At the end of two days, the decision will be yours to make, just as it was mine."

"Mam, I never told you, but I've always thought that the stories were make-believe. You know, like fairytales."

Mam sighed. "I wish they were. If only...if only humans had been kinder to animals and to each other, perhaps we would not have needed the island." Mam yawned. "It's getting late and we both need our sleep."

Villia held her mam's hand. "What does she look like, this Ancient One?"

"She takes many forms. She might be a ladybug that lands on your hand or a bird that sings to you as the sun is rising. She's even been known to be a tree or plant. And once she became a boulder so children could climb and play upon her. Rhiannon has watched over you since you were born. In fact, you have met her many times. You will know her and your destiny through your feelings. Always trust your feelings."

"What about school?"

"Consider it a holiday. We'll leave early and take the flatbottom boat. It's a short trip; a couple of hours, no longer. Remember that the island is invisible to all, except to a Flatbottom."

∞

Villia lay in bed her with eyes wide open. Surely her mother didn't expect her to sleep. Sometimes her brothers and sister would make fun of their mother, calling her crazy or just plain weird. John, who was taking a class in psychology and already regarded himself as an expert, had pronounced her delusional. A few weeks later he called for a powwow. Most of the time the kids wouldn't invite Villia, but this time they did.

"I've got it," he said, tapping his book on abnormal psychology as if it was the Bible. "Mam and Tad have what is known as a *folie à deux*. It's what our family has suffered with for generations."

"What's a *folie à deux*?" asked Villia.

John cleared his throat, sounding and looking very professorial. "It's like a bad case of chicken pox—one kid gets it, and then another kid gets it, and then another ..."

His class of three was mesmerized, and he relished every moment of it. Villia remembered the chicken pox and especially the itching!

"Except," he continued, with Freudian authority, "it's craziness. Please allow me to explain. One person sees something that's not there, but they believe so strongly that another person begins to see it. And then it becomes real for both of them."

Angie said, "That describes Mam and Tad, all right." All the kids nodded in agreement except for Villia.

Could John be right? What if I catch this foley-ah-dew tomorrow?

She slept fitfully that night, plagued by nightmares: flying beasts carrying her and her siblings off to a mountaintop aerie, her skin broken out in livid sores that looked like chicken beaks, and finally being locked up in an insane asylum.

Her mother shook her awake. "Happy birthday, sleepyhead! Time to wake up, my twelve-year-old."

She sat up. The house was quiet, no sign of her siblings. In her half-awake, half-nightmarish state, she wondered if they had been carried off during the night.

"Where are all the kids?" she gasped.

"It's past nine—you slept through the morning turmoil." Her mother sat on her bed. "Your brothers and sister wished you a happy birthday and left a gift for you."

She sat up. "Really?"

"Yes, really. And they really do love you. Now, a quick shower for you and donuts for your birthday breakfast. We'll be staying on the island for the night in a lovely hut made just for us."

"Who will take care of my sister and brothers?"

"They'll be staying with Aunt Jane and Uncle Arthur for the weekend."

Aunt Jane and Uncle Arthur were Tad's sister and brother-in-law. They spent most big holidays together and always brought gifts that no one liked.

"They sent you a birthday present; I'm sure you will just love it."

Villia scowled. "Wanna bet?"

"Now, don't be that way," Mam scolded. "Would you like to open your gifts now?"

Villia nodded.

She unenthusiastically ripped open Aunt Jane and Uncle Arthur's gift, wrapped in wrinkly leftover Christmas paper. "A Patti Playpal doll. Boy, am I going to get teased about this one!"

The 36-inch "companion doll" stared at Villia with a simpering expression. "They must think I'm eight."

"Shush! You'll be grateful and write a nice thank-you note."

"Oh, all right. Can I hide her?"

"Well ... as long as you bring her out for our Thanksgiving dinner. You don't want to hurt Aunt Jane's and Uncle Arthur's feelings, do you?"

Villia sighed. "I guess not."

"Good girl. Now, before you open the gift from your sister and brothers you need to open the one from me and Tad."

Their gift came in a card. Inside the card was a brand new ten-dollar bill, fresh from the bank.

"Every twelve-year-old should have some spending money."

Villia hugged her mam. She knew about fifty ways to spend it.

"Turn the card over," said Mam.

On the back in Mam's elegant cursive handwriting was a note: "You may now have your ears pierced."

"Oh, Mam!" Villia threw her arms around her mother. "Will Angie do it?"

"Over my dead body!" her mother replied, using one of her pet phrases. "Dr. Martine will do it in his office. Now, open the gift from the kids."

"Pearl earrings! Just like Grace Kelly wore in *Rear Window*."

Mam's face suddenly changed to the forbidding look usually reserved for her three eldest children when they had disobeyed her. She didn't mind the kids going to the movies, but she had a prudish streak when it came to horror movies and movies containing adult themes—as all of Hitchcock's films did. *Rear Window*, she knew, concerned voyeurism, and had its fair share of sensuality. Not suitable for her children!

"*Rear Window*? When did you see that?" she demanded.

Whoops. Would Mam now get the spoon heretofore reserved for Villia's siblings? She hung her head and whispered. "When you thought we were seeing *Peter Pan*."

Mam frowned and shook her head. Not a good sign!

After considering the importance of this celebratory day, her frown changed to a smile and laughter followed.

"Take your shower and be sure to thank Tad. He was against pierced ears, and it took more than a bit of convincing to get him to agree."

Whew! Narrowly saved from the scourge of the spoon.

Villia flung her arms around Mam's neck and bussed her cheek. "You're the bestest, Mam!"

∞

Villia tried to stay awake during the voyage to the island, but the sea was calm and the gentle rolling movement of the flatbottom boat soon had her drifting off to sleep.

Mam woke her, but not in the jarring way she did on school days. With six people and one bathroom, they had a tight schedule to follow, and Mam went so far to post a timetable on the door.

"We are nearly there," Mam murmured. "Visit with your tad before we dock." She busied herself with checking the provisions. Villia stood next to Tad as the mist that had hidden the island slowly began to dissipate.

"Thank you, Tad, for letting me have my ears pierced."

Tad stared toward the island. "Always thought only fast girls had their ears pierced. But your mam convinced me otherwise." He looked at her and the smallest smile crinkled the corners of his mouth. "I know you're a good girl ... and I also know times are changing." He leaned over, giving her a quick peck on her cheek. "Happy birthday, Villia. You're growing into a fine, lovely young woman."

The preteen beamed. "Tad, tell me the story of how I got my name."

"Well, your mam was carrying you and she was bigger than a house. But don't tell her I said so.

She had a hankering to see this operetta called *The Merry Widow*. We were kind of poor but I bought the best tickets I could afford. Well, the show starts and there's lots of singing, of course, and then in the second act the star of the opera—playing Hanna, the main character—started singing a beautiful aria called 'Vilja.' Your mam suddenly doubled over in pain. I urged her to leave, because after three kids, I knew number four would come quick-like. However, your mam can be stubborn and she wouldn't leave until the song ended. We rushed out and grabbed a cab. Got to the hospital and darn if you weren't born in the elevator! Your mam took one look at you and said, 'Her name is Villia.' And that's how you got your name. It wasn't until much later, when your mam ran across a piece of sheet music for the aria in a notions shop, that we found out the correct spelling is V-I-L-J-A—we had just spelled the name phonetically on your birth certificate."

"I like my spelling better. Can you sing the song, Tad?"

He laughed. "If I did, you would never want to hear it again. I'll get you the record. The Vilja in the aria is described as a witch of the woods."

"What! I'm named after a witch?" said Villia, aghast.

"Your Mam says a witch of the woods means a wood maiden—a fairy, if you will. And what with the Flatbottom history, the forest and all, your Mam said the name was a perfect fit."

Mam joined them and put her arm around Villia's waist. "Look yonder. Tell me what you see."

"A beach, and a thick jungle beyond..." She gasped. "Mam! Tad! Two monkeys are standing on the dock!"

Tad laughed. "Chimpanzees, to be precise. They're waiting to catch the dock lines." Tad tossed them the ropes. "One for each of you!" he called out, but that didn't stop the chimps from arguing over who caught which line first and who should tie them to the posts.

Villia's jaw dropped. "Mam, they're talking!"

"Of course they are. All of the animals do." Then she whispered, "Even the slugs and snails."

Tad shouted to the chimps: "Hey, you two! Stop the arguing and help with the gangplank so we can get out of the boat."

"Those are the twins, Frick and Frack," Mam explained. "They bicker all the time."

Villia looked at her. "Is this real? Am I dreaming? I see a unicorn... no *two* unicorns. And a dragon! Will it breathe fire?"

"Only if you want to roast marshmallows. Perhaps we will sit outside this evening and make s'mores."

A thunderous chatter arose from the jungle as the inhabitants came first in pairs and then in groups to welcome Villia.

"The animals are here to greet you, as is Rhiannon, the Ancient One."

"Where is she? How will I know her?"

"You won't be able to miss her."

After they departed from the boat, the animals stepped aside to create a clear path. As the trio passed by, Villia heard them welcoming her in distinctive voices.

"Welcome to the Island of the Blue Moon!" said a giraffe, her voice soft and flutelike.

"Greetings, daughter of the Keeper!" cried a dragonfly, whose voice suggested the tintinnabulation of a waterfall.

"She's here! She's here! She's herrrrrre!" sang a quartet of dormice, their mellifluous voices blending like a children's choir.

Villia held tightly to Mam's hand. "Mam, what do I do?"

"Say hello and wave to them."

She did. It was then she noticed fairies flitting all around her, as tiny as Tinkerbell, arrayed in gossamer gowns, their skin in all colors of the rainbow. Villia was beguiled by their loveliness.

"Oh, Mam, the fairies! They're so colorful."

"Yes, they come in every color to represent all who live on earth."

"Mam, this is the best birthday ever!"

A woman stood waiting at the end of the path that led from the boat dock. No one had to tell Villia it was the Ancient One, Rhiannon. She was tall and slender, and of regal bearing, with hair the color of cornsilk and eyes as clear and blue and bright as a mountain lake. A lovely ivy chaplet encircled her brow. Her bare feet, the toes adorned with gemstone rings, peeked out from the hem of her pure white linen tunic, cinched at the waist with a purple sash. A serene smile blossomed upon her flawless oval face. Rhiannon held out her hand. And without any hesitation, Villia reached for it as she had as a baby.

She sure doesn't look ancient, Villia mused. *She looks exactly like Grace Kelly!*

"Thank you for thinking of me as a movie star. I've always wanted to act on the big screen."

Villia was confused, for the Ancient One's lips had not moved, yet she had heard her words in her mind.

Sensing Villia's confusion, Rhiannon spoke: "I can speak aloud if you wish. Or, you can allow your mind to be opened to this way of communicating, which is called telepathy."

"How do I do that?" Villia wondered.

Rhiannon laughed. "You just did."

They continued on another path that veered to the north until they came to a lake. "Take off your shoes," commanded Rhiannon.

Villia glanced at the Ancient One's own bare feet; she figured it was some weird island custom. Shrugging, she complied. Two Barbary macaques had followed them through the treetops. The wooly monkeys jumped down, grabbed Villia's shoes, and scampered away.

"Stop!" she shouted, but they had already disappeared into the jungle.

"My mam will kill me for losing my shoes."

"Lose them, my dear? They are taking them to the hut. They will be shadowing you while you are here on the island. They are quite overwhelmed by their new assignment, and I think a bit shy. I wouldn't be surprised if they didn't polish your shoes until they look brand new."

"Where did they come from?"

"Their ancestors came from what is now known as France, and they enjoy celebrating their heritage. The female's name is Edith, after Edith Piaf, her mother's favorite singer."

"Mam plays her music all the time. And the male?"

"Napoleon."

Villia couldn't suppress her giggles. "Is there any way I can have my private thoughts back?"

"Yes, picture yourself in a movie theater and the screen is black."

Villia concentrated; the strain was evident on her face.

"Very good," said Rhiannon. "Your private thoughts are now your own."

"By the way," said Villia, "how do you know about movies? I mean, being a goddess and all that?"

"I go on occasion. I was with you when you snuck into the theater to see *Rear Window*."

"You were?"

"Yes, I was the kid sitting behind you. Remember when I threw popcorn at you?"

"You mean that bratty boy?"

"Yep! That was me having a bit of fun."

They walked for a while along the shoreline, letting the water wash over their feet.

Rhiannon stopped and picked up a fallen branch. She pointed it upwards. "This is the Tree of Superlative Fruit. If you are ever hungry, all you have to do is hold out your hands."

"Like this?" Villia asked, cupping her hands.

The tree began to sway, bending its supple branches towards her outstretched arms.

Villia heard the tree whisper: "Welcome, Villia," as a piece of fruit fell into her hands.

"The lions are particularly fond of this fruit."

"I thought lions only ate meat."

"It's forbidden on this island."

"What would you like this fruit to taste like?"

"Pizza," she said without missing a beat.

"Now bite into it."

"Dang! Best pizza I've ever tasted."

Rhiannon laughed, and for a moment Villia thought that all the stars in the sky had decided to twinkle at the same time.

"Here on the island no one eats flesh or meat, as humans have chosen to call it." She paused, adding, "I believe you have some doubts."

"It's just I haven't heard it called flesh. To call it flesh makes it real, and that makes me sad."

"You are a thoughtful and perceptive child. I like that." Rhiannon regarded Villia with a benevolent smile. "I can see your black screen flickering. You are safe here; ask what you wish."

Villia's eyes widened. "Do you mind if we use our voices? I'll have to get used to the telepathy way."

"Not at all. Life should be around choices whenever possible."

Villia cleared her throat. "Do you live forever? I mean, it's a magical island so no one should have to die."

"We live a very long time on the island, but still we face death."

"You too?"

"Yes, I have my death date."

"You know the actual date?" Tears came unbidden to Villia's eyes. She found the idea of her own "death date" most distressing.

"Knowing when is not bad. I've had eons of time. Sometime far into the future I will tell you what the other Keepers since the time of Branwyn have not known."

Villia asked, "A secret? Can't I know now?"

"You will have to trust me to know when the time is right. Knowledge is a gift that has to be timed properly. Let me put this another way. You know the doll you got from your aunt for your birthday?

Villia gasped. "How did you know about that?"

"I am all seeing and all knowing. If you had received that doll a few years ago, it would have been perfect. The doll hasn't changed, but you have. Now, I believe you have a question to ask."

"Won't you get old and sick and wrinkled?" Villia blurted out.

Rhiannon suddenly metamorphosed into a thousand-year-old woman with skin as translucent and thin as tissue paper.

Villia gasped and backed away.

"Don't be afraid. When it is my time, I shall pass peacefully and be renewed."

"But, but ... you're a goddess, for crying out loud!"

"Perhaps we have jumped too far ahead. Let us not dwell on what you humans think of as death and enjoy our island tour. However," she added, "I'm probably not the best tour guide—better fix that." In a twinkling she had changed into a young woman wearing a T-shirt that said:

ISLAND OF THE BLUE MOON
TOUR GUIDE

Wow!

Rhiannon drew an outline of the island in the sand. "There are three mountains on the island. Look in this direction." She pointed to the north. "Each mountain has its own magical properties that trickle down through three rivers. Each river then flows freely into a lake. During your stay here, you will bathe in the three lakes: the Lake of Sorrow, the Lake of Dreams, and the Lake of Wisdom. Only then will you be able to decide if you wish to be the Keeper."

Rhiannon pointed to one circle in the sand; as Villia watched, it took the form of a blue lake. "This is the Lake of Sorrow."

Villia asked, "But if no one really dies, why would there be sorrow?"

"There is great sorrow throughout your world, and not only around what you think of as death. For example, there is poverty, war, cruelty toward those who are different. The list is long. When the island was created we took a solemn oath to live in a state of harmony. We discovered that by doing so our hearts became open and filled with compassion. We began to take in the pain from your world and replace it with prayers for a peaceful and loving future."

"I don't think it's working."

Rhiannon cocked one sculpted Grace Kelly eyebrow. "What do you mean?"

"I get teased a lot at school about my name."

"Yes, I have seen it. Yet, several children have defended you."

"So that's how it works?"

"We can only send out our prayers; we cannot force the changes."

Rhiannon drew another circle in the sand. "This is the Lake of Dreams."

Villia said gleefully, "It's in pastel colors." She swirled the sand with her hand. "I just mushed all the colors together."

Rhiannon laughed. "I forget you are still a child."

"What does that lake do?"

"It gives us hope by showing us how the world could be." She sighed. "If only kindness could replace hatred, what a world it could be."

"I think I'd like that lake best."

Rhiannon made another circle in the sand. "Now, the third lake is called the Lake of Wisdom."

"I like that lake, too," said Villia. "But why is it gray?"

"One of your ancestors, Huw by name, selected the color. He was the second Keeper and a physician. He thought that knowledge and wisdom could help us gain understanding. He also had a sense of humor and wanted the lake colored to represent the region of the brain called gray matter."

"Do I know of him?"

"Huw was Branwyn's eldest son. He was of a gentle heart and saved many lives."

The Ancient One became still. "Which lake would you like to go into first?"

"Can I think for a minute?"

"Of course. Take all the time you need."

Villia sat down on a nearby boulder, her head in her hand.

"Welcome, Villia!"

She leaped up, her eyes searching for the source of the husky, booming voice.

Rhiannon said, "Surprise! Everything in the universe is a living entity."

Villia faced the boulder. "I'm so sorry. Did I hurt you?"

"Not at all! We boulders are made for sitting, climbing, and jumping off of. We also—and I say this with the utmost modesty—hold many things together. Like the mountains. Come sit, relax; do your thinking."

She sat back down. "It's hard to know which lake to go into first. Are the temperatures all the same?"

"They will be as you desire," answered Rhiannon.

"Hmm, I could sure use some help with math. Could the Lake of Wisdom help with that?"

"Of course. But why limit yourself?"

"I don't understand."

"If you enter that lake with only one thing in mind, you will get that and only that. But if you allow yourself be open, the lake will discover what you need and provide it."

"So, it's not like a genie? You know, granting three wishes?"

"Not at all. Come, take my hand. We shall walk to the Lake of Wisdom; it's not that far."

∞

Villia never forgot that day. Alas, the Lake of Wisdom did not transform her into a math whiz, but better than that, she began to see the world through an unclouded lens of awareness.

And so it was with the other lakes. She entered the Lake of Sorrow and for a moment her heart was opened, and she could feel the pain of the world. For that brief time, she thought she would die in recognition of mankind's cruelty.

She sobbed and Rhiannon held her. "I'm sorry," the Ancient One said. "You have to know. Without feelings there can be no change. Come, let me take you to your mam."

Mam held her and let her sob. "Mam, did this happen to you?"

"It happens to each of us. By entering the two lakes you have discovered knowledge and sorrow.

Tonight, when the community has gathered, you will enter the Lake of Dreams. Only then will you achieve full awareness. Then and only then can you make your decision to assume the mantle of Keeper, or not."

∞

That evening before the sun fully set, the inhabitants of the island gathered around the Lake of Dreams. Villia, who had been given a simple linen robe like Rhiannon's to wear, waded into the lake. The water was warmer than the other lakes and Villia fell into a dreamlike state. She saw the world not as one filled with suffering as she did with the Lake of Sorrow, nor with the wisdom of all the sages throughout time, as with the Lake of Wisdom. She saw clear waters flowing freely, fields overflowing with crops. Fear had disappeared from the earth. She was provided with a vision of how the world could be: a place of healing and compassion.

When Villia walked out of the Lake of Dreams, Rhiannon was there to meet her and took her hand. Mam and Tad, clad also in linen robes per island custom, stood on either side of her. There was no need for words; all present knew her answer.

The four of them walked to the clearing next to the Lake of Dreams and stood upon a simple dais made of stone and wood. The animals bowed down before Villia. Rhiannon removed the chaplet from her head and placed it upon the girl's brow.

"Villia Flatbottom," said the Ancient One with great solemnity, "I pronounce you the next Keeper of the Island of the Blue Moon."

With a glance from Rhiannon, the animals burst into cheers. She, Mam, and Tad embraced Villia, each in turn. A beatific smile blossomed upon the girl's face.

Villia returned home a changed person. Her sister and brothers, sensing in her a perception and serenity far beyond her tender years, stopped their relentless teasing.

∞

Villia put her memories away and returned to the present. She let Pooch out before calling Ebrill.

"What, don't I get to say hello?" the dog protested.

"That's the last thing I need. Now, scoot!"

Pooch scooted.

Remember to call her April.

Villia dialed April's office number imagining that she would be at her desk, taking multiple calls while snapping multiple orders. She had once asked April how she managed it all. "It's just multi-tasking," she scoffed.

"April here."

"April, it's Mam."

"Hold on one minute, I have to close the door."

Villia could hear a chair moving, then the tap, tap, tap of April's Kate Spade shoes on the willow oak flooring, and the clicking shut of the glass office door framed in snakewood.

"Mother?"

"Yes, I'm here."

"I have a favor to ask. I'm scheduled to go to Europe for three weeks. It's a once-in-a-lifetime opportunity to branch out into international real estate. This could put me on the cover of real estate magazines throughout the world."

"You know I'll do anything to help you."

"Here's the issue. I scheduled the kids for summer camp during those weeks and if everything was going according to plan, I wouldn't need your help. But wouldn't you know it, I got a call from the camp administrator that camp has been delayed for one week. You know all the rain they had around Big Bear?"

"Yes, I do keep up with the news," Villia said, a trifle testily.

"The roads leading to the camp are unsafe. Sinkholes! Wouldn't you just know it! Repairs are in progress and they told me it should go smoothly, but they had to postpone the session for a week.

Could you, would you keep the kids for a week, and take them to the bus drop-off?"

"Of course I will. But what about Michael?"

"Ha! Michael is up to his ears in patients. You'd think there was no other heart surgeon in the world." Her voice softened. "He's planning on joining me in Paris and truth be told, we could really use that time together. Things have been a bit rough between us, for a while now. And time alone in Paris—well, I'm hoping it's just what our marriage needs."

"I'm sorry you and Michael are having problems, April."

Villia heard her daughter sniffle. "Thanks, Mam, for calling me April. I'll have everything packed and be over tomorrow morning around nine."

They said their goodbyes, and Villia placed the phone back on its cradle. April had called her Mam instead of Mother. Could it be a new beginning or simply an old habit coming alive?

She thought back to the time when there was a little girl named Ebrill whose eyes grew wide with wonderment when her mam told her stories of a magical island teeming with mythical creatures. All that was lost when her name became April, and family ties were replaced with dreams of popularity and success.

Villia felt her life force waning, as it had for several months now. She needed to return to the Island of the Blue Moon and bathe in the

Lake of Dreams. Her energy would be restored, but her responsibilities as the Keeper of the Island would continue to weigh heavily upon her.

She threw her shoulders back and wiped her tears away. How many times had she seen her mam do the same? But there was no time to mourn the past or worry about the future. She had less than twenty-four hours to get ready for the children, Emilee and Ethan, and then there was the preparation for her trip to the island. Oran had checked the sailboat, but she would need to check it once again.

She felt overwhelmed and wished Oran was here to soothe her. She had once confessed to him,

"Sometimes I feel as if I'm adrift on the ocean in a dingy, without oars."

His advice rang true, then as now: "Most people get overwhelmed because they're worrying about the future. Focus on one thing at a time." He had advised her to create a Things to Do list. Her first one had more than twenty entries.

"I want you to only hold onto the first item on your list and let the rest go." She had followed his advice and saw that it worked.

Now she took out her most recent Things to Do list, filled from top to bottom. "Cleaning" occupied the first ten entries.

"Focus," she reminded herself.

Removing dust bunnies could wait, and so could cleaning the closets. She crossed out the entries until the number one item on her list was to inventory her remaining stock of herbs and curatives. Some grew in the greenhouse located next to the original adobe house; others could only be found on the island.

The greenhouse had been a surprise Christmas gift from Oran. She chuckled when she thought of her not so subtle hints. Catalog pages and Post-its were left at strategic places throughout the house, car, and boathouse. All spoke of her heart's desire.

Oran had not disappointed her. She had opened the padded envelope—free from the United States Post Office—that contained photos of the greenhouse, plus accessories. She had jumped up and down— that was ten years ago when she still could jump up and down.

"How ever did you know?" she exclaimed.

Oran grinned and hugged her until she became breathless. They knew each other's ways of being, and the joy in feigning surprise was well practiced and treasured.

Focus, she reminded herself. Adobe...herbs...curatives.

She would tackle that first, then hit Trader Joe's. She remembered April's final admonishment: "Mother, I know how much you want to spoil them but please go easy on the junk food. Promise?"

What a dilemma for a card-carrying grannie. Villia danced around the kitchen, stacking dishes in the sink, wiping down the counters and most of all thinking about those two adorable, precious grandchildren of hers.

Emilee was, as Oran was inclined to say, full of piss and vinegar and tenacity bordering on stubbornness. Emilee had her mother's tendency toward knee-jerk responses, but unlike April, she remained open and unguarded.

Ethan was a thinker rather than a doer. He had inherited April's red hair and Michael's compassion. Villia thought of him as a philosopher in training, although she worried about how life might break his heart.

She smiled inwardly, thinking about Emilee and Ethan. What fun they could have over the next week! *Let me set aside all my worries and put my job as a grannie at top of the list. After all, what is a grandma's role? To spoil, of course!*

CHAPTER 3

Villia Flatbottom removed the black iron keyring from the black iron hook that hung next to the kitchen door. Out of the corner of her eye, she saw the velvet pouch lying on the kitchen counter. She gasped. Had it just moved or was that merely a figment of her imagination?

She had forgotten about the pouch until reminded by Edgar and Annabelle, and now her curiosity was aroused. *I wonder what Rhiannon, the Ancient One, has up her sleeve this time?*

With Pooch by her side, she walked out the backdoor, down the creaky wooden steps and into the yard.

Oran, a devotee of obscure facts, had done the math shortly after they moved into the house.

"The property is the equivalent of four football fields," he said over coffee. "I figured that out while you were in the shower."

He sat back in his chair and beamed. She smiled, her eyes filled with love and acceptance. How lucky she was to find someone who could be as quirky as she.

Every time she walked to the old adobe, she thought *four football fields*. At times her imagination would paint a picture of herself standing in the middle of a football field in full regalia, surrounded by cheering teammates as she scored the winning touchdown.

Villia paused by the brick patio shaded by two weeping willow trees, planted years ago as seedlings purchased by mail order.

Oran had scratched his head, saying, "They look like plain twigs to me."

She knew they would grow into magnificent trees. She didn't know how she knew, but she had felt their energy when she had lifted them from their protective box. She soaked the roots overnight in water and planted them the next morning. Every morning, just as the sun was rising, she would rush outside to look at her twigs until one day she saw a slip of a branch forming. She ran to get Oran.

"Come see, Oran! It's life!"

Oran knelt next to Villia. "Well, so it is. I would have never guessed it. I'll never doubt you again."

"There's life here too," she said, lifting his hand and placing it on her belly. "Our first," she whispered.

And Oran Flatbottom, a man of the sea, who had fallen in love with a woman who was as quirky as he, wept.

Villia continued walking past the vegetable garden and the empty chicken coup, until she reached the adobe house. Thickets of Catalina cherry trees surrounded the 150-year-old house, providing privacy as well as succulent fruit. She wasn't sure when the trees were planted; they were among the countless things in her life that had simply always been. She sat on a nearby bench and closed her eyes to take in their fragrance, accompanied by the melody coming from songbirds nestled in the trees.

Beauty surrounds us if we stop, look, and listen.

She and Oran had packed a picnic lunch in late spring and plucked fruit from the trees.

Oran said, "The cherries are delightful...everything on earth gives us something. But I think we humans have forgotten that you cannot take without giving something in return."

That was her Oran, quirky at times and reflective at others.

The Ancient One had once told her, "You and Oran are the perfect example of yin and yang."

"How so?" she had asked.

"Oran is your anchor, and you are Oran's deliverance from reality."

Before entering the adobe, she stopped to turn on the drip watering system, then closed her eyes to say a prayer of gratitude to any

Deity that might be listening: "Thank you for all you provide and for sharing it with us. Please watch over Oran and bring him home safely."

She stayed in a state of tranquility until she felt Pooch pressing against her leg.

"Keeping me on task, are you?"

Pooch smiled. "Someone's got to do it!"

She jingled the keys and said, "Wait here and be a guard dog."

"Fair maiden, my sword is by my side. *But,* perhaps a little snooze is in order before I take up such an onerous duty." Pooch lay down, resting his head upon his paws.

Villia shook her head in disbelief before turning her attention to the adobe house. The house was born from sun-dried bricks made from clay soil, sand, and straw. Impacted by the weather, the bricks would swell and shrink, yet the house continued to stand, but not without the Flatbottoms' consistent care.

Oran had maintained the house by following the techniques used by all the Flatbottoms that came before him. Villia's tad had shown him what needed to be done. "This is one thing I won't miss," he had said with a smile, showing Oran how to make mud plaster. "Clay soil, sand, water, and straw, in these proportions." He continued mixing the ingredients in the oversized tub. "Now, use your trowel like this," he said, making horizontal strokes. "You see how bricks bond to plaster? Just like a marriage. We'll wait a couple of days and then seal them with whitewash."

Oran had asked, "How so, like a marriage?"

"I figure Mam and me, we're like this adobe. The rain comes, the sun beats down, and sometimes we feel like we'll crumble. That tells us we need to take a look at the damage and repair it before it collapses. This house is exactly like a marriage."

Two-feet-thick walls kept the house warm in winter and cool in summer. The original thatched roof had been replaced years ago with clay tile. Earthquakes came and went, yet the house remained standing. Villia glanced over at the King development. Signs of deterioration were showing on the roofs, doors, and shutters. She shook her head. *Such a shame.*

She heard Pooch snoring. *Some guard dog you are!*

Attached to the entrance door was a warning sign she had made using Bruce's woodburning kit; it was something she remained proud of, having only burned her fingers twice. It read:

BEWARE THE WITCHES AND SPELLS.
THOSE UNINVITED WHO DARE TO ENTER
WILL NEVER BE SEEN AGAIN.

Oran had admired her handiwork but told her in the gentlest of ways, "Any snoopy child will be enticed."

Oh, I suppose Oran was right. The sign had weathered over time, and she had a momentary thought about taking it down.

She straightened her shoulders and stretched to her maximum height. She might have wrinkles and had suffered from her siblings labeling her a Munchkin, but by all the gods and goddesses, she still had a purpose. *I am like this sign—weathered and worn but still of value.* She touched the sign. "Stay, old friend; we will get through this life together."

She looked at the four door locks and wondered which Flatbottom had felt the need for such tight security. They certainly would be a deterrent for anyone trying to break into the house, she thought, as she fumbled with the unmarked keys. After several attempts, she swung the door open with a heavy push.

The room was dark except for the sunlight shining through the east-facing barred window, casting a crisscross design over the hand hewed wooden floor. There was enough light, she thought, as she stood in the doorway; no need to turn on the one modernization insisted upon by Oran: a single overhead electric lamp.

When her eyes became accustomed to the change in light, she saw two pairs of moccasins lined up next to the door.

Once, when she had taken a barefooted Bruce and Ebrill into the adobe house, she had pointed to the moccasins. "Never walk barefooted in here," she'd warned.

"Why, Mother?" a five-year-old Ebrill had questioned. "Because of a spell?"

Villia had to hold back her laughter. "No, because of splinters. You see, the floor is ancient and has become splintery. I don't want you to get pieces of wood in your feet."

The room began to spin, and Villia grabbed onto a chair to keep from falling. What kind of mother had she really been? Had she become delusional thinking that her beliefs would also be her children's? She believed all the signs that said they were tightly connected and chose to ignore those that said they were in trouble.

Oran had even joked about Villia and Ebrill being joined at the hip. They ate breakfast under the kitchen table, and Ebrill took in everything she told her about fairies and the long-forgotten animals that lived on the Island of the Blue Moon: an island that was only visible to those humans who carried the Flatbottom name.

Was I merely naïve in thinking it would last?

She tried to remember when it began to change between her and Ebrill. Was it in middle school? No, by middle school the damage had been done and the fragile mother/daughter relationship was shattered. It started after the first day of fourth grade at Lincoln Fifth Avenue School.

∞

Ebrill had been off-the-wall excited at the thought of fourth grade and couldn't stop pirouetting in her new dress and shoes bought at Macy's—a far cry from Sears, where they usually shopped.

"Please, Mam," she had begged, "can I get taps?"

They stopped at the shoemaker, and for the next two days tapping was heard throughout the house. Ebrill offered Mam and Tad a wide grin as she danced in the kitchen before dinner.

Owen whispered, "Can you turn her off?" They laughed, knowing that later this would be a memory to warm their hearts.

School began the following day and calm reigned over the house.

"It's awfully quiet," observed Oran.

"Enjoy it while you can," Villia replied. "I'm picking Ginger Rogers up at three."

Villia pulled Bessie, their 1955 Chevy, behind the long line of expensive new cars. Mothers gathered in clusters, clad in their outfit of the day. There was the fitness group that proudly showed off their sweat lines and burgeoning biceps. The all-organic group chatted as they held onto snack bags designed and filled by Kids Snacks, the newest store in town. The "gotta get the kids into the best college" group met with catalogs and suggestions on how to put their kids on the path to success. Bragging was offered at no additional cost.

Villia, having toiled in the garden this hot September day, was still dressed in her dirt-covered lightweight sweats and gray T-shirt. Equally dirty sneakers completed her ensemble. From time to time she noticed one of the groupies staring at her. A quickly averted eye gave her to know the woman wasn't admiring her bumpkinish outfit.

Gads, I should have at least washed old Bessie. Bessie was a salesman's model. "Basic," said the previous owner, which meant no armrests, no back seat, and no ashtray. Villia didn't mind the no ashtray part, but no back seat? As a bonus it came with a few dents and faded paint. She and Oran looked at each other and with one voice said, "Sold!" It was what they could afford, and Oran found a back seat at the auto parts yard. It didn't match the rest of the upholstery, but what did match in their lives?

Villia spotted Ebrill, and her heart swelled. She will be tall, she thought, like her tad. Tad and mam...she liked that they used the Welsh names for father and mother.

She waved at Ebrill. She looked cute in her Duran Duran T-shirt and Guess jeans with neon pink leg warmers—all thrift store finds—but the smile from this morning was nowhere to be found. When the girl clambered into the car and Villia tried to hug her, she pulled away. Villia hoped it was just that the day was long and she was tired.

Villia said, "I thought we would stop for some ice cream."

"Okay," Ebrill mumbled.

"How was school?"

"Okay."

"What's wrong, Ebrill?"

"Mam, would you call me April?"

"Of course, that's what your name means. But perhaps you'll tell me why."

"We had to tell our names to the class and talk about ourselves. And the kids laughed when I said mine: Ebrill Flatbottom! Dang, what a nerdy name! And then they started whispering. And the girls wouldn't eat with me at lunchtime." She paused, smacking her bubblegum furiously. "Mam, why do we have such a funny last name? And Ebrill sounds funny too. I don't want to have funny names."

Villia remembered her own tortuous teasing when her classmates learned her name was Villia Flatbottom. And when the teacher asked her what Villia meant, she said, "It means nothing." The kids all laughed, but she didn't want to tell them that her name really meant "a witch of the woods."

"April," Villia said, "you asked a worthwhile question but sometimes finding the right answer takes time. Let me think about it. Now, what if we put aside that big question until tonight when Tad and Bruce are home? For now, let's push all our worries aside and pig out on ice cream."

April bounced up and down in the seat. "Can I have a hot fudge sundae?"

Villia licked her lips. "You bet. I think I'll have one too!"

That afternoon before dinner, Villia and Oran formulated a plan.

"It's time for April and Bruce to know the truth," said Oran. "No more pussyfooting around with fairy tales. We'll face the situation head-on. Tomorrow I'll check out the flatbottom boat and make sure she's ready for the trip. This weekend the kids will pay a visit to the island and know the truth. Once they see its beauty and the animals...can you imagine their faces when they hear a singing dragon?"

"Or crows that talk?" Villia added.

"Yes, exactly. There's an old maxim that's been said in many ways and by many different people, but I learned it in Sunday school: 'Then you will know the truth, and the truth will set you free.'"

∞

The Flatbottoms gathered around the TV set watching a rerun of *The Andy Griffith Show* and balancing paper plates filled with pizza.

Oran turned off the TV, patted his stomach, and groaned. "Full as a tick."

"*I'm* not filled up," said Bruce, shoving another slice in his mouth.

Oran shook his head in disbelief. "Son, remind me to have you checked for a tapeworm." He turned to his only daughter. "April, I heard you had a bit of a difficult day, my girl."

"I told Bruce about it, and he said it happened to him too."

Villia turned to Bruce and said, "You never told me...*us*."

"Can I have another slice of pizza?" he said, still chomping on the last piece.

Bruce was in middle school and beginning to show signs of an erupting puberty. Insatiable hunger, his voice cracking, and a bit of dark fuzz gracing his upper lip were the first signs of manhood. Bruce, her quiet, steady, thoughtful son had his own direction and his own dreams.

"I'd like to hear about it now," said Oran. "That is, after you've finished masticating that poor slice of pizza."

Bruce held up a wait-a-minute index finger, chewed vigorously, and swallowed. "I know our name is unusual," he began, "and Mam told me it was given to us for a very special reason. I always thought it was just a family story, like a fairytale. I never got teased about my first name, like Ebrill has, but Flatbottom? Yeah, I've taken some flak for that. Might as well hang 'kick me' signs on our backs! Mam...Tad...couldn't we just change our last name?"

"Son," said Oran, "the story behind our name is not a fairytale, and this weekend Mam and I will be proving it by taking you to the island. Now, suppose you tell us who gave you 'flak' about the name Flatbottom?"

Bruce spat out his words. "It was that troublemaker, Dawley."

"The sixth?"

"Yeah, he's a bully just like all the rest of the Dawleys. He starts the teasing about our name and some of the other kids join in. Then he goes around bragging about it. Plus, he brags about everything his ancestors have done, even if it's cruel stuff."

"Did you talk to a teacher about the bullying? Or your principal?"

Bruce gulped down his glass of milk. "And be a snitch?" He got up from the floor and sat in the overstuffed chair and a half. "You and Mam have told us not to fight and to use our words instead. So, I used them."

Villia held her breath. "Would you care to tell us what words you used?"

"I think it's best if I take the fifth."

Oran and Villia exchanged a secretive glance that they hoped their kids didn't catch. They didn't.

"And did the words that you care not to share, stop it?" asked Oran.

"Yep. You might say the case has been resolved."

Villia said, "By the way, Bruce, have you selected your law school?"

Oran chuckled.

"Yes, Mam. Either Yale or Harvard. Can I go back to eating now?"

∞

Oran filled the tub with hot water, adding bubble bath until the bubbles reached the top of the tub.

Villia felt the water with her fingers. "Perfect. Thank you, love. Remind me to keep you for the next hundred years."

"That's it? Only a hundred?"

"Hmm," she replied, sticking one toe into the steaming water and easing her way into the tub. "Maybe longer if you'll do me a favor. Would you check on the kids? I'm still dizzy from our conversation."

"Of course." Oran entered the L-shaped hallway. As he approached the junction that led to April's and Bruce's rooms, he heard April rapping on Bruce's door.

"Bruce, are you up?" she said softly.

"Yes, barely," he grumbled.

After April entered Bruce's room, Oran inched close enough to hear their muffled conversation, and to see through the crack between the door and the jamb.

"Bruce, what did you say to Dawley VI?"

"If I tell you, do you promise not to tell anyone? And I do mean anyone."

"Cross my heart and hope to die, if I have told a big fat lie."

"I told him my mother's a real witch, and she'd cast a spell and turn him into a toad."

"Think he believed you?"

"Yeah, he looked scared to death. Of course, my little threat was just hearsay. It wouldn't hold up in a court of law."

April giggled. "Bruce, I do hope you become a lawyer."

"I will. A good one, and I'll go after the Dawleys of this world. What about you, April? What do you want to be?"

"I want to be rich and live in one of the big houses at the top of the hill with a view of the ocean." She reached her arms toward the ceiling. "And all those kids who laughed at me will be sorry. I'll be so rich, and I'll have the biggest car and servants and—"

"Whoa, exactly how will you get rich?"

"Oh, I'll marry a lawyer or a doctor."

Bruce grinned. "You know what I think? I think you'll get rich on your own. You're a real go-getter, sis. I admire that about you."

In a sudden burst of sisterly affection, April kissed his cheek. "I love you, Bruce—you're my best friend."

"I love you too, April." He lay down, yawning. "Sleep tight..."

"I know, I know. Don't let the bedbugs bite."

Caught off guard, Oran stood behind the bedroom door as April opened it. He inhaled deeply, hoping that would make him invisible if discovered. But April headed for her own bedroom without a backward glance. Oran exhaled and tiptoed to the bedroom he and Villia shared.

Villia was in bed with a book propped on her bent legs.

"How was the bath, my love?"

"Healing. I'm as relaxed as a bowl of Jell-O. Thanks for checking on the kids," she said, reaching out to Oran.

Oran got into bed, sinking into the comfort of her encompassing arms. "How are you at keeping secrets?"

She crossed her heart. "Cross my heart and hope to die, if I just told a big fat lie."

"Like mother, like daughter," he murmured, pulling her even closer and revealing all.

CHAPTER 4

Even though the island was less than two hours away, Villia packed a lunch, snacks, and drinks.

"Why can't we take the sailboat?" asked April, staring at the flatbottom boat. "Is it even safe? It looks old and creepy."

Villia saw April's hands tremble while droplets of perspiration appeared on her face. She knew they heralded the beginning of a full-blown anxiety attack.

"Come sit by me, April," she said softly, patting the bench upon which she had placed three cushions. "Bruce, perhaps you could put down your law book and sit with us."

Bruce sighed, closed his book, and sat next to Mam.

"This boat was built by your ancestor, Dylan Flatbottom, around 150 years ago. Tad believes there is some unique property to the wood. Being a romantic at times, I'd like to believe that Dylan put so much love into making the boat that it has the strength to withstand storms and earthquakes and even fires." She paused. "I know you don't believe and aren't interested, but perhaps someday you or your children, or even your children's children, will want to know the love story of Dylan and Branwyn. If that time ever comes, you will find Branwyn's journals and letters in the old trunk that's kept in the adobe house.

"I will say this much: the journals are about two young people who fell desperately in love and had to cross an ocean so that they could be together. Their story and this boat belong to you and all the Flatbottoms for generations to come."

Bruce said, "We read Shakespeare's *Romeo and Juliet* in my English class. Some of the girls cried."

"And you, Bruce?"

"Well, have to admit, it had a sad ending."

"Branwyn and Dylan's story rivals *Romeo and Juliet*, except with a happier ending."

Oran, at the wheel, cried out, "Island ahoy!"

Villia grinned. "Your tad loves to shout that. He's been doing it ever since he first laid eyes upon the island. Come, let's join him."

Tad said, "I love this part of the journey. See that mist hanging over the island? Keep your eyes on that slight break in the mist, that bit of clearing."

Bruce looked intensely. "Yes, Tad, I do see a bit of a break in the mist. Wait! Wait! I see some trees."

April's mouth twitched and her eyes remained downcast. Bruce elbowed her. "Look, April. Trees and a dock. Oh, my God, I see an elephant and a tiger and a giraffe. Tad, are you sure no one else can see it?"

Tad said, "Check the charts and tell me if you see an island anywhere near our position."

"Well, if it's invisible and not on the charts, why wouldn't a ship run into it?"

"That's the magic of the island."

April gazed outward. "I hate it here. All I see is a mound of sand and a broken-down dock. No trees and no animals. It's a desert island."

Villia took April's hand as they faced the island. "I'm confused," she said. "Oran, what do you see?"

"Paradise." He pointed toward the island. "Check out that palm tree, and tell me who is hanging out there."

Villia said, "Birds and squirrels and..." She laughed. "Oh, it's Two-headed Rosie!"

"Yep, Rosie the Rose-breasted Grosbeak; the bird with two heads. And what is she doing?"

"She's singing a duet. Soprano from one head and tenor from the other."

"Can you hear the music?"

"Loud and clear."

"And the song is?"

"'The Impossible Dream' from *Man of La Mancha*."

"Now, what about you, Bruce and Ebrill?"

Bruce said, "It's a nice island, Mam, Tad. But all I see are ordinary animals and trees and two plain old songbirds; I guess they're twittering. Come to think of it, it looks a lot like pictures I've seen of Hawaii."

As they approached the dock, April began to swat at her arms. "I don't see anything but swarms of insects." She sobbed. "I hate it here. I want to go home and be like the other kids. I don't wanna be a Flatbottom."

Instead of the day becoming a day of enlightenment, as Villia and Oran had planned, it became their worst nightmare.

Oran, confused about April's response, tapped Bruce on the shoulder. "Look up there, at that tree. Do you see a bird?"

"Yes, Tad. I see a bird. Maybe it's an eagle. It's staring right at us."

"April, what about you?"

"There's a vulture sitting on a dead tree, but who cares?" With an angry cry, she swatted her arm. "The insects are eating me alive! I want to go home, I want to go home, I want to go home ..."

Villia said, "I don't understand. Come, we'll walk to the hut. It's where Tad and I spent our honeymoon. And next to it is the most beautiful body of water: the Lake of Dreams. A few drops of water from the lake and the bites will disappear."

They walked the path from the dock to the hut.

"Look!" Villia cried out. "The hut's been decorated with flowers." She put her hand in the lake. "Ah, so clear, cool, and pristine! Come, April, put your arms in the water and your bites will disappear."

"I'm not putting my arms in that filthy water," she sobbed.

Villia looked at Oran.

Bruce said, "Tad, I don't know what's going on, but I hardly see a lake—it's more of a puddle. Look at April's arms. She's covered in bites! I think we should leave."

Villia said, "Oran, take the kids back to the boat. Get the first aid kit and find the witch hazel— that'll sooth April's bites. I'll follow in just a few minutes."

Villia sat on the soft Irish moss at the edge of the Lake of Dreams. She looked at the water and saw the Ancient One's reflection behind her.

Rhiannon sat down, dangling her feet in the water. "You still have much to learn. The island is different for everyone, even the Flatbottoms. People see it not only with their eyes, but also with their heart and soul."

"I don't understand."

"Do you see that tree over there?"

"Why, yes."

"Describe it to me."

"It's one of my favorites. It's an Australian tea tree."

"And why is it your favorite?"

"It gives so much and asks so little. Its essential oil has antibacterial and therapeutic properties and is used in skin products..."

"And it's poisonous if ingested."

"That's true."

"Come closer to the Lake of Dreams and see how others see the tree."

Villia looked deep into the lake. At first all she saw was clear water, so clear that she could see to the bottom. Then the tree appeared.

"This is your vision."

"Yes. A graceful tree with a spreading canopy and smooth, silvery gray bark. It's in full bloom, with delicate five-petaled white flowers, and songbirds perching on its branches, singing their hearts out."

"Watch closely," said Rhiannon. "This is Bruce's vision."

The tree's blossoms disappeared. The birds were no longer there.

Villia blinked her eyes in disbelief. "It's just an ordinary tree with all its specialness gone."

"Bruce can only see an ordinary island—pleasant enough but not enchanted. Keep looking. This is Ebrill's vision."

Villia sobbed. "It's black and decayed. Dead! My heart hurts for my baby."

"It can be bitter when you see through another's heart. Ebrill has the ability to see everything, but refuses to believe. She had to create something she could fight against so that she can survive in her familiar world. Every tree, every bit of foliage, became dead. Every animal, the rainbow fairies, the singing dragon, and even the unicorn turned into biting insects. Look again."

"Oh, it's a magnificent Old World yew, with a hollow base you could drive a Winnebago through! The twisting trunk is covered in fantastic burls—they're like the faces of wood spirits with mossy beards. Why, it must be thousands of years old!"

"That is Oran's vision. Do you understand more clearly now?"

"I think so, but my heart aches. I don't know if I can stand it."

"Look at me, Villia. How do you see me?"

Villia wiped away her tears. "Why, you change forms all the time."

"Then you see me as I truly am in the moment, and that is why you are the Keeper. I will tell you a little secret: Oran only sees me in this way."

The air around the Ancient One shimmered, and Villia was startled to see Glinda, the Good Witch of the North, from *The Wizard of Oz* standing before her.

Rhiannon laughed, and the sound was like the music of water burbling over river stones. And when she spoke, it was in Billie Burke's unmistakable lilting voice. "Oran only sees the good in me, and in others. It is you who must change. Accept your children for who they are, not for whom you wish them to be."

Villia looked down at her bare feet. Never a need for shoes when she visited the island. There were no stones where she walked, only the soft, sponge-like sensation of moss under her feet.

"Will I have enough time to learn it all?"

"Of course not. I was created thousands of years ago, and I too am still learning. Take your children home, safe in the knowledge that even I have no control over destiny."

The trip home was silent; each member of the Flatbottom family tried to find a place on the boat that belonged only to them: Oran at the helm, focused on the sea; Bruce, his head buried in the book *How to*

Take Law Exams in a Nutshell; Ebrill and Villia inside the cabin, with Ebrill trying not to scratch her insect bites and Villia trying to soothe them.

Taking out a bottle of tea oil and a wad of cotton from her first-aid kit, she began to daub April's arms.

"I'm sorry for your suffering," Villia said softly. "I'll never ask you to go again."

April looked up, a little girl whose eyes spewed dragon fire. "You lied to me. All your stories—what a bunch of bull! Just leave me alone." She turned away from her mam, never to fully return.

Remembering the Ancient One's words, Villia left April to stand next to Oran.

"Oran, we need to talk."

∞

They trudged up the steps from the dock to the rickety house built on stilts. Four hearts filled with sadness, hopes dashed, and a family falling apart.

Tad pointed to the dining table. "Let's all sit down. Your mam and I had a long talk on the way home. Villia, it was your idea—you tell them."

"You have both suffered because of me, and I have the deepest regrets." She wiped the tears that flowed freely down her cheeks. "I thought you would see the island as I see it, but I was wrong. This week, Tad and I will go to school to see about getting your last names changed on your records. If necessary we'll see an attorney. From now on, you may use Tad's original name: Davis." She gestured toward her children. "Introducing Bruce Davis and April Davis!"

Bruce smiled; April jumped up and hugged her mam.

"How are those bites, Ms. Davis?"

She held out her arms. "They're gone."

Villia nodded. "What we are doing about your names doesn't change who you are to me, to us. I will always be your mam and Tad will always be your tad. Tad and I will keep our thoughts about the island just between ourselves, as it should be. Now, let's all freshen up; the day is still young and we're going to Marineland to swim with the dolphins."

∞

The years went by, and they never spoke again about that day when they had ventured out to the island. Like the dust bunnies on the kitchen floor, they were swept under an emotional rug.

To no one's surprise, Bruce fulfilled his dream of becoming an attorney. April thrived as April Davis, although not in the way that Villia had hoped. April became popular in school, and as her popularity grew her attachment to her family waned. She hung out with the in-crowd, girls from wealthier families who were given everything before they even asked for it.

April got her wish: she married Michael Preston, a physician, and lived in one of the largest homes in Sherman Oaks, a suburb a few miles north of Beverly Hills. She became a realtor, selling high-end McMansions to the friends she had made in high school and college. April discovered that she didn't have to rely on a wealthy husband to be successful, although being married to a well-known pediatric heart surgeon gave her the status she longed for.

Villia and Oran were invited to the housewarming party of April and Michael's own McMansion. A cookie-cutter replica of every other house in the sprawling neighborhood, Villia thought of the house as a vulgar testament to materialism gone mad, with nothing unique to recommend it, and no love evident in the bones. The interior was likewise sterile, with every picture and plant placed just so, like a hoity-toity magazine spread, and the designer furniture daring rather than inviting one to sit. The catered affair boasted enough champagne and caviar to choke a horse. High-powered men and women clustered in Gucci-clad knots, making business contacts or bragging about their new Porsches.

Oran and Villia, wearing their Kmart best, didn't stay long. They were misfits there as much as April had been a misfit on that long-ago day when they had sailed to an invisible island and lost a piece of their hearts.

They said their good-byes and April gave them a "mwah" kiss on each of their cheeks. "Must you leave so soon?" she said distractedly, her eyes drifting toward a potential client she'd been stalking all evening.

They were silent on the hour's drive home. Once in the house, Oran and Villia Flatbottom wrapped their arms around each other and sobbed.

∞

Villia had never forgiven herself. Why hadn't she seen the signs? Was she so consumed with the island that she had neglected her children, especially April? She had oftentimes entered the Lake of Dreams with the single desire of repairing her broken relationship with her daughter. And yet, her prayers were denied and her relationship with April remained distant.

She glanced around the two-room adobe house. *More than 150 years of use, wear, and change.* Generations of Flatbottoms had lived here, eventually building the house she and Oran now lived in.

The story began with Dylan and Branwyn. She was well versed in family lore about Dylan, Branwyn, and their three children. There were also stories passed down about another child, an orphan, found by Dylan and made one of theirs.

Her ancestors had only taken from the earth materials needed to survive. The original floors were made of earth and hard-packed with cow's blood for stability. Their beds laid on the floors—mattresses stuffed with straw or cotton, then covered with cowhide. Were they less happy than April residing in her McMansion? Villia doubted it. In fact, she rather believed they were probably infinitely happier.

She had once read that five thousand bricks would be needed to build an ordinary two-room house such as this. She thought of the work that had to go into creating the bricks—the collaboration of collecting, mixing materials, and placing them in forms. Yet, when she entered, it was anything but ordinary, first because she could feel the living energy from the past, and secondly, because it was made extraordinary by its contents.

As she stood in the center of the room, she felt the sense of purpose that invigorated the house and kept it alive. She remembered seeing a cooking area when she was a child, but that had been permanently removed to allow for repairs.

A twelve-foot table nearly spanned the width of the main room. Two chairs completed the monastic furnishings. Floor to ceiling shelving brimmed with glass bottles and jars whose contents were of various and curious origins. Her hobby of late was combing thrift stores for vessels such as these; she wasn't above scavenging for specimens of whimsical shapes and colors in the neighbors' recycling bins, or even the city dump, waiting to be sorted, crushed, and molded into new shapes. How like life, or at least life as she believed it to be. She picked up a bottle, wondering how many lives it had lived, and vowed to give it fresh purpose.

She had no romantic thoughts of having been a princess in a previous life, but held on tightly to words from the Ancient One. To believe that there was life everlasting, in some form, was enough to satisfy her.

She walked over to the domed top oak trunk adorned with burnished brass lock and hinges and leather handles. It had been made by Branwyn's grandfather, a casket maker by trade, as a wedding gift to Enid, Branwyn's mother.

The trunk was in surprisingly good condition, as were its meager contents: two parcels wrapped in plain brown paper and bound together by a frayed length of twine. They seemed lost inside the cavernous trunk. She lifted them out and read the inscription on the topmost parcel, written in her mam's elegant hand: *Branwyn's Journals. A chronicle of your ancestors.*

Villia knew how easily she could get distracted and began to feel anxious about getting everything ready before tomorrow morning. She began to return the journals to their resting place but hesitated. Instead, she tucked them into her tote bag. *Perhaps it's time for me to revisit the past.*

What time did April say she would be over? Was it nine or ten? *April's always running a bit late. What's an hour or so, after all?*

She walked over to the shelves that held rows of jars filled with herbs for curing illnesses and broken hearts. She unscrewed the tops of the bottles, peered inside and sniffed, setting aside those whose contents would be returned to the earth as compost. She made mental notes of the herbs that needed to be replaced from her greenhouse and those she would gather once she was on the island.

There was a small bookcase next to the trunk. Behind its locked glass doors were opaque jars with twin strips of tape forming forbidding X's across the already tightly screwed lids. They were filled with gifts, special potions from the Ancient One, and were only to be used in what Villia deemed times of crisis.

Under normal circumstances Villia could contact Rhiannon simply by sending out her thoughts, but with her mind currently in such a chaotic state, she decided she'd best resort to their backup method of communication.

Unlocking the door, she removed one of the jars, stripped off the tape, and unscrewed the lid. A vapor arose, infused with the scent of lilac. In a trice, the ancient one's face appeared inside the jar.

"Villia, what a pleasant surprise!" said Rhiannon. "If you're contacting me the old-fashioned way, I know something's up. Tell me about it."

"I'm just feeling...well, overwhelmed, what with Oran gone and the grandkids coming, and the Resetting Ceremony only a couple of weeks away."

"Yes, it is a hectic time," Rhiannon agreed. "During this lull before the storm, I'm taking my summer break and retreating to my castle for rest and relaxation. Can you imagine? I've gained ten pounds! How vain of me—a goddess who, after thousands of years, still worries about her figure."

Damn, does everyone get a vacation except for me?

"You've had your screen down, Villia. Something you don't want me to know?"

"Just a grumble or two."

"How was your visit with Annabelle and Edgar? They aren't the easiest to entertain."

"Quite informative."

"They do love their job. They always come back to me a bit plumper; I do believe you're spoiling them with your treats, Villia. But that is neither here nor there. I'm eager to spend some time together during the Resetting of the Calendar Ceremony. Villia, we are in difficult times. You are the last Keeper and the community is concerned. The emotional waves are high, and the waters murky. There are rumblings among the gods and goddesses. Some would like to see the island disappear forever; others believe that it serves a purpose. There is bickering and jealousy among them. Not unlike you humans, after all."

"Rhiannon, I am tortured over our dilemma. How can you go away during this crisis?"

"You know I do my best thinking and planning at the castle. The time may come for drastic measures. That's why I sent you the parcel via Edgar and Annabelle. I bet you haven't even looked at it yet."

"You know me too well."

Villia reached into her wide jacket pocket and removed the velvet pouch. She peeked inside to see what looked like confetti in the colors of the rainbow: red, orange, yellow, green, blue, indigo, and violet.

"It's pretty," Villia commented. "But what's it for?"

"You hold in your hand an Elixir with the power to make the island visible to outsiders. It is only to be used under the gravest of circumstances. Administer one tablespoon for adults and one teaspoon for children. Be careful with the dosage—too much and they may see more than they bargained for. Remember, it will make the island visible to friends and foes alike. Ta-ta for now. My massage therapist calls."

The vision of Rhiannon faded until it disappeared.

Per Edgar and Annabelle's earlier instructions, Villia emptied the confetti-like Elixir into one of her mother's clear Ball Mason jars. She remembered that Mam entered a canning frenzy every spring and summer. How she hated to see the jars of string beans lined up on the kitchen counter.

"Enough for months," her mother would murmur as she filled jar after jar after jar. Villia shivered at the memory.

Villia next sealed the lid, affixing two pieces of tape across it for extra protection. She then placed the jar in the bookcase with the other potions, where it would be safe from sunlight. She also placed the "emergency contact" jar back in the bookcase, and then locked it.

CHAPTER 5

The rest of the day was a whirlwind of shopping and cleaning. *Dorothy and her tornado have nothing on me*, she thought. Her good intentions to read the journals were put aside as she dashed to Trader Joe's, studied each and every label, then stopped cold at the ice cream freezer. Ebrill's words echoed: "Mother, easy on the junk food. Promise?"

How can organic ice cream be considered junk food? She topped off her basket with one of each flavor and, while standing in the check-out line, spotted a display of Trader Joe's Cookie Thins. One of each flew into her cart: Meyer Lemon, Triple Ginger, and Toasted Coconut. She could see the scene now; perhaps they would watch *The Sound of Music—I'll have to find the video* she mentally reminded herself—while Emilee and Ethan daintily spread a bit of ice cream on their very favorite cookie. Perhaps they could add a sing-along. She hummed "Do-Re-Mi" all the way home and up the steps to the kitchen door.

Villia unpacked the bags and spread their contents on the table. She stopped, looked at the array of food and said, "Oh my God, what have I done?"

Reassured that it had only been a temporary psychotic break, she managed to fit the ice cream into the freezer and squeezed the cookies into the overflowing cupboard.

She gave the house a quick once-over and paid special attention to preparing April's old bedroom for Emilee and Ethan.

Exhausted, she climbed into bed and said a brief prayer: "To any deities listening, please keep April out of my freezer and cupboards." She arranged the covers and pillows the way she liked and patted Pooch's head before reaching for Branwyn's journal and opening it to the first page. The date—March 13, 1847—written in a childish scrawl, became unfocused as she felt her eyelids flutter, then close.

CHAPTER 6

Villia woke to Pooch's snoring and the sun streaking through the bedroom window. She had dreamed of being Alice in Wonderland and drinking a magic potion that made her very small, and then eating a magic cake that made her very tall, and then very small again after taking another sip of the potion.

If only it had ended with her being taller. Fuzzy-brained and now stuck with an earworm from the White Rabbit—"I'm late! I'm late! For a very important date!"—she swung her legs over the bed and, for a moment, viewed the distance from her feet to the floor. *Damn, in my next life I'm coming back taller or else! At least April got Oran's genes.*

Then it hit her: April and the kids. This morning. Nine a.m. Was she late?

She breathed a sigh of relief; she had a whole hour. Best not to fritter it away in daydreaming— an oft-heard accusation leftover from childhood; while she still denied it, she knew it to be true.

She saw the journal lying on the bed. Damn, another good intention fallen by the wayside. *Focus and prioritize, Villia.* She needed time for breakfast and to steel herself for the great April tsunami.

She followed her morning routine and took her breakfast under the table. Pooch joined her.

"Lover of Cream of Wheat," Villia said, putting a spoonful of the coveted cereal in Pooch's doggie bowl. One swipe of a tongue the size of a snow shovel and the cereal disappeared.

Villia rubbed his head. "Now, I'm counting on you to help entertain the kids. I have no idea of what to do with them for a whole week."

"Well, you could lock them in a closet and shove an organic pizza under the door every now and then," Pooch suggested snarkily.

"What a mean thing to say! They're not bad kids. Actually, I'm hoping this will be an opportunity for us to grow closer." She added under her breath: "And I think it will be good for them to be out from under April's materialistic influence for a while."

"I heard that," said Pooch.

"Humph! You hear everything. I do trust you'll be on your best behavior while they're here."

"Cross my paws and hope to die, stick a Milk-Bone in my eye."

Villia sighed. "Just my luck—I have a talking dog, and he's a comedian."

"Sadly, since you are the only one who can hear me, my talents don't reach their full potential."

The clock chimed the half hour. Thirty minutes to splashdown.

She heard a key in the lock, a shove on the door, and the threesome burst inside.

April's voice rang out: "Mother, we're here!"

Villia Flatbottom peeked out from under the table. Her spoon teetered in the near-empty ceramic bowl before falling to the floor. Pooch didn't waste a minute before cleaning the spoon and cereal bowl.

"Mother, why are you under the table?" April tapped her foot irritably.

"Because my mother and I used to eat our Cream of Wheat right here, and right here I shall be.

Besides, you're early."

The children bounced under the table and began to sing the Cream of Wheat song, taught to them by their Grannie the last time they visited.

"Lots of lumps?" they asked in unison.

"Why, of course! Lumps my mam made for me and lumps it shall always be." She whispered to the kids: "I think your mother is annoyed with me. Come, let's not upset her."

And with that, Villia Flatbottom untangled her legs and scooted backwards while holding her hands on top of her head to prevent any banging. She dared not chance losing any additional gray matter.

Pooch, the dog of many breeds, jumped on April and slobbered her hands with his Bernese Mountain Dog kisses.

"Yuck! Mother, could you please keep your wooly mammoth at bay?" said April with distaste as she washed her hands at the sink. "I'm early because I've got a plane to catch and you know that morning traffic to LAX." She dried her hands and added: "Could we sit *at* the table and talk?"

"Of course. Emilee and Ethan, have you had breakfast?"

Emilee said, "Just a breakfast bar."

"I'm starving," said Ethan.

"Look inside the breadbox and you'll find muffins. Milk is in the fridge."

"Is it organic?" asked Emilee.

"I milked the cow myself. Coffee, April?"

"No, I'll grab a Starbucks at the airport. Mother, please, can we focus? I've really got to get going!"

Villia sat at the table while April shuffled through a stack of papers. "I've created a portfolio for each of the children—their routines, allergies and emergency numbers."

Villia felt her attention commandeered by the White Rabbit's song that refused to leave her brain.

"You have my cell phone number; call if anything comes up...*anything*. Mother, are you paying attention?"

Villia nodded.

April's voice softened. "Michael will be joining me in Paris." There was a slight catch in her voice. "We really need this time," she whispered. "Things are tense between us."

She cleared her throat and stood up. "Emilee, Ethan, I'm leaving. Are you under the table?"

Emilee said, "We're in the forest and Ethan is about to get eaten alive by a grizzly."

Ethan was making little sobs.

"Emilee, stop teasing your brother."

"Hold on, Ethan. Grannie is coming to shoo that grizzly away."

April threw up her hands. "I give up! Please, Mother, don't fill their heads with stories about that ridiculous imaginary island."

Villia muttered, "You still haven't forgiven me, have you?"

"It's inconsequential," she said, surveying the room with a realtor's greedy eye. "Mother, why aren't you selling this house? Five acres in Palos Verdes, with its own natural harbor, a boat dock, and boathouse to boot. Why, why...it's worth millions! I could have it appraised when I return. Think about it. You could live like a queen. Travel if you want. See the world. Invest. Why, I could develop this property myself!"

For a moment Villia fancied she saw dollar signs appear in April's bulging eyes, just like a Scrooge McDuck cartoon she remembered from her childhood.

"I can tell you're not listening. Just this once, don't let me down. Camp, next week. The bus and clean clothes. And make sure you follow their food lists."

"I promise. Now have a good trip and leave all your worries right here with me."

April shouted out as she left the house: "Bye, kids! Be good for Grannie!"

Villia flipped through the portfolios. *Children's lives reduced to schedules, diets, and fears of possible calamities. I failed my child.*

"Grannie, Grannie!" she heard from under the table. "We want a story.... *puh-leeeeze!*"

April was adamant about not talking about the island, but what about reading from a journal written by an ancestor? Surely that couldn't do any harm.

"Emilee and Ethan, I have a story idea. How about the two of you come out from under the table, help with some chores, and then I'll have a surprise story for you."

She saw two faces peeking out from under the table.

"Chores?" Ethan frowned.

"Why, yes, but guaranteed to be fun."

"How can a chore be fun?" asked Emilee suspiciously.

"We'll pick wild blueberries that grow along the fence and afterwards we'll sit under the trees, eat the blueberries, and watch our fingers turn blue. Have your fingers ever turned blue before?"

The kids shook their heads.

"Are blueberries on my allergy list?" asked Ethan.

Villia pretended to look. "Not that I can see."

Emilee chimed in: "Will the blue go away before Mother returns?"

"Guaranteed!"

"What's our story surprise?" asked Ethan.

"I am the very proud owner of a journal written more than 150 years ago by your ancestor, Branwyn. If you help with chores we'll spend time every day learning about her adventures."

"Can't we go to the mall?" whined Emilee.

"We'll see."

"For Mother and Father, we'll see means no," Ethan moaned.

"For me it's a true maybe. Now, let's get moving. If you pick enough berries we'll bake a pie for dessert."

Their hands did indeed turn blue, as well as their faces and shirts. *Strike one! I've ruined their Neiman Marcus shirts. At the rate I'm going, we might have to hit the mall before the week is up. Wonder if April will notice they're wearing Old Navy when I give them back to her?*

She was certain it was midnight, but the clock said nine p.m. She threw out a telepathic message: "Liar!"

Baths, bedtime snacks, and two kids in bed. Not bad for an old fart; these two were easy-peasy. *I don't know why April complains so much.*

"We were so busy baking we didn't get around to Branwyn's diary. How about a bedtime reading?"

"Yes, Grannie, yes!" Emilee enthused.

Ethan said, "Read slowly so the story lasts way past our bedtime."

Villia smiled. *These are delightful children who just need their imagination tickled a bit. And I'm the one to do it.*

"Branwyn's adventures start, I suppose, when she was born. And that's true for everyone, for life should always be an adventure. She began to keep a journal when she was twelve—"

"I'm almost twelve!" Emilee interrupted.

"No, you're not!" Ethan protested. "You're only ten!"

"Going on eleven! And *you're* only eight!"

"And three quarters!" Ethan growled.

"Children! Do you want me to read this to you, or not?" Chastened, the kids sprouted halos and went mute. "Now, get cozy and be as snug as bugs in a rug."

Ethan and Emilee snuggled into their beds, pulling the covers tightly around their necks. Villia opened the first journal and began to read.

CHAPTER 7

March 13, 1847. Hello, my journal! My name is Branwyn Rees, I'm twelve years old and I live on a farm near Newtown, Wales. My mam gave you to me for my birthday. And a new set of pencils! I'm going to ask for a pen and inkwell for my next birthday. Mam told me a journal is a good place to write about what I see, do, and feel.

Tad gave me a horse and a brand new saddle. I love my horse; I've named him Enfys, which means Rainbow. You see, when I was born Mam told me a rainbow appeared in the sky and she said that was a sign that the gods and goddesses had blessed me.

I had to pretend I liked the saddle, but it was a sidesaddle for girls. Tad says I must be a proper lady, but I like to wear trousers and ride with my older brothers, Phillip and Simon. Even though I am only twelve, I can outrace them anytime! My tad, who prefers to be called Father, is named Lewis and wants us to grow up to be proper Brits, speaking the King's English and having stiff upper lips, whatever that means. My mam's name is Enid, which means a soulful, quiet woman. And that she is. Although, at times, I think she is also sad.

I was baptized in the Church but Mam believes in the old ways—in gods and goddesses, and that everything in the world is made up of spirits. Even rocks! It might seem strange to others, but I believe it because my mam said it is so.

Mam has a secret place in the attic filled with herbs and potions.

Tad never goes up there, and my two brothers don't know anything about it either. Mam says the attic is only for us women because we are healers.

When I was little, I think five, I got very sick and they had to send for the doctor. He shook his head, put his hand on Mam's arm and said, "I'm so very sorry."

Mam said she didn't cry, but went up to the attic and made a potion handed down by her great-great-grandmother. The next morning my fever was gone and I was hungry!

Mam tells me that we are always surrounded by light, but all too often we shut out the light and only see the dark. And that can be why we get sick.

I had a birthday party today, with twelve children, all family friends and cousins except for my best friend, Dylan. Dylan is two years older; we grew up together and we go to school together.

I can't remember ever being without Dylan. He and his tad work and live on our farm, and when there is little farm work to be done, they take to the rivers to catch fish.

Tad wasn't happy about Dylan being at my party, and I heard him having cross words with Mam. He thinks Dylan is beneath our family. "We are landed gentry!" he shouted. Mam responded quietly to his sharpness, as is her way. But she can be like a boulder that sits on top of a high mountain, impossible to move. Mam said, "It matters not, as long as Dylan is of a good heart."

I will cry if I can't have Dylan for my best friend.

Before my party Tad took me aside and reminded me to call him Father or Papa like the British children do. He told me soon, I will go to a finishing school to learn how to be a proper lady.

I'm not sure what being a proper lady means. I hope it doesn't mean I can't climb trees with Dylan or ride my horse wearing pants and using the same saddle as my brothers.

Goodbye for now, dear journal. I think we shall be the best of friends.

∞

"Well," said Villia, "that's the end of Branwyn's first entry."

"Read more, Grannie!" urged Ethan.

"Yeah, Grannie, don't stop now!" Emilee echoed.

Villia was pleased to see their interest but maintained a poker face. "One more, then it's lights out."

$$\infty$$

April 20, 1847. Dylan had to leave school before summer break to help his tad with the farm work. Dylan is fourteen, and must now work instead of going to school. He doesn't seem to mind; he likes to see things grow and he loves being on boats and fishing.

He held my hand as we walked back to my father's lands; he to work in the fields and me to the big house we live in. Dylan's hands are rough from working so hard, but his heart is soft and tender.

We walked down the same path we have taken since my first day of school and stopped to rest at the willow tree. Usually, we would climb the tree to sit together on a strong limb, but today we only stood under its canopy.

I will never forget our words.

Dylan said, "I know the ways of the land and the ways of the sea. I can read, write, and do some numbers; that's more than my tad can do. I'm not ever going to be a fancy gent like your tad and brothers, but I can make my way in this world."

He looked down and scuffed the dirt with the toe of his shoe.

"Branwyn," he said, "I want to go to America."

Usually Dylan calls me Bran, but when he's serious his voice deepens and he uses my full name.

I felt my throat tighten and I couldn't swallow. "Why, Dylan?"

"A man can be free there. Here, I will always be like one of your tad's plough horses and nothing more."

"When will you go?"

"I'll have to work first to save for the crossing. I got a job working on the flatbottom boats. You know how they go down the river to the sea?"

I couldn't speak for the lump in my throat and only nodded my head.

"I want to learn all that I can about building and sailing boats." He stopped talking and looked in my eyes. "Bran, can we still meet, sometimes? Maybe after Church?"

"Mam usually gives me freedom after Church. We only go to please Tad. Dylan, soon I'll be leaving for finishing school. My tad wants to make me into a lady."

Dylan paid me the highest compliment when he said, "Bran, in my eyes, you already are a lady." Then I saw his eyes fill with tears. He leaned over and kissed me on my cheek. "I'll be here every Sunday after Church, waiting for you." His face turned bright red. "Branwyn, after I go to America, will you wait for me?"

I didn't know what to say but I knew my heart would always belong to Dylan.

We walked to where the road split, Dylan going to his world and I to mine. I turned and said, "I will wait."

That night when Mam came to tuck me in, I told her about Dylan. She said, "You are still young, and your heart may change."

I started to tell her no, but she hushed me.

"Or it may not. Be true to your heart, no matter what. Be true to your heart."

I thought Mam was very sad. She didn't cry, but it was the way she spoke her words.

Villia closed the journal. "All right, my darlings, it's way past your bedtime."

Emilee's eyes widened. "It's a love story. Oooh, I just love, love stories! Did Branwyn and Dylan marry, Grannie?"

"Well, why don't we just wait and see? We'll read more tomorrow. Perhaps instead of television. What do you think?"

In unison, Emilee and Ethan screamed, "Yayyyyy!"

CHAPTER 8

Villia stretched and yawned loudly. She turned over to look at the clock. Almost nine a.m. Pooch, asleep at the foot of the bed, was breathing heavily and his back legs were twitching.

Well, she thought, *aren't we a couple of slugabeds! Is this what it's like getting older?* Villia stretched, looked at the clock again, and snuggled back under the covers. No need to get up just yet; she and Pooch had the house to themselves and the whole day ahead ...

She bolted upright. She'd forgotten about Emilee and Ethan! The quiet was deafening. She knew the dangers of kids and a quiet house.

Her bedroom door creaked open. Emilee and Ethan stood there with dark blue grins plastered across their faces.

"Surprise, Grannie!" said Ethan, balancing a plate filled with lop-sided blueberry muffins.

"Surprise, Grannie!" said Emilee, holding a steaming cup of coffee.

Villia wasn't sure if she should laugh or cry. Traces of flour clung to their hair, faces, and pajamas. Blueberry stains made for some unusual, interpretive patterns against their white, Chinese-inspired cotton pajamas sporting mandarin collars and wood buttons.

More ruined outfits! Oh, well. "My goodness, how did you manage this wonderful feast?"

Ethan said, "Mother sent us both to culinary classes for kids, and I knew how to use your oven."

"And I," bragged Emilee, "found your recipe box."

"Well, you both did a fabulous job." She patted the bed. "Come join me. I'm assuming you've already eaten."

"How can you tell?" asked Ethan.

"Just a hunch."

"Grannie, will you read some more from the journal?" asked Emilee, sitting on the edge of the bed.

"Emilee loves a love story," said Ethan, doing one of his famous eye rolls.

Villia sipped her coffee to wash down the bite of muffin she'd taken. "No eye rolling allowed in this house. Use your words instead."

"You sound just like Mother," chimed in Emilee.

Could it be, my Ebrill/April has some of me inside her?

"Here's the plan for today. I'll have my coffee—delicious, by the way. And a muffin or two—equally delicious—and then we'll have chores. And then we'll spend time with Branwyn's journal."

Emilee protested, "Chores again?"

"Yechh!" Ethan concurred.

"Ah, my dear grandchildren, life is run on chores." *Even if I hate them myself. I must take advantage of this captive labor.* "By the looks of the two of you, I think it shall begin with kitchen cleaning, followed by showers. I believe a picnic lunch under the willow trees will be the perfect spot to learn more about Branwyn and Dylan."

There is an unwritten rule in the Flatbottom family that every picnic must begin with a blanket placed upon Mother Earth, followed by the grand unveiling of an overflowing wicker picnic basket. Emilee and Ethan, while spreading the blanket underneath the willow tree, had a bit of an argument over where it should go, but finally settled on a place where the shallow tree roots were most exposed.

"A willow tree is where Branwyn and Dylan meet, so the blanket has to go under the tree even if there are bumps," explained Emilee.

Ethan added, "Bumps it is, because life can be bumpy. But see, Grannie? In between the bumps are places to sit."

From the mouths of babes.

He paused, and Villia waited for more words of wisdom. "As long as you have a small butt."

Both kids broke out in giggles, which Villia was helpless not to join in.

Villia opened the wicker basket and gazed wide-eyed at its contents. She had purposely looked the other way while Ethan and Emilee foraged in the kitchen and packed lunch.

"You both did a marvelous job! We shall have a glorious feast, along with a toast to Branwyn and Dylan. Now, before we read from the journal let's see what surprises we have in this basket."

"I couldn't find plastic wrap," said Emilee.

"That's because it doesn't exist in our house. I do see that you discovered wax paper. Excellent! So, are you kids really allergic to almost everything in the world?" she asked as she pulled out sandwiches wrapped in wax paper.

Ethan glanced around, as if looking for spies. "Promise not to tell Mother?" he said sotto voce.

"Maybe..."

"Almond butter is on the list, but we trade with our friends in school all the time."

"I see we have almond butter sandwiches, along with Grannie's homemade apricot jam and her famous homemade bread. Plus, apples, cookies, chips, and water. And speaking of cookies, how did three boxes of Trader Joe's Cookie Thins find their way here?"

"Oh, we saw them in the pantry and just couldn't resist," said Emilee. "Not on our suspected allergy lists, thank goodness."

Ethan added, "Grannie, do you have an ice cream thing? Because your freezer has more than the grocery store."

Villia blushed, ignored the question, and dug deeper into the basket.

"Oh, and look at this...how did Hershey's Kisses find their way into the basket?" she said with a wink.

"Uh-oh—chocolate's on our allergy lists," Emilee lamented.

"Yeah, big time," Ethan agreed.

"If you break out, I'll call 911," Villia said, passing out the food. "Now, who would like to give the toast to our ancestors?"

"I will, I will!" yelled Ethan.

"I wanted to do it," Emilee sulked.

"Too bad. I called dibs." Ethan raised his stainless steel water bottle up high. As Kermit the Frog said, "Take a look above you, discover the view. If you haven't noticed, please do, please do."

Villia chuckled. "That's very appropriate, Ethan. A sendoff for Bran and Dylan, who, although facing separation, must each find their way. I shall skim through a number of short entries. Hmm.... she hates homework and despises vegetables." Villia continued to turn the pages. "Ah, here we go, the next entry that picks up on Branwyn's story is in early summer."

July 2, 1847. I hate my life. Everything I love is being torn away. Tad came into my room and saw me writing in my journal. He scowled and said I shouldn't keep secrets from him. I fear he will steal my words and dreams away.

Mam said it's best if we hide my journal in the attic and then I can write in it when Tad's away.

Late this afternoon, I met with Dylan and he told me he is saving all his earnings for his voyage to America.

"Look, Bran." He held up a leather pouch stuffed with coins and bills. "Soon it will be enough for a new start in America. I can work my passage across, and with enough money I'll be able to buy my own boat."

He was so happy and I was so sad.

He reached out and touched my face.

"You look so sad. Please don't be. I know we're young, and I know we'll be far away from each other, but will you wait for me? Will you be my betrothed?"

He took a ring made of bone from his pocket.

"Would that I could give you a gold ring, but 'tis far too dear. I myself carved this ring from the antler of a stag. I was in the forest last fall and saw a white buck shedding his antlers by rubbing them against a tree. I hid in a bower till he left. It's said the antler of a white buck is filled with magic. Will you take this ring?"

"Dylan, keep it safe for me. The time will come when I won't have to hide it from my tad."

I felt no one could tell me who to love or who to marry. My tad could beat me, but he could not make me stand up in church and say "I do" to someone I do not love.

I pointed to the sky and said, "Look, the sun is beginning to set. I promise to wait no matter how many sunsets I will see or how many suitors my father will force upon me."

Dylan took my hand in his. "Branwyn Rees, I pledge my heart to you for all eternity. Once I'm in America, I promise to write and send for you as soon as I can." He slipped the ring in his pocket. "I'll keep it safe until we can become husband and wife."

And with that he kissed me, not on my cheek as he did before, but the tenderest of kisses on my lips. It was then I knew there would be no man in my life except Dylan.

Villia stopped reading. "I read this journal many years ago and had forgotten about the intensity of their love. Perhaps I should read ahead to make sure it's age appropriate."

"Grannie," said Emilee, "you can't leave us with a cliffhanger. Keep reading! Branwyn's journal is positively binge-worthy."

Villia was bemused. "Binge-worthy? What in the world does that mean?"

"You mean you've never heard of binge-watching a TV show? Boy, Grannie, you are behind the times, just like Mother says." Emilee's hand shot to her mouth. "Oops. I probably shouldn't have said that. Sorry!"

"Apology accepted," said Villia, who was a trifle insulted. "Suppose you enlighten your old-fashioned grandma about this binge-watching thing."

"Here's how it goes. You have six seasons of a series to watch. And each season has maybe twelve episodes. Each season leaves you hanging. Instead of having to wait months and months for the next season, you save them all up and do a marathon of the whole series. It's loads of fun! I do it with my best friend, Shawnta."

"And your parents know about this?"

"Grannie, did you tell *your* parents everything?"

"Point well taken. And you, Ethan? You've been awfully quiet. Is Branwyn's journal, well, too spicy for you?"

"So far, so good."

Emilee tittered. "That's one of Ethan's favorite idioms. Collecting them is kinda his hobby."

Ethan smiled shyly. "I found Father's book on famous idioms and...and..."

"Go on, Ethan. Grannie won't laugh."

"I memorized most of them." Ethan closed his eyes. "Page 128. James Kelly's Scottish Proverbs, 1731: 'So far, so good. So much is done to good purpose.'"

"Why, that's marvelous, Ethan!" said Villia. "And your parents know of this hobby?"

"Grannie, did you tell your parents everything?"

"Seems like we just covered that, but I'll take the fifth on that one. I think we can continue on one condition. If you feel at all uncomfortable, you'll let me know. Agreed?"

"Agreed!"

Oh well, the road to hell is paved with good intentions. Here goes!

"There is a long gap between entries, and it looks like a couple of pages were torn out."

Emilee said suspiciously, "Why would she tear out pages?"

"There are some things we may never know. Perhaps she wrote something she regretted or didn't want anyone else to ever read...not even us."

Emilee made a fist and pounded the ground. "I hate secrets! When I become an FBI agent I'll solve everything—even Branwyn's missing pages."

"I think you shall be a wonderful FBI agent. Perhaps the next entry will offer some explanation..."

∞

November 1,1847. I have missed you, my dear journal, but I had to wait until Tad left the house before I could once again write upon your pages.

I am most unhappy. Tad would not let me return to school to be with all my friends. He said it was filled with ruffians and I need to be with my own class of people. I got angry and spoke out. Oh, I must confess I shouted, "My own class?"

I got a hard slap across my face for yelling and now I'm being tutored at home until it's time for me to go to finishing school.

I have three tutors: one for music, one for manners, and one for poetry and literature. Tad says he will make a proper lady out of me if it's the last thing he does. I find it so difficult to concentrate on my studies. My tutors have administered several painful and humiliating canings on my palms when they've caught me mooning over Dylan. When Dylan and I have our children, I swear we will never stoop to such a barbaric practice!

The tutors are away on Sundays, and after Church, I meet Dylan under the willow tree. Dylan is changing. He is taller and has soft golden fuzz on his face. I touched his cheek and told him there were a few hairs that felt like the bristly brush I use on my horse, Enfys. We both laughed, but the next week the fuzz and whiskers were gone. He told me his tad had shown him how to shave. Again I felt his face; it was smooth, and I wished he would kiss me again.

I am changing too. My chest, once as flat as Dylan's, is beginning to blossom. Mam sat me down one day and explained what it means to be a woman. Most of what she told me I already knew from watching farm animals. But then she said, "Only women can bring life into this world." And then I felt special.

Tad and Mam have been talking about sending me to Mrs. Strickland's Finishing School for Young Ladies. I think I shall indeed be "finished" if I must leave my home and Dylan. Mam told me that she went to that very same school and met the most wonderful friend. She said, rather sadly, that they don't see much of each other anymore.

Mam's eyes welled with tears because she misses her friend so very much.

How will I live without Mam and Dylan? I hope Tad decides not to send me away.

∞

Villia stopped reading. "There is a final entry in this journal and then nothing but blank pages. Any thoughts or feelings?"

Ethan picked up a napkin and dabbed his eyes. "I would hit my father in the stomach."

Emilee said, "Really? If our father was like Branwyn's tad, you'd be dead!"

"Then I would throw up all over his feet."

Emilee looked at her grandmother. "Ethan hates to vomit."

"What would you do, Emilee?"

"I'd run away. I wouldn't go to some stupid school. I'd stow away on a ship and find Dylan wherever he was, and we'd live happily ever after."

"You are both very creative, and filled with passion. I would expect no less from my grandchildren."

"What would you do, Grannie?"

"I would take my life's journey, no matter how many twists and turns it may take." Villia's mind drifted away. *I do believe that is what I have done...*

"Emilee to Grannie...Emilee to Grannie..."

After a long moment Villia detected the child's hand waving in front of her face. "Oh, pardon me, I did go to la-la land, didn't I? I do believe you two have given me much to think about. Let me see, according to this next entry, Branwyn is now thirteen. Shall I continue?"

Emilee scrunched up her face. "Well, duh! This is better than any old Lifetime movie."

∞

August 31, 1848. Today, I am being sent away to finishing school. Mam said, "Don't throw the time away. There are things you can learn that may help you later on."

I turned away to hide my tears. Mam turned me around hard by my arms and said sternly, "Look at me."

I cried. "Dylan has left for America and now I'm being taken away from you."

I looked into Mam's eyes and I could see they were red from crying.

"This is but a skirmish. Don't fall into a trap; you must play the game well, my girl. You will be watched and your father will know of every slip. Trust me, I will not let you down."

Tad called me into his study to say goodbye. He sat behind his desk with a half-empty decanter of port wine and a full glass by his side.

"Your mother's job is to see you off to school and visit upon occasion to make sure you become a proper lady. My job is finding you a suitable husband. By suitable, I don't mean someone you will love. Marriage has nothing to do with love; it has to do with conveniences and duty. Duty to your family and to our future wealth."

I longed to yell at him. Was I nothing more than one of the animals sent to the slaughterhouse or to be traded? As much as I hated him, I said nothing, for if I told him what was in my heart, it could come back to Dylan's tad, Mawrth, whose livelihood comes from my father's farm.

Tad had the oddest smile on his face, as if he was gloating over my predicament. "I am glad to see that you put that childish journal away. You must face reality. No more wearing your brother's old trousers and running wild."

He slammed his fist on the table and looked at me. "You will be tamed. Girls are of little use, other than marrying into wealth and bearing heirs. That is your fate. Make the best of it. Now go."

My hands were clenched in rage as I turned to leave and I could feel bile rising in my throat.

Mam was waiting outside his study. I could tell that she had heard everything.

"It's time," said Mam. "The coach is waiting outside. I will visit you every few months and if a letter comes from Dylan, I'll bring it to you."

Mam took you, my dear journal, away from me—my only link to my thoughts and feelings about Dylan. "Your journal will be safe with me," she said. "I shall bring it with me when I visit."

I reached out for you. "Please, Mam, just a few more minutes with my journal."

Mam handed you to me. "I'll tell the coachman to wait. I promise you, I will not let you go the way your father plans."

I wrote this entry, the last words I will be able to write until I return on holiday.

Farewell, my journal. I am now on my way to Mrs. Strickland's Finishing School for Young Ladies.

Emilee asked out of the blue, "Grannie, why is your last name Flatbottom?"

"I want to know too," echoed Ethan.

"My goodness, but you are an inquisitive pair!"

"Emilee is a super snoop."

She elbowed her brother.

"Ouch!"

"I like to think of myself as a detective. A *superlative* detective."

Ethan said, "We're curious 'cause we saw one of Mother's old report cards and *her* name was Flatbottom."

Okay, Villia, get yourself out of this one.

"I suppose in my time, in the prehistoric era before binge-watching was a 'thing,' we would say 'stay tuned.' Now, enough of this lazing around." Villia slapped her legs and stood up. "There are chores that must be done."

"Again?" the two kids asked in unison.

"I think you'll like this one."

"I'm suspicious," remarked Emilee.

"Have either of you noticed the cats that visit us?"

They shook their heads no.

"Well, then, have you seen the fence that surrounds our property?"

They nodded yes.

"One day, some years ago, a few blocks came loose and made a gap that went unnoticed. No one came to repair them, and it seems that the feral cats liked our property better than the housing development. I keep their food outside of the old adobe in bearproof trash cans. You, my dear grandchildren, will now learn how to set out the food and water for some dozen cats."

"Aren't they dirty?"

"Probably no dirtier than us after we've been picking blueberries, or any other animal that's out and about."

They trudged past the willow tree to the adobe house.

Ethan whispered to Emilee, "This is the witch's house from 'Hansel and Gretel.'"

"Is not! Grannie, what's this? A playhouse?"

"It is most definitely not a playhouse, and it is most definitely off limits."

"I might be allergic to cats," said Ethan.

"Piffle! So far your allergies seem to have disappeared." Villia made a sweeping gesture. "See these bowls? Line them up all along the fence next to the water spigots. Then we'll fill them with the best cat food money can buy. You kids do that while I dash back to the house and grab a few cat treats."

Once back in the house, Villia stopped to take a breather. *Breathe in, breathe out.* She could feel panic rising throughout her system. *The kids are keeping me on my toes. Close call with the kids asking about the adobe house. I may be having a sugar drop.*

She opened the freezer door. *Gad, I really overdid the ice cream thing.* She reached for the box of Mini Stroopwafel Ice Cream Sandwiches. She surveyed the label; words began to pop out in three dimensions: mini...created in Gouda...thin waffles...10 ounces for the entire box! She selected four to match the number of locks on the adobe house. She took a healthy bite of the first one and closed her eyes, letting the butter fat and sugar ooze through her system. Then she scarfed down the other three without blinking. Reinvigorated, she scooped up the cat snacks and returned to her outdoor project of keeping the kids out of trouble.

∞

She stopped...she looked...she wasn't sure if she should laugh or cry.

"I see by your appearances that the water spigots are working just fine," she commented, taking in their head to toe mud splatters.

"We had a mud fight while you were gone," said Ethan sheepishly.

"Yeah, and I lost," Emilee muttered.

Villia knew that "are we in trouble?" look. She reached for the hose and, turning it on spray, pointed it directly at Emilee and Ethan.

They laughed and frolicked, slipping and sliding in the mud.

"She started it!" said Ethan, a big grin plastered across his face.

"No, he started it!" said Emilee, trying to hide the laughter that was bubbling up.

"Either way, it's a job well done that deserves some treat, but not until you rinse and dry off."

The children exchanged incredulous looks.

"A treat? You mean you're not mad?" Emilee asked. "Mother would absolutely *kill* us if we got this dirty at home!"

"Your mother has a lot to learn about children," Villia muttered. She sat down on one of the chairs next to the cherry trees. "As soon as you're dry, come join me. The cherries aren't ready yet, but I have apricots and homemade granola bars. And..." She reached into a Trader Joe's shopping bag. "Ta-da! I have Branwyn's second journal."

CHAPTER 9

The children capered about merrily, chanting, "Read it! Read it!" as Villia unwrapped Branwyn's journal. "Patience, children, patience! It's quite fragile, you see. It has been wrapped in this brown paper for many years. I remember my mother reading it to me, just as I'm reading it to you."

"Did you read it to Mother?" asked Ethan.

She shook her head. *I wanted to, oh, how I wanted to share it with her.* "Not everyone is interested in the same things. It's important to offer your children a taste of many things in life and then let them follow their own dreams. What about your dreams?"

Ethan cast his eyes down and murmured, "I want to be an ice sculptor."

Villia lifted his chin up with her fingertips and looked into his eyes. "A worthy calling. Say it proudly!"

Ethan grinned. "I want to be an ice sculptor!"

"There, that's better." She looked at Emilee. "If memory serves, you want to be an FBI agent."

"That's right! I didn't think you'd remember."

"Child, you cut me to the quick! Your grannie is not so old as that. Both very interesting choices. Now, dig in!"

"These are great snacks, Grannie," said Emilee. "I'm not even asking if they're on my allergy list."

"Me neither."

"The granola bars are one of my favorite recipes. We'll bake more tomorrow. I battle with the squirrels for those delectable fruits, and most of the time I lose. I was lucky to get five ripe apricots." She laughed. "Save one for me!"

"Here's a juicy one," said Ethan. "Catch!"

Villia held out her hands; Ethan tossed and she caught.

"Mmm, dee-lish!" said Villia, after taking a bite. "Now, shall we see where life takes Branwyn?"

"Yes, let's!" said Emilee.

"I hope it doesn't get too mushy," Ethan declared.

Villia opened the journal to the first entry. "Let me see ... Branwyn has been at Mrs. Strickland's Finishing School for Young Ladies for a few months and has now returned home for the Christmas holiday."

∞

December 13, 1848. Hello, my dear new journal. I'm home! Mam thought I should start over fresh and got me you! I have been away for four miserable months. Mam came to visit me one time and told me she was planning on spending a few days afterwards with her old school friend, Madam Izobelle Latham.

On my first day at Mrs. Strickland's all the new students gathered together in the main parlor. We introduced ourselves and sat down for tea.

She corrected us for slumping and I got the most corrections. At least I was the best at something. Mrs. Strickland frowned and I had to wonder if she would ever smile. "The goal of this school is to help you become refined wives and mothers," she declared in a nasally voice dripping with snobbery.

I almost choked on my tea but remembered Mam's words to play the game.

"No gulping," she said, looking directly at me. And that was just the first day.

I hate this school! We are drilled relentlessly on how to dress, to be respectful to our elders and to never raise our voices under any circumstances. The unspoken attitude is that women should be seen and not heard. Also, and most disconcertingly, we have to learn how to build up a man's ego by flattering him. We are being groomed to be servile, empty-headed, second-class citizens, with no purpose in life but to please the male sex. Oh, how these tedious exercises make my blood boil!

Tea time is not about slurping my tea, gulping down cookies and running outside to ride like the wind. No, we must practice receiving visitors for tea "with utmost gentility," as that insufferable Mrs. Strickland terms it. And all the while I'm pouring tea from the kettle into a cup, I'm praying my stomach doesn't grumble. I couldn't seem to get the pouring quite right and cracked at least three teacups. The other girls giggled at my clumsy attempts.

I hate what I have to wear—a corset that makes me feel as if I will faint or, worse, that I should retch. Would you believe the school insists that I ride sidesaddle? Mrs. Strickland says that is the only way a "decent" woman rides a horse. Forgive me, dear journal, but I wish a horse would trample her!

Mam said I will have to keep up the pretense of being a lady because Tad will be watching me. I can pretend as long as it leads me to Dylan. While I am home on holiday I will go to the willow tree and imagine that Dylan is here with me.

My brothers are also home for Christmas. They are both studying at Oxford University and have given up believing in the old ways. Tad talks to them all the time, asking who they know and what they will bring to our family in the way of a dowry.

The other night during supper, Tad looked at me and, for once, he wasn't scowling. "The school has molded you into a proper young lady, and I'm pleased," he remarked. "Soon, I will find a suitable husband for you."

Then he turned to the boys and said, "You see, women have their place in society. Between the three of you we shall increase our land holdings and, more importantly, our status in the world."

My brothers both politely clapped. I was fuming but as Mam had said, "Play the game well."

Mam didn't flinch, but she cast her eyes my way; I knew we had our secret, but had not yet a plan.

∞

Emilee asked, "Did they get a plan?"

"You must wait to find out. It would be like reading the end of a novel before you have finished the beginning and middle."

Ethan snorted. "Emilee does that all the time."

"I can't help it," said Emilee. "I get stomachaches if I have to wait."

"All about instant gratification, eh? One day you'll appreciate the sweet agony of anticipation."

"Huh?"

"Never mind."

Ethan whispered to Emilee. She whispered back.

"What's the whispering about?" Villia asked.

"It's kind of a secret, and Ethan's not sure if he should tell you."

"What did you tell him?"

"I told him to spill."

"You heard your sister: spill."

Ethan, hands in pockets, eyes on floor, rocked the toe of his right shoe. Finally he blurted out: "Some of the kids at school call me a name."

Villia could feel her blood beginning to boil.

"You know my allergy list, Grannie?"

"Yes."

"It's really a list of foods that can make me fat. The kids call me pudgy-wudgy."

Villia stroked her chin in thought. "So, the allergy list is your mom's way of trying to protect you."

"I guess, except it doesn't work."

Emilee chimed in: "Mother went to school and talked to the principal and the teachers, but the kids are sneaky. They know how to call other kids names without getting caught."

"You know it's not nice to call people names, don't you?" Villia asked.

"Sure! Mother taught us that," said Emilee.

Well, good for her. "I was looking at your camp registrations. Ethan, you're in the camp for...overweight children."

The boy hung his head. "You mean the fat camp. That's what everybody calls it."

Emilee said, "And I'm in the gifted kids camp. I don't want to go! I know it's an honor and all to be called gifted, but it makes me feel funny. I don't want anybody to think that I think I'm better than them. Does that make sense, Grannie?"

Villia smiled. "Certainly it does, my darling."

"We talked it over last night," said Ethan. "Grannie, can we cancel camp and stay with you?"

"We'll do extra chores," Emilee volunteered. *"Puh-leeeeze?"*

She looked at Emilee and Ethan, who at this point looked like two mud-splattered lost waifs, then glanced at the journal, still open and sitting on her lap.

"I think that's a bit of a stretch, even for me. Camp stays in place. Look, you can either moan and groan or make the most of the time we have together. What's it going to be?"

Ethan sighed. "Under protest, I vote for making the most of our time together."

Don't let me burst out laughing. Under protest? I'll have to email that one to Oran.

Emilee said, "I vote for that too."

"Well, it's unanimous them," Villia agreed. "At least *this* little democracy works!"

Perhaps there was a reason for this journal coming back to life after all these years. There are lessons for the kids and reminders for me.

"In spite of hosing you down, you're both quite caked with mud," Villia remarked. "I think you need a second hosing before you set foot in the house. Let's do that and then get cozy. There'll be a chill in the air in about an hour; it happens most evenings, being so close to the ocean. Makes for a perfect evening for a fire and reading words from the past."

The children sprang upon Villia and smothered her in hugs and kisses.

"Now look what you've done! Gone and got me dirty!" she cried in mock protest.

Ethan grabbed the hose. A mischievous fire glowed in his eyes. "Then I guess we'll have to hose you off too!"

CHAPTER 10

"You both did a great job of cleaning the kitchen and yourselves," Villia remarked. "In fact, everything sparkles, including me."

"We didn't fight once," said Ethan.

"Indeed! You've done so well, I think tomorrow we'll have a lesson on clothes washing."

"No mall?" sighed Emilee.

"Are you pouting?"

"That's how she gets her way," Ethan said sarcastically.

"Is not!"

"Is so!"

Villia held up her hand and shushed her bickering grandchildren.

"Would you like to know something about your mother when she was just a bit older than you?"

Their eyes grew wide and their heads bobbed.

"There were malls, but can you guess where we shopped?"

They shook their heads no.

"Thrift shops. Your mother was extremely talented in discovering previously worn clothing, and creating something new and exciting. I always thought she could have had a career in designing clothing."

"*Our* mother?" they asked in unison.

"Yes, your mother. It was her senior year and we were looking for her prom dress. We went from store to store and those we could afford were not to her liking, and those she liked we couldn't afford. We were both getting desperate when I suggested we drive into the older part of Palos Verdes. I hadn't been in 'old town' for quite a while and was surprised at the changes; it had become quite upscale. I parked and what did we see but a sign for a resell store: MONA'S LA CHIC: OUT FROM THE BACK OF THE CLOSET.

"I said, quite impulsively, 'Let's go in.' At this time, however, your mother was very anxious so I suggested we have lunch first and then think about seeing what they might have before we went home. We decided to dine at the Yellow Vase, and I'm glad we did. The restaurant's sophisticated atmosphere and its delectable quiches served to calm April down considerably. After she'd chilled a bit, your mom was in a much better frame of mind, and the Yellow Vase became one of our favorite dining destinations on special occasions.

"We walked back to Mona's La Chic and I suggested again that we go in, just to browse.

The owner, Mona Chapman, was there. Your mother blurted out her frustration, and Mona was most understanding. She took April's hands and said, 'I worked in the garment industry for years. And I saw the waste. Expensive gowns worn once and then tossed in the back of the closet. I also knew that not all women and girls who need a dress for a special occasion can afford to pay retail prices.'

"'I had this idea: why not contact all the people I worked with for years, and ask them to donate those garments that were gathering dust. They did, and Mona's La Chic was born. You pay what you can afford. Come with me, I think I have just the dress for you.'

"She turned to me and, pointing to a most comfortable-looking sofa, said, 'Please wait here while April and I find the perfect dress.' I must say, I was happy to relax; shopping is not my strong point. I couldn't hear what they were saying in the dressing room, but the tone was soft and earnest. Finally your mother emerged wearing a lovely dress and smiling from ear to ear.

"Mona said, 'April loves this dress and has a couple of ideas for making it uniquely hers.'

She referred to her appointment book. 'If you come back next

Tuesday at four p.m. our dress designer, Jeffrey, will be here. He'll work with April to alter the dress to her liking.' Well, that's exactly what happened. Your mother had the most beautiful dress at the prom, and she looked absolutely stunning in it."

"Wow," said Emilee, "I can't picture Mother even wanting to go to a prom, much less dancing and having a good time. She's so...?"

"Tense?" said Villia.

Emilee nodded. "I was thinking uptight, but yeah."

Villia spoke from a deep place. "It can be hard to think of our parents as being young and filled with dreams. This might be the perfect time to return to the distant past, which may be our lesson for the present."

She opened the journal. "There are a couple of letters tucked in the back." She held them up. "The paper seems fragile; we must be careful not to damage these words from the past. The first one is from Dylan to Bran when he arrived in New York..."

∞

October 5, 1848

Dear Bran,

I have arrived in New York and planted my feet upon American soil.

I missed you something fierce on the voyage, but I was kept so busy on board the ship, the days did seem to slip away.

I sailed on the *Europa*, a steamer. She's a fine ship and proved herself by taking the treacherous seas with determination and speed. The seas were rough and most of the passengers were seasick. But we made New York Harbor in record time.

Captain Meade put me to work in the galley. I didn't mind the dirty work; I will work my way up wherever I go. As it turned out the cabin boy got sick and I got his job, which had me scurrying from bow to stern performing errands at the Captain's behest.

Captain Meade knows my tad and he has a shipbuilder friend by the name of Yoder, who lives in Pennsylvania. Remember the map I showed you of the United States? Pennsylvania is right below New York. And guess what? Mr. Yoder's shipyard is building flatbottom boats like the ones we used to navigate our rivers. They use them here too. But they are unacquainted with the practice of making them seaworthy by outfitting the flat bottom with a keel; in Wales we accomplish this by fixing a log to the flat bottom with chains. I think I can show them a thing or two! In a week's time, I'll be heading to Pennsylvania, which is not too far from New York, about a two-day journey by coach.

New York is like nothing you have ever seen, loud, crowded and oh, the big city smells! Most unpleasant. I've heard stories about the gold rush in California and I may be heading there after I save enough money. "Go West, young man!" is the rallying cry for adventurous spirits seeking their fortune. You know gold holds no appeal for me, dear Bran, but I want to see for myself this so-called land of milk and honey.

As you may know, California is as far from New York as you can get; if you went any further west, you would drop right into the Pacific Ocean! I hear there are places in California where the sun shines all year long. Would you like that, Bran?

My love, I worry that your tad will force you to marry before I can send for you. When the moon was full, I would gaze out upon the sea that was taking me further and further away from you. I took solace in the knowledge that, although we are worlds apart, the moon glowed no less brightly for you than it did for me—a beacon of our undying love.

Please wait for me. I will work day and night to save for your passage.

Yours forever,

Dylan

∞

"The other letter is Bran's reply," said Villia.

"What's she say? What's she say?" demanded Emilee, jumping up and down.

"Hold your horses! Let me get it out of the envelope..."

∞

December 22, 1848

Dear Dylan,

It has been months since you wrote your letter. It first went to your tad, then to my mam, and lastly to me, when she visited me at this accursed finishing school, which remains the bane of my existence. I trust you have not been too worried about not receiving a speedier reply, but we must keep my tad from discovering our dreams and plans. Because we are being so cautious, the time that passes between my letters may be longer than either one of us desires.

I put your letter to my lips and breathed it in, then held it to my heart as if it were you.

I hope you know during this time of separation that you have my heart.

My brothers are home from Oxford. They seem fine with the preposterous idea of an arranged marriage. I suppose it is a singularly masculine ideal. However, I know you don't feel that way; how sad that my boorish brothers shall never know the love that we have. I would rather be poor and know that you will always be by my side than to be rich and see my life slip by.

Is there truly a place where the sun shines all the time? I shall have to find California on our map.

I breathlessly anticipate the time when we shall be together again. With all my love,

Bran

∞

Ethan said, "Boy, it sure took a long time to get somewhere back in the olden days. We went from Los Angeles to New York and it only took five hours. I remember because I watched two movies and had a snack, and then we were there."

Emilee sniffled. "Ethan, you are so unromantic. Bran and Dylan loved each other and were kept apart because of hatred."

Ethan ignored his sister's comment. "Grannie, is that how you got your name—after the flatbottom boat? Is there a story around that?"

"Indeed, there is. I do believe there will be more about that in the journal. But for now, I think a comfortable bed and sleep sounds quite wonderful."

Villia kissed Emilee and Ethan good night. Oran had reassured her that the sailboat was in excellent shape, but it had been years since she had taken it out on her own. She needed to get a feel for it and make sure it was stocked with supplies for the island.

The kids might enjoy a day at the beach, dipping their toes in the ocean and letting them actually see the flatbottom boat.

God, she was bone tired. What a peculiar phrase, to be bone tired! As if your bones could become more tired than the rest of you.

She wasn't sure if it was from aging, or the added responsibility of caring for the kids. She felt as if she was in a circus performing a high-wire balancing act while throwing juggling clubs high into the air and catching them without falling. One careless move and you plummet to the floor below.

CHAPTER II

Villia woke to gray skies and mist. Not exactly a perfect day for the beach, but the day was young and the June gloom would burn off.

The house was quiet—too quiet. There were strange noises coming from the kitchen.

She bolted up. "Christ, it's the washer and dryer!"

Dashing into the kitchen, she saw the laundry organized into colors, whites, and gentles—and folded to boot!

Emilee said proudly, "We thought we'd surprise you by doing our laundry."

"I can see your mother taught you well."

"Actually, it was part of our homemaking class."

"Did they teach you how to clean floors?"

"No, is there a trick to it?"

She looked at the dust bunnies scattered around the kitchen floor.

Free labor was her first thought, but she became distracted when Ethan said, "Mother called this morning. We told her we were having a good time."

Emilee added, "We decided not to tell her about the journals."

"Why?"

"Grannie, we hear our parents talking. Well, mostly Mother talks and Father listens."

Ethan spoke in a hushed voice. "Sometimes Mother cries."

"I'm sorry," Villia said with a catch in her voice. "Tell me, what did your mother have to say?"

Ethan shrugged. "She just wanted to see how we were doing and if we were being good."

"I told her we helped in the garden and made you breakfast," Emilee added. "She said she was proud of me."

"And me, too!" Ethan put in, not to be outdone.

"I'm also proud of you both. The day is flying away, and I thought we might go down to the beach. Remember you asked about the flatbottom boat?"

The kids nodded like two bobblehead dolls.

"Well ... Gramps and I have it."

"What!" they exclaimed together and traded gobsmacked looks.

Emilee asked, "Is it as old as Noah's Ark?"

"Well, not quite."

Ethan began: "Will you bring the journal with us—"

"—and can we sit on the boat while you read to us?" Emilee finished.

"Oh, I think that can be arranged." Villia looked at the floor. "Up for another chore while I fix lunch?"

∞

The three beachgoers took the flagstone steps from the house to the boathouse.

"Your gramps fixed these before he left. My grandfather helped my father to build this walkway years ago. I was about ten and loved to hang out with them. Of course, I'm sure I was more of a nuisance but they never let on."

"Like us?" asked Ethan.

"Well, you keep me on my toes, but that's exactly what you are supposed to do. Do you want to know what my grandfather said about the flagstone?"

"Yes, I love your stories, Grannie," said Emilee.

"Me too," said Ethan.

"My gramps had a really deep voice." Villia deepened her voice as much as she could. "'You want to invest in something that will last,' he said. 'Flagstone is nigh eternal.' He was right, you know, and not only about flagstone."

"What else was he right about?" asked Ethan.

"It took me years to understand what my gramps meant." She brushed the sand off the steps. "This flagstone has endured the wind, rains, and ocean spray, and over time it's shifted and loosened in the sandy soil. You see, this one is a bit loose, but it's still strong and only needs some gentle repairing. Much like the people we love."

"Maybe like Mother and Father," Emilee suggested.

Villia winced. "Maybe."

They continued down the steps. "Here we are," said Villia, standing in front of the boathouse. She juggled her keys until she unfastened the four locks and, with a mighty push, opened the door.

Villia, Emilee, and Ethan stood in the cavernous boathouse.

Sunlight streamed through two skylights bathing the otherwise shadowed area in natural light.

"It's still chilly," remarked Villia a sudden shiver washing over her. Before tackling the beach, let's climb aboard the flatbottom boat and read more of the journal."

They did.

Emilee said, "This is such a cool boat. Father keeps talking about the time he helped Gramps."

Villia smiled. "I remember that day. Your gramps had his Merchant Marine buddies over to work on the boats, although I'm not sure how much work they actually accomplished." She winked. "They took the flatbottom boat out and returned with the ravenous appetites of teenaged boys. I don't think I have ever seen your father looking so relaxed and happy."

Ethan added, "Our father loves to sail. He always says when he retires he wants to sail around the world. But Mother won't go."

"Mother said she had enough of the sea when she was young," said Emilee. "Do you know why, Grannie?"

Villia hesitated. "I think that's a question for your mother when she gets home."

"Always a mystery," mumbled Emilee.

"What's for lunch?" asked Ethan, settling onto the deck bench.

"Hungry already? It's barely eleven."

"It's fun to eat while you hearing a story. Plus," he said, lifting his T-shirt, "I think my tummy has gotten smaller since I've been here."

"Personally," said Villia, "I think it's all the running around and chores. Plus"—she paused for effect—"you've grown at least an inch."

"I can do more chores," replied Ethan, flexing his biceps.

"That can be arranged. Now, let's see. Cheese sandwiches on homemade bread for Ethan. Mustard and a dab of mayo. Peanut butter and jam for Grannie. And egg salad for Emilee."

"With olives?"

"Of course, exactly the way you like it. And now for the *pièce de résistance*: chips, apples, and cookies for all. Now, where were we?"

Emilee prompted: "You had just read Dylan's and Bran's letters."

"Yes, that's right. It's a bit of a miracle that they survived all these years. Here's another letter from Bran to Dylan. Let me see, it's dated January 1, 1849 ..."

Dear Dylan,

The Christmas Holiday flew by and now it's New Year's Day. I hope you have made some friends in America and weren't alone during the holidays.

Mam and Tad had a Christmas party with over thirty guests, including Lord Bishop, who owns the farm next to ours. It's the largest farm in the county. The lord has a son, Arnold, at least ten years my senior. I could tell by the way the two fathers were chatting that something was a-brewing. Tad kept pointing out my virtues and I felt like a horse at the monthly livestock auction!

Arnold tried to engage me in conversation. I shunned him because he wasn't you and besides, he smelled of whiskey and grease from the lamb and beef Mam served for supper.

I thought of you when the servants brought out *cyflath*. I know how much you love Welsh toffee; I shall make it a point to bring some when I sail across the sea to your side.

I am trying to be strong, dearest one, but I fear I may not be able to stand up to my tad. Oh, Dylan, send for me soon! I cannot wait for us to be together again.

Love,

Bran

∞

Emilee sighed theatrically. "Grannie, this is better than a Lifetime movie."

"That's the second time you've made such a statement. I've seen advertisements for Lifetime in magazines and on some of the TV stations Oran and I like to watch. It doesn't seem suitable for children your age. Exactly how much of this sordid fare are you watching?"

Emilee looked puzzled. "Sordid fare?"

"Junk," Villia clarified.

Emilee laughed. "Oh, Grannie, you're so retro! But in a cool way. Sarah, our housekeeper, likes Lifetime. And if Mother and Father are out for the evening I watch it with her. By the way, Grannie, why don't you have cable?"

Villia put down the journal. "Answer this question for me: have you been bored? Because I can give you about thirty things to do."

Emilee smiled. "I love what we're doing."

Ethan said, "Me too. Read more, please."

Villia placed the journal on the deck table. "Look, the sun is out. We'll read later. It's time to run along the beach and collect seashells. You mother used to love doing that. Building sand castles too. Your mother was quite talented. I do believe I have some photos showcasing her creations tucked away. Are you both too old for sand castles?"

Ethan said, "It's sort of like making ice sculptures."

"Why, yes, it is. Your mother was very artistic and imaginative in her own way. Now, shall we? Last one to the beach is a rotten Dawley!"

∞

Emilee ran up and down the shore, dodging waves to collect seashells.

Ethan made a roadway in the sand and began building a sand castle.

Villia, watched as Ethan and Emilee darted into the ocean, then retreated back to the safety of the shoreline. She felt the weight of responsibility and sighed with relief when they turned toward other interests; Ethan building a sand castle and Emily collecting shells. Emilee returned with her bucket overflowing and began to line the shells up in the dry sand.

Villia remarked, "They're quite beautiful. I see you found sand dollars."

"Mother loves them best. She told me the legend of the sand dollar."

"There are many versions. Which one did she tell you?"

"That they are coins lost by mermaids."

Villia chuckled. "That's directly from your mother's mermaid phase. Oh my, how she loved thinking about becoming a mermaid." Villia pointed toward Ethan. "Ethan looks like he knows what he's doing. Don't tell me he took a class in building sand castles?"

Emilee said, "Okay, I won't tell you." They both laughed. "Father says Ethan's behavior borders on obsessive-compulsiveness."

"Oh, I rather think he's just an intense little fellow—very talented and detail-oriented." Villia scrutinized her grandson's handiwork. "Emilee," she asked, "what is that circular area made of rocks surrounding Ethan's castle?"

Emilee casually examined shells from her bucket. "Remember when we told you that Mother sometimes cries?"

"Yes."

"We heard her one night. She was telling Father about this horrible island she had to visit when she was a kid. She said it was dead and filled with biting insects. It's why she hates sailing.

I think it got stuck in Ethan's brain. That's why he always creates castles on an island. The rocks represent the shoreline."

Villia was at a loss for words. *That was the worse day of my life.* She wished she could put it to rest, but the guilt from that day would never leave.

The rising tide threatened Ethan's sand castle.

"We'd best be going," Villia said, motioning to the kids.

Emilee said, "I had the best time, Grannie."

"Me too," Ethan agreed, "except I hate to see my castle swallowed up."

"I brought my camera," said Villia. "We can get a photo before the sea reclaims it."

"What is that?" asked Ethan, pointing to the camera.

"This is an old-timer's smart camera, called a Polaroid. It will develop the photo on the spot."

"No way!" said Emilee.

"Way! Why don't you both stand next to the castle?"

She snapped the picture and waited. The kids watched as the photo gradually appeared.

Ethan exclaimed, "Whoa, that's cool, Grannie!"

"We'll have to take another one. And this time keep your tongues in your mouths."

The first one with funny faces was followed by two children holding hands and smiling. A bit browner than they were when the day began, and with more than a bit of sand clinging to their bodies. But their smiles were broad as if they were surrounded by an aura of happiness.

Villia believed there was nothing like a day at the beach to relax and wear children out.

Later, at home, she thought Ethan was going to plant his face in his dinner plate. Emilee pleaded with her to stay up late by claiming she wasn't tired at all, but when she couldn't keep her eyes open past ten, Villia had to practically carry her to bed.

Villia was exhausted too. She thought back to when she had been married only a short time, couldn't get enough sleep, and was troubled by nausea. She went to their family physician, Dr. Sokol, a gnome of a man who was no taller than she, exactly five feet tall. At least he was someone she could make direct eye contact with. He had tufts of bright red hair and the palest blue eyes she had ever seen. He examined her and said, "Six weeks."

"Six weeks to what?" she had asked innocently.

"Villia, I have treated your entire family. Why, I even brought you into this world. Did you not have any idea that you might be pregnant?"

"How did this happen?" she exclaimed.

He laughed. "I thought your mother gave you the birds and bees lecture."

"Oh, Dr. Sokol, of course I know the physiology, but...but..."

"Hmm, let me guess: you didn't believe it could happen."

"No, it's not that," she said through happy tears. "I just never thought I would be so *blessed*."

$$\infty$$

Dr. Sokol came out from the delivery room, his hand extended. "Congratulations, Oran, you have a son. Villia tells me his name is Bruce."

"I'm a father." Oran whispered.

"Yes, indeed. This waiting can be hard. Times are changing and soon, fathers will be allowed in the delivery room. Grab some breakfast and stop at the gift shop. Your wife and son will be in a room by then." He lowered his voice. "Just don't buy the whole place out."

Oran wasn't the only crazy father buying out the gift shop. Was it too soon to buy Bruce a tiny baseball mitt? Loaded down with absolute necessities, he returned to the maternity floor and found his way to Room 147.

Villia was sitting up in bed holding Bruce.

Oran gasped. "He's beautiful and so are you."

"The nurses insisted on combing my hair and putting on a bit of makeup. I think they were afraid you might faint otherwise."

"I do admit I was worried. Dr. Sokol thinks they'll be letting fathers into the delivery rooms."

"About time," Villia retorted.

"I called everyone and bought cigars. I wasn't sure how many. Do you think a hundred is enough?"

"Barely," she quipped.

He bent over to kiss Villia and placed a bouquet of flowers and balloons on the side table.

Oran put his finger in Bruce's hand. "Hello, Bruce. He's got quite a grip. I can tell he knows me."

"Of course he does. He's strong and smart. Look at how serious he is. He shall be a scholar; I can tell. Oran, I had the strangest thing happen. I had a vision just after Bruce was born. I was standing on the beach watching Bruce playing in the sand and I saw myself holding an infant girl. I told Dr. Sokol and he said he gave me some medication to help with the pain and I must have had a lovely dream. I knew it was a prediction that our next baby will be a girl and we shall name her Ebrill."

"Next one? Already?"

"When it pleases the gods and goddesses."

Three years later, Dr. Sokol laid Ebrill on Villia's chest. "She's a beauty. Oran and Villia, you both did well."

Oran bent down and kissed his beloveds, first his wife and then his daughter. Ebrill began to make sucking noises and Villia put her to her breast.

Oran was about to burst with pride. "She's quite smart, isn't she? I can't wait to tell everyone."

"Call our parents, darling," said Villia. "And I know you want to call your friends."

"First, I want to get a photo." Oran took out the Polaroid camera.

Dr. Sokol said, "Here, let me get the three of you." The flash went unnoticed by a suckling Ebrill.

Villia thought, "She's so attached to me already. It's you and me through thick and thin, my little one."

Ebrill loved the beach and the water. She adored collecting sea-shells and making sand castles. And then there was her mermaid phase, complete with a red wig and flowing plastic tail.

But things dramatically shifted. She went from loving the sea to not wanting to set foot on a sailboat. She had let her daughter down, disappointing her because of who she was—a weirdo, apparently. Could she ever earn April's forgiveness? Or as a radio talk show therapist she sometimes listened to often said, could she ever forgive herself?

∞

Tomorrow, Villia would wind things up by finishing the second journal. As she recalled, the perfect ending to the story, Branwyn leaving Wales for America to be with her love, Dylan. She could picture herself closing the journal and saying, "And they lived happily ever after."

April had been very direct about her not mentioning the island. Perhaps she was right. Emilee and Ethan didn't have to know the rest of the story, or that a third journal even existed. She would not betray her daughter—again. *I've had enough surprises for a dozen lives. No more!*

CHAPTER 12

Ethan and Emilee had fallen into Grannie's routine. While Emilee had initially called it "dorky," it had a calming effect upon the kids.

They sat under the dining table for breakfast. Pooch, despite his earlier snarkiness, had taken to the two kids and, without an iota of guilt, had abandoned Villia. He spent equal time on Emilee and Ethan's beds and had joined in their roughhousing with surprising good humor, even allowing Ethan to ride him like a horse.

"I'm going to miss you both, but I think Pooch will miss you even more."

"Can we take him home?" asked Ethan.

"LOL," said Emilee.

Villia cocked an inquisitive eyebrow. "LOL?"

"It's internet lingo, Grannie. It means 'laughing out loud.' Mother will never allow us to have a dog or a cat. She can't stand the mess."

"Perhaps you can visit more often."

"I'd like that," said Ethan.

"Me too," said Emilee.

"We do have today and tomorrow to be together. There is one thing I must do the day after tomorrow. It's my day to help at the homeless shelter during lunchtime. You're welcome to come with me or you can stay home." She smiled. "You have both earned my trust."

The siblings looked at each other, appearing to communicate tele-pathically. "Thanks, Grannie, but we'll stay," said Emilee, speaking for both of them. "We can do some chores while you're gone."

I knew I'd win them over. Villia kissed the tops of their heads, which required her to lean over only slightly. *I do believe they have grown since they've been here,* she mused.

"That brings us to today. How would you like to go out for an early dinner?"

"How early is early?" asked Ethan.

"I was thinking around three."

Emilee asked, "Where to, Grannie?"

"A wonderful Italian restaurant. *Dove il Mare e la Terra si Incontrano.* Translation: Where the Sea and the Earth Meet. It's been in the Savino family for several generations. You eat there once and you become family. Your gramps and I used to go there when we first met. And later we would take your mom and Uncle Bruce. Your mother loved that restaurant, and now the two of you can have the same dining experience. At three o'clock it will be quiet and uncrowded."

"What did Mother like to order?" asked Ethan.

"She was very selective."

Both kids rolled their eyes.

"I'm choosing to ignore the eye rolling. Order first, and then we will see how close you come to your mother's taste. Until then, what say we get dressed and feed the cats?"

Dove il Mare e la Terra si Incontrano was a hidden gem, situated behind a commonplace strip mall. They walked behind the stores and entered through a dark wooden door, blinking to adjust their eyes to the low-light atmosphere after being in the bright sun.

"Mrs. Flatbottom!" A young man wearing slacks, a button-down shirt, and bowtie came over and held out his hand. "So good to see you. It has been so long!"

"Anthony? Is that you?" She took his hand. "I hate to greet you with such a trite phrase, but my, how you've grown! It must be at least four years since I've been here. How are your parents?"

"Retired. My sister and I are now partnering in the operation of the restaurant." He smiled at Emilee and Ethan. "And who might these charming young people be?"

"My grandchildren, Emilee and Ethan." They stood gawking at Anthony until Villia elbowed them, whereupon they chorused: "Pleased to meet you."

Anthony grinned. "It is entirely my pleasure. Do you want your usual table, Mrs. Flatbottom?"

"You remember?"

"Of course! Follow me."

They walked to the table facing the beach.

"The window is open a bit to allow for the ocean air," said Anthony. "Please let me know if it gets too chilly." He handed them menus. "May I start you off with some drinks?"

Ethan and Emilee looked at Villia. She smiled, knowing what they wanted, and simply nodded.

"Root beer," said Ethan.

"Mountain Dew," said Emilee.

"A double expresso for me, Anthony," said Villia.

I think we'll be in for a long and sleepless night. Oh well, I might as well be hung for a sheep as for a lamb.

When Anthony returned with their drinks, Emilee ordered lasagna and a salad with vinegar and oil dressing.

Ethan went for pizza and a salad with Thousand Island dressing.

Villa over-ordered. The thought of cooking for their last days together seemed abhorrent. What could be better than leftover lasagna, polenta and ribollita, soup made with cannellini beans, kale, a variety of vegetables, and thickened with leftover bread? It was Oran's favorite and hers as well.

When Anthony left to put in their order, Ethan asked, "Did we guess right?"

"Not even close. Your mother had a taste of her own. And none of us ordered her favorite: bottarga."

"What's that?" asked Emilee.

"Smoked eggs from the rat of the sea."

"Gross!" said Ethan, pretend-jabbing his fingers down his throat.

"Disgusting," Emilee concurred.

"Grannie, are you're teasing us?" challenged Ethan.

"Oh, no. I think your mother wanted to try something different and she seemed to enjoy it. Have you heard of caviar?"

"Yes, Mother says it reminds her of..." Emilee's voice trailed off. "Sometimes she'll sing dippy songs from when she was in high school. She'll smile and then sometimes she'll cry a little. Not major crying, you know?"

Villa nodded.

Ethan chimed in, "Trickling tears." He demonstrated by making a sad clown face. "It only happens when she's had too much wine."

"Grannie, are you crying?" asked Emilee.

Villia wiped her tears with a napkin. "Sorry, guess I got carried away. I was remembering those days when your mother was in high school. She was very involved and—happy. Sometimes memories stir up our feelings."

Ethan tenderly put his hand on her arm. "I think I know how you feel."

Anthony brought their food with the assistance of a second server. Dish after dish was placed on the table until Villia was certain she could hear the table groaning. "Anthony, do you think we overdid it a bit?"

"Not one morsel too much, Mrs. Flatbottom! *Buon appetito!*"

Villia was taken aback at how quickly the day went and how little bickering there was between Emilee and Ethan. In spite of the caffeine rush, they had both fallen asleep during the ride home. It felt as if a blanket of comfort had settled over the occupants of the rickety house built on stilts. She had an eerie feeling, one she had experienced before, a signal that underneath the quiet, a storm was brewing. By the time they got to Palos Verdes, the fog had risen from the sea, blanketing their home.

Later that evening they nibbled on leftovers, fruit, nuts, and a few cookies in between chores.

She even got Emilee and Ethan to sweep the kitchen and dining area.

She stood in amazement: the dust bunnies had disappeared.

∞

At Villia's urging, Emilee and Ethan changed into their pajamas before settling into the den's oversized chair.

"Plenty of room for a sister and brother! Let me get a photo of the two of you." Villia aimed her Polaroid. "Now, don't move! Your mother and father will love this."

She thought, *Snug as two bugs in a rug.* Emilee looked softer and Ethan less anxious.

She opened the journal and began to read.

∞

September 1, 1849. I am getting ready to begin my second year at Mrs. Strickland's Finishing School for Young Ladies. While I long for my lost freedom, there is a certain feeling of peace from being away from my father's outbursts.

Most of the girls attending the school are excited about future marriages and don't seem to mind that their lives will be arranged for them.

A new girl, Maryanne Lapanze, joined my age group, but no one wanted to sit next to her or room with her. They said she was too "different" and beneath them. Perhaps most damaging was the fact that her mother and father act upon the stage. Her parents are Shakespearian actors and perform in plays around the world. Rumors ran around the school like a dog chasing after its tail. Tongue-waggers spread one bit of gossip after another, but the final blow was that her family was "bohemian," and therefore beneath their social class. Mrs. Strickland called me into her office and told me that I would be sharing my room with Maryanne. I think I am also seen as being too "different." I consider it a badge of honor!

Our friendship began during gymnastics when we looked at each other and knew we were thinking the same thing: the exercises were barely enough to keep our blood flowing. Maryanne now shares my room and I have my first real friend at school.

Maryanne likes to climb trees and run free the way I do. She said her parents won't make her marry. She wants to go on to an institution of higher learning and become a doctor. Imagine, a girl going to medical school! She has five sisters and they have the same freedom as boys. Maryanne has accompanied her parents on their travels and when we get into our beds at night, she entertains me with stories of foreign lands.

I told her about my love for Dylan, but said nothing of our wish to marry. I wonder if my life will be as exciting as Maryanne's? I can't wait until I can travel to America to be with Dylan.

Villia paused. "There are many short entries about school. They're on scraps of paper that were later pasted onto the journal's pages. I think that's how Branwyn got around the not having her journal with her. Shall we skip ahead a bit?"

"Yes, Grannie...do fast-forward," Ethan said with a wide grin.

Villia smiled at the faster pace that was so natural to her grand-babies but, at times, was pure torture for her. She thumbed through the pages, mumbling as she went about the various topics. "Teas, dance class, the proper setting of a table, and an afternoon on learning to take command of servants."

Emilee overheard her. "Poor Branwyn and all the women of that time: held back by misogyny," she remarked airily. "Please read on, Grannie."

Villia smiled at the apparent worldliness of her granddaughter.

March 10, 1851. Mam paid me a surprise visit. I thought at first it was to celebrate my birthday, and while that was partly true, there was another purpose as well.

I hadn't seen Mam for several months and was taken aback at her appearance. She looked thinner, older...as if she wasn't well.

When she hugged me and wished me a Happy Birthday, I thought she would never let me go. She spoke in the softest of tones. "We have to find a quiet place to talk. I've told Mrs. Strickland that I am taking you into town for a private celebration and that we will be spending the night at the Jolly Giant Inn."

Mam lowered her voice until it sounded like a breeze wafting through tall grass. "Mrs. Strickland thought we would be in horrible danger, two women alone at an inn, but I told her I had my pistol with me."

I had to laugh, because Mam was the best target shooter in our county and could outshoot any man around.

I packed a few belongings and we got into a carriage for the ride into town. The air seemed fresher, more alive. Much like it must feel when someone is released from prison, I fancied.

It was a quiet time at the inn, with a few travelers eating an early supper before retiring. Mam had ordered a sumptuous repast which was brought to our rooms shortly after our arrival. At first, we spoke of things of little importance; the girls at school call it chitchat. Mam shared the town gossip, which made me smile. The she told me that my brothers were doing well, and that Tad was pleased at their arranged unions.

Her voice, which heretofore had been lightsome, became suddenly serious, and I could see that she had brought more than birthday wishes.

Mam went to her raggedy valise and brought out a letter.

"From Dylan," she said. "I wish I could have brought it to you sooner. Read it first and then we shall talk."

I held the letter in my hand. "Have you read it, Mam?"

"Yes, I hope you will understand. I had to know Dylan's intentions in order to make plans."

I simply nodded and began to read in silence.

∞

January 30, 1851

Dearest Bran,

It has been months since I have heard from you. I have been horribly worried, but I spoke to my landlady; she told me it can take months for letters to travel back and forth between continents. And even worse, she said that letters get lost all the time. I pray that nothing has happened to you and that you are well.

So much has happened since I arrived in America.

I traveled from New York to Pennsylvania and was hired by Yoder Shipbuilders. At first, I did the most menial of jobs, sweeping, fetching tools and running errands. Then one day, I showed them how to change the flatbottom boat so it could be seaworthy. Mr. Yoder was pleased and wanted to give me a permanent job, but I had a hankering to travel to San Francisco, California. After a few months of hard work at Yoder Shipbuilders, and saving all that I could, I left for San Francisco. San Francisco is a busy seaport in western California, where I quickly found employment in another shipyard.

There are many jobs available out here, mostly related to the gold rush, but I have my heart set in another direction. I don't want to be underground, breaking my back on the fool's errand of striking it rich with a bonanza; I want to be on land and sea with you by my side.

Dearest, I have sent this letter and your passage money to my tad, who in turn will share this letter with your mam.

I know this will go against your tad's marriage plans for you, but I beg you to not give up on our dream of becoming husband and wife.

Now, I must leave the arrangements to your mam, who I know will be taking a great risk by doing so. Once we are bound together in marriage, she will be my mam too and I will love her with all my heart.

If all goes well, and I pray it will, your mam will send your travel details to me by telegram.

Waiting for you,
Dylan

∞

I felt my heartbreak over Dylan's fears; had he not received all my letters? I gasped back into reality and blurted out, "By telegram? But Mam, the cost is so dear."

"We'll choose our words carefully." Mam smiled. "It'll be worth every pound. Your father believes I am here to arrange your return home."

"Why? What will be happening?"

"Your father has agreed to a union between you and Arnold Bishop. There is to be a betrothal party."

"It might as well be my funeral."

"Neither will occur," Mam said firmly. "I will not have you suffer as I have suffered. I can only imagine the sacrifices Dylan had to make to secure your passage, but I can't have you go in steerage. The unsanitary conditions are appalling. Those poor people! So strong is their need for freedom they will sacrifice anything. I shall make other arrangements to make certain my daughter is safe."

Mam grew pensive, and at length remarked, "You do realize that you will be cutting off ties with your family and friends, perhaps for a lifetime of hardship?"

"A minute with Dylan in the most humble of homes will be better than a lifetime in a palace without love."

Mam withdrew a silk pouch with her valise. "I've saved this nest egg prudently over the years from household money. Your father never knew. I had to learn to be clever. I thought, one day I'll need this. I never thought it would be used to send my daughter away from me."

I rushed over to hug my mam and buried my face in her bosom as I did when but a child.

She returned my embrace and when she released me, I saw her smiling, yet tears were streaming down her cheeks.

"It's strange how we can have more than one feeling at the same time," she said, wiping her tears away. "I have been planning this for months, knowing that I could never allow you to marry without love. We have a brief period of time to put our scheme into place. You must listen carefully to what I have to say."

I sat on the chair, my back as true as a die, and decorously folded my hands in my lap. Realizing I was automatically following my finishing school indoctrination, I made a great show of slumping in my chair, much to Mam's amusement.

"I have spoken with Mrs. Strickland and told her about your marital plans," she said. "She was thrilled to hear the news, regarding it as a feather in her cap, to see one of her pupils 'marry well.' I would like to be there when she hears the news of your escape."

I joined Mam in hearty laughter.

"In a week's time," she went on, "a carriage will arrive at your school. Your headmistress believes it will be to take you home for your betrothal party, but you will not be coming home. Do you understand?"

I nodded. "Where will I be going?"

Mam held up a silencing hand and continued.

"Your father goes to inspect the crops tomorrow and will be staying for two weeks with the farm manager. He will spend his time hunting, drinking, and bragging about his good fortune. Coffers filled and land acquired—by selling his daughter."

Mam set her tea cup down angrily. She stood and began to pace around the room, all the while describing her plan for me.

"You are to pack only what you might need for a home visit. Make certain you leave enough of your belongings so that suspicion is not aroused. I will make certain that everything you need for your voyage to America will be waiting at your destination, the home of Madam Izobelle Latham. As I've mentioned, we were roommates at school and the very best of friends."

Mam seemed to go into a dreamlike state. "Izzy has a most unusual talent; perhaps she will share it with you. You will spend a few days with her and she will see you to the boat that will take you to America."

"But why, Mam? Why would you do this?"

She gazed at me and her eyes filled with tears. "Before your father..." She hesitated for a long moment. "Let us just say I was in love once, and only once. I have never forgotten the ways of the heart."

∞

The next few days of school were filled with excitement about what everyone thought was my pending engagement. There was a tea with gifts for me, including a nightgown to be worn on my wedding night. That created a lot of giggling and blushing amongst the girls. I was overwhelmed by their generosity and ashamed because I was lying. That night I packed, leaving many things behind as if I planned to return, as Mam had instructed. Maryanne hugged me and I hugged her back so tightly that she said, "You're not going away forever, silly goose. And once I graduate I can visit you."

I could say no more, but would live with the remorse of having betrayed a friend whom I had come to love over the last few months.

So it was that on the seventh day following my mam's visit, a carriage arrived at seven in the evening. I felt that the two sevens were lucky charms boding well of my life to come.

Villia stopped reading. "Well, my loves, I don't know about you but I am ready to fall over. What say we stop for tonight?"

Ethan was blinking like an owl, barely able to keep his eyes open. Yawning prodigiously, Emilee managed to say, "Can we finish tomorrow?"

"Yes, we'll call it a marathon pajama day. We'll eat leftovers and popcorn and finish the journal."

CHAPTER 13

It was the silence that woke her. Villia bolted out of bed toward the children's bedroom. Strangely there were no creaks or groans from the house, or the sound of chattering or bickering from the children. Their bedroom door was the way she had left it, opened a crack. She peeked through the opening to see Ethan and Emilee in a deep sleep. She breathed a sigh of relief. Two angels, she thought.

She whispered into Pooch's ear while petting his head. "No Cream of Wheat today. Let's make pancakes instead. And, we'll eat at the table instead of under it."

"Where do *I* sit?" asked Pooch.

"Still a comedian, eh? At your mistress's feet, as it should be."

Grannie had promised the kids a pajama day and so it would be. The fridge was filled with all kinds of leftovers. She would throw the calorie counter and allergy chart out the window...at least for this special day.

The chill from the sea air crept through the gaps in the windows and doors. Shivering, she started a fire in the kitchen fireplace. She let Pooch out after giving him a few doggie treats.

"No barking," she warned. "The kids are zoned out."

Pooch gave his doggy smile of understanding.

"So many things wrong with this house," she grumbled out loud, "including the furnace that needs to be replaced."

Maybe April was right—perhaps she and Oran should consider selling the property and building an up-to-date house. For a moment she allowed her mind to drift to a modern kitchen and a spectacular bathroom. Other Flatbottoms had sold off parts of the original acreage; why shouldn't they?

Oh, Villia, that is so not you! In a heartbeat, she banished any thoughts of selling and gathered the ingredients for her buckwheat pancakes. Reaching for the coffee pot, she thought out loud, "Maybe I should buy one of those single serve coffee makers. But then how would I recycle the grounds?" She put all thoughts of modernization away.

"This is the life," she concluded. "Not a real worry in the world and everything going along according to schedule. To think that Ebrill had her doubts."

Emilee and Ethan shuffled in, eyelids drooping and looking half-asleep.

"I could sure use some coffee," said Emilee.

"Your mother lets you have coffee?"

"Not exactly."

"Emilee drinks Mother's coffee when she's not looking," Ethan volunteered.

"Just a sip, tattletale."

"How about hot chocolate while I whip up pancakes?"

"Thanks, Grannie."

"Me too!" Ethan chirped.

∞

The kids, still clad in their PJs, lay on the den couch, the head of each resting on an arm of the couch, their feet touching somewhere in the middle.

Villia, snug in her robe that fit like a second skin, sat on the oversized chair, her cup of coffee placed upon the side table, well within her reach.

She picked up the second journal and turned to the next entry.

Smiling, Villia held up the journal for the kids to see. The page was filled with hearts and flowers, with only one line written in block letters.

MY JOURNEY TO AMERICA AND DYLAN

"Bran was artistic...like me," Ethan observed.

"Yeah, that page is real pretty," said Emilee. "It doesn't look much different from something I might draw in a notebook myself."

Villia nodded. "Proof that children 150 years or so ago were not so very different from modern children. Now, lend me yours ears—"

"Why, are yours broken?" laughed Ethan.

"Shut up or I'll break *yours*," said Emilee, elbowing her brother hard. "Go ahead, Grannie, we're all ears." Ethan grinned and started to say something; she shot him a warning look.

As total silence reigned, Villia began reading.

∞

March 18, 1851. I began the next part of my adventure at Madam Latham's home at 45 West Morley Street, in the town of Cardiff. Cardiff is located near the sea, bringing me ever closer to Dylan.

The coach ride was several hours long and I must admit that despite the excitement I was lulled into sleep. A bump in the road woke me and shortly afterwards, the coach stopped. I peered through a gap in the curtained window at the inky black sky festooned with millions of twinkling stars. A waxing gibbous moon cast its pale blue glow upon a thatch-roofed cottage surrounded by flowers and a lush green lawn.

Accompanied by the coachman, I walked along a brick path leading to the house. When we got to the entry door, I beheld a most unusual knocker in the shape of a woman's hand. I felt rather foolish holding hands with a stranger, even though it was made of brass. The coachman, seeing my hesitation, rapped the hand against the wooden door and barked, "It ain't alive, miss."

The door opened, revealing my second surprise for the evening. The woman standing just beyond the threshold wore a velvet dressing gown, not unlike the one my tad wore. Her chestnut brown hair was not long like mine or Mam's, but was cut to the gown's collar and swept back from her forehead. Her skin was tanned as if she spent hours outside in the sun. I thought perhaps she tended to her garden or was otherwise athletically inclined.

For a moment I had a rush, remembering how I would wear my brother's pants and ride Enfys, who remained my favorite horse.

The woman smiled and held out her hand. "I am Izobelle Latham."

I took her hand and curtsied. "Madam Latham, thank you for allowing me to stay with you."

"No need for formality. You may call me Izzy if you wish; it's a nickname given to me by your mother." She smiled and her dark brown eyes, so very large and luminous, echoed the warmth of her smile.

I smiled back, but I wasn't quite sure I was ready to breach formalities just yet. I decided calling her "Madam Izzy" might be a good compromise.

"You must be famished," she said. "Please come inside."

I stood in the foyer as she reached into the pocket of her dressing gown and handed some coins to the coachman. "Thank you, Hugo. I shall expect you to return next week at the appointed time."

Hugo tipped his cap. "Will do, Miss Izzy. G'night."

With the door now shut, I could see fully into the foyer. A sense of welcoming washed over me. I thought of our home, so drab and forbidding with its heavy velvet drapes and outsized, dark brown furniture. This room, even in the candlelit dimness, was filled with a brightness that came as much from the senses as it did from the light-colored furniture.

Above the receiving table was a painting of a horse fair. I stopped to admire it.

"A gift from a very talented friend of mine, Rosa Bonheur," Madam Izzy remarked.

"It reminds me of Enfys, my horse that I leave behind."

"A painter has done their job when their art reminds us of life, even if we do feel sad. I will let Rosa know. Now, please join me in a light repast."

She took hold of my hand and guided me through double doors to the library, which, as I was soon to discover, held much more than books.

"Come sit by the fire," she said. "We shall eat and then I will show you to your room."

Madam Izzy rang a small bell and a servant girl, no older than I, entered the room pushing a tea cart filled with delicate sandwiches and desserts.

"Thank you, Nancy. Nancy, this is Branwyn."

Nancy held out her hand and gave mine a firm shake.

Tad would have never treated a servant with the respect shown by Madam Izzy, nor would any of our servants be so bold as to shake hands with someone regarded as a superior.

My eyes widened at the sight of fresh strawberries. My mouth watered at such a delicacy! But not wanting to appear greedy I picked up a single strawberry and took a delicate nibble.

I was surprised once again when Madam also picked up a single strawberry, but instead of taking a small bite, as I had been taught at Mrs. Strickland's, she put the entire strawberry in her mouth.

She closed her eyes, savoring the delicacy. "Ah, sometimes it fills good to be greedy."

Had she read my mind?

She asked if I wanted coffee or tea. I preferred tea; she took coffee.

"Some complain that coffee steals their sleep," she said, pouring my tea from a white enamel carafe painted with delicate spring flowers. "I don't find that to be true. Work the body hard during the day and you shall sleep well at night."

I could see by her sturdy build that this was a woman who lived by her own words.

Madam Izzy continued. "Your mother and I have discussed your situation and I am quite delighted to be part of your adventure. It's been many years since Enid and I put our heads together like this. I must admit, I have enjoyed my small part in this undertaking.

"Your mother and I were oftentimes in trouble at Mrs. Strickland's. Not that we were bad, just not always compliant, mostly at my urging, but your mother became a willing follower. Tell me, does Mrs. Strickland still have that ridiculous rule about not eating after six?"

"Yes. She believes in a twelve-hour daily fast."

Madam Izzy shook her head. "She had no sense about the needs of the growing body, only how girls should be molded into ideal wives."

She laughed lightly and her eyes sparkled.

"Your mother and I would occasionally sneak into the kitchen and forage for food. We thought we were being ever so clever by not leaving crumbs or clues. But Mrs. Strickland discovered the missing food; I'm quite sure she counted every morsel in the pantry. The entire school was denied food until the culprit confessed. I wasn't about to confess but I pretended to faint from hunger and that frightened her enough to feed us."

I never knew this about Mam, that she could have done something so risky and naughty. I thought it would be impossible to love my mam more, but after Madam Izzy's story, I did.

"How did you manage afterwards?" I asked.

"My dear, one of the advantages of being the only child of a wealthy man was that I had a great deal of spending money. I bribed one of the groundsmen into smuggling victuals from town into the dormitory. I purchased enough for all the girls, eliminating the possibility of a tattletale. This arrangement became routine, to the point the entire class began to fill out, as it were. Mrs. Strickland, who was never any the wiser, attributed this development to our becoming women. But enough nostalgia," she said, standing. "Let me take you to your room."

I followed Madam Izzy up the stairs to my room.

"I believe you'll find everything you need."

And at that she bade me good night and closed the door behind her. I was too tired to do anything but change into my nightdress and sink into the comfort of the bed. I thought of how lucky Mam was to have found a friend who was not afraid of breaking oppressive rules. My eyes would not stay open and I slept until I heard a grandfather clock strike the hour of nine the next morning.

There was a knock at the door and Nancy entered my room.

"Madam Izzy would like you to come down for breakfast." She held out a most beautiful silk kimono similar to one I had seen in a Japanese travel brochure.

"I'm not dressed," I sputtered.

She said nothing but continued to hold the robe, and while I felt quite foolish, I slipped into its silky texture. I followed Nancy down the stairs to the dining room where Madam Izzy was engrossed in a book.

Apparently she had been up for some time, because the blouse she wore showed traces of grass stains and dirt.

She closed the book and signaled to Nancy to fill my cup with tea. "I have many flaws," she said. "One of them is getting up at sunrise and working in my garden."

I didn't think of that as a flaw, but I remained quiet.

Once again, there was a large bowl of strawberries set upon the table. I took several at once and placed them on my plate. I then followed Madam Izzy's example from last night by putting one whole in my mouth. The juice flowed from the ripe fruit and the taste was extraordinary.

Madam Izzy glanced up and lightly applauded my breach of etiquette.

I glanced down, slightly embarrassed by my greed. That was short-lived, however, as my eyes wandered to her book.

"*Wuthering Heights*," she said, following my gaze. "Written by a female author, Emily Brontë, now deceased, God rest her soul. Originally published under the masculine pseudonym Ellis Bell." I felt she made this observation with some distaste. "I doubt that you have read it; such daring and original prose isn't something you would find at Strickland's. This is my second reading." She slid the volume toward me; I picked it up and thumbed through the pages. "I think you will enjoy it. It's a love story, albeit quite a tragic one." She smiled. "Please know that your mother and I are committed to your romance with Dylan enjoying a happy ending."

"Thank you," I managed to squeak out, overwhelmed by her erudition.

"We have a few days to spend together and I hope that you shall not be bored. Perhaps you can think of our time together as the prelude to your journey to America."

I couldn't see how anyone could be bored in Madam Izzy's company, but not being certain of how to respond I simply thanked her for the book and remained quiet.

"Your mother was quiet too. But after a while with me..." She laughed. "After you bathe and dress we shall walk in the gardens and talk."

We finished breakfast, and Nancy accompanied me upstairs to a bathroom the likes of which I had never seen.

"This is Madam Izzy's latest addition," Nancy remarked. "She likes to be as modern as possible."

Nancy pointed to the flush toilet and showed me how it worked. She was well informed and I could tell she derived pleasure from explaining it all to me.

"There are cisterns in the attic that hold fresh water for the bathroom. Waste from the toilet is taken away and the toilet is once again filled by the cisterns." She then went to the tub and turned on the two faucets. "Hot and cold water at your disposal."

Mam and Tad had updated our house with a water closet, but this room was "*le pièce de résistance*," as Nancy announced with a dramatic flourish.

Nancy proceeded to fill the tub with water. I watched wispy clouds of steam rising as hot water gushed against cold porcelain. She added drops of lavender oil to the water and left to ready my clothes.

I soaked for what felt like an hour, adding more hot water, which flowed most freely from the spigot, when I heard a gentle tapping at the door. Nancy came in holding a large towel. She turned her head after motioning to me to stand up. I had never been naked before another person except for Mam, but I complied. She left me to dress and I saw that the clothes she had brought included pants not unlike my brother's castoffs that I used to wear, except they were cut in a style only worn by elegant gents and sewn from fine cloth.

I joined Madam Izzy, who held me at arm's length and turned me around. She lifted my hair, and stared for a moment at the back of my neck. I was highly embarrassed, as I had never had another person look at me with such scrutiny.

"We shall talk as we walk," she said.

I now had the opportunity to see the gardens at midday.

Groundskeepers were busily at work, trimming and sculpting the shrubs into fanciful shapes. I could not help but stare at what appeared to be reproductions of Greek statues, some of which I had seen in a book one of the Strickland girls discovered hidden away in the school library. We giggled and blushed at the sight of the naked male bodies until Mrs. Strickland, following the sound, discovered us. Without a word, she gathered up the book and told us sharply to go to our rooms.

As we continued on, the groundskeepers removed their hats and waved in greeting.

Madam Izzy waved back, sometimes stopping to chat and admire their work.

We soon came to a gazebo covered in climbing roses in yellow, pink, and red. A table, just large enough for two, was in the center, set for tea and coffee.

With a hand gesture, Madam Izzy indicated that I should sit. As if reading my mind, she said, "The human body is not meant to be ashamed of. Rather, it is meant to be seen as the work of nature and admired." She smiled, adding, "I owe you an apology for examining your neck this morning. You reminded me of your mother when she was your age, just before she left school to be married. Your resemblance is quite uncanny, and I was curious to see if you shared the same birthmark on the back of your neck. To my great pleasure, I see that you do."

"Mam says it means we were kissed by angels."

"Yes, I would agree."

She poured tea into a cup and, remembering how I took it, added two lumps of sugar and a small squeeze of lemon. She then prepared herself a cup of coffee and reared back in her chair, the very picture of ease, comfort, and self-confidence. I somehow knew I was in the presence of a grand raconteur and waited breathlessly for her to begin.

"Your mother and I were the two misfits at school." She laughed melodically, as if her senses were suddenly flooded by sweet remembrances. "I came to Mrs. Strickland's school because of my father's status with the government. It was expected that I, his only child, would marry and marry well. After all, what else was there for a woman? I must say, he didn't fail due to his lack of trying. I was just quite adept at finding flaws with each suitor. At twenty-two, I was labeled an old maid, which suited me—not the label, but that my father would no longer attempt to find a suitable husband. After he died, I inherited his estate, lock, stock, and barrel, with the understanding I should operate it without restrictions, as I saw fit. As my father had frequently pointed out, with great pride I believe, my wit and intelligence were the equal of any man. Without a guardian to impede my every move, I have been free to follow my natural inclinations."

She sipped her coffee and set the cup on the table. "What do you know of your mother's family?" she asked.

"I know that my grandfather made his fortune as a coffin maker. Not an ordinary coffin maker for the masses, but works of art, carved with such detail and beauty that royalty and the wealthy came only to him. Some ordered their coffin well in advance of the time they might die, just to make certain it was there for them when needed."

"Coffins are something that everyone eventually needs," Madam Izzy said wryly.

"I also know that cholera took my mother's family, except for her and her father."

"That's correct. And without a mother your grandfather did what he felt was best: he sent her away to boarding school. Enid and I were only eleven when we first met. We dreamed of a time when we might not be held back by the restrictions of men.

"Your mother and I were each born with a special gift. I had the gift of second sight, and your mother the gift of healing through natural remedies. We had planned that once our formal education was completed, we could move away from our families, who only wanted to control and stifle our gifts. Ah, those childish fantasies! Your mother wanted to use her talent to heal others and I, to forecast insight about the future."

"You mean as a fortune teller?"

"Not if you mean reading tarot cards or tea leaves and making vague predictions, as most charlatans do. No, my gift—or curse—is to see the future. Specific scenes, details. I rarely spoke of it lest I be labeled a witch. Even though those accused of witchcraft are no longer put to death, fear and hatred can still cause the kindest neighbors or dearest friends to mercilessly persecute the eccentric in their midst.

"At night, as your mother and I lay in our beds, we would whisper our deepest secrets to one another. Your mother told me about how her family had practiced the ancient ways and that before her mother had died, she had learned about the healing properties found in nature. I, in turn, told her that I could see the future, something I had never told anyone else.

"We began to weave daydreams of owning a home together and creating a place for curing people according to the ways of nature and intuition. Sadly, when your mother graduated her fate was not to go adventuring with me, but to submit to an arranged marriage."

"What happened?" I asked, teetering on the edge of my seat.

"Your grandfather had become wealthy as a casket maker, but as often happens, greed takes many forms. Money alone was not enough; he wanted status. And your father, while having status and vast holdings of property, was deep in debt and in need of money. It was a match of convenience, not love."

I became overwhelmed with sadness at the thought of Mam's suffering.

Madam Izzy's voice took on an otherworldly quality as she said, "Destiny has a peculiar way of guiding us to where we need to be."

I thought the remark strange, almost as if it had been pulled from some deep, painful place.

Madam Izzy ended the conversation by telling me that she was having a few guests for an after-dinner party she called a soirée. It was a word I wasn't familiar with; sensing this, she explained it to me.

"We shall gather for stimulating conversation and the sharing of talents, such as music and reciting poetry. You may wish to rest beforehand, as we generally stay up quite late."

She stood up, ending our visit rather abruptly, and we returned to her home.

I was filled with thoughts about our conversation. I wondered what my future might hold. Dare I ask her to share her gift with me?

I retired to my room and, as Madam Izzy had suggested, began to read *Wuthering Heights*; I was instantly enchanted by Miss Brontë's elegant and impassioned prose. I heard a soft knock, whereupon Nancy entered the room carrying a dinner tray. Placing the tray on the table next to the chair which I had found so comfortable, she excused herself and departed, only to return in a moment with a garment.

"Madam wishes you to wear this."

It was a bright red velvet gown far more elegant than anything I had ever owned.

Nancy said, "Everyone will be dressed up and Madam did not want you to feel out of place."

I was too excited to take much refreshment. After a few distracted bites I joined Madam Izzy and her friends in the drawing room. There were an even dozen including me; I was immediately amused by their dress, or perhaps I should say costumes. Each wore a garment or a hat or some other accessory representative of a character from Grimms' Fairy Tales. Madam Izzy herself had on a long golden wig that almost touched the floor. I immediately knew she was one of my favorite characters, Rapunzel.

I remained unsure of the character I was dressed as, or the role I was to play in this gathering.

"You look lovely," Madam Izzy said. "And this will complete your costume." She held a red cape with a hood in her hands and placed it around my shoulders. I now knew I was Little Red Riding Hood.

The guests applauded lightly, smiling and giggling as if they were young children watching a Punch and Judy puppet show.

Madam Izzy took hold of my hand and introduced me to her guests, first as the characters they represented and then by their actual names. The costumes were lavish and the guests inhabited their roles with panache and élan.

Snow White's stepmother sent shivers up my back. She gazed into a jeweled framed mirror, stared at me and said, "Magic mirror in my hand, who is the fairest in the land?"

Her imperiousness gave way to self-deprecation as she looked at me and said, laughingly, "Why, you, my dear, are the very fairest in *this* land."

Lastly, we stopped in front of a gentleman, about my tad's age, dressed in a long-sleeved shirt, with leather waistcoat and trousers. He carried with him an old-fashioned flintlock rifle and scowled at me with a furrowed brow.

Madam introduced us. "This is the hunter who saves Little Red Riding Hood from death at the jowls of the ravening wolf. In real life he is Captain Angus Blair. In his own style, he will be instrumental in saving you from a fate worse than death."

At this point, all the guests laughed and the captain, whose scowl had become a smile, took my hand and bowed.

Madam Izzy said, "Tonight, you shall be the guest of honor."

Remembering Madam's earlier description of a soirée, I gasped: "But...I have no talent."

"Of course you do; it is only waiting to be revealed."

She then guided me to a small table with two chairs in the center of the room and bade me to sit next to her.

A hush fell upon the room. She nodded to her guests, who seemed to follow a familiar routine. The oil lamps were dimmed until the only illumination came from the candelabra atop the grand piano and the fireplace that warmed the parlor this chilly night.

The room became silent and all movement ceased, as if every character had suddenly become a figure in a museum.

Madam smiled. "Is there anything you wish to ask me?" I felt my face turn a bright red. She sensed my discomfort. "You have nothing to fear, I only wish to give you that which you desire."

She took my hands. "Close your eyes and I shall close mine."

I did as I was told, although I was uneasy about what might be revealed. We sat that way for what seemed like hours but was in actuality but a few moments. Her hands became preternaturally warm, which unsettled me. Despite that discomfort, or perhaps because of it, I felt myself entering a dreamlike state.

"You and Dylan will have a long life together, and a most unusual one," she said. "You will travel further than you expect." After a long pause, she continued. "I see several children born to you, and a forest. A forest teeming with flora and fauna of every description, and the chatter—the chatter from the creatures inhabiting the forest is deafening. Most unusual, most unusual. The forest is not without its perils. Beware the forest, unless invited."

I could feel her hands trembling.

"I see another child who shall come to you but not be of you...wait a moment, not from your body. A girl, and you shall name her Rhianwen."

Rhianwen? What a peculiar name, I thought but feared to speak out loud.

"I am seeing the Moon Goddess Rhiannon. The queen of Faeries. The Goddess of rebirth and wisdom. She will be part of your lives...yours and Dylan's, and all the generations that follow."

She shuddered, and the warmth from her hands became so painful that I tried to pull away from her grasp, but her hold upon me had become too powerful.

"I've only had this happen once or twice, but never has it been so strong."

Suddenly her hands went limp and as her hands dropped, so did mine. When I opened my eyes, Madam Izzy's face was a picture of mingled exhilaration and exhaustion. She leaned toward me and whispered enigmatically, "Your talent shall be found within this forest."

She stood and briefly bowed her head. I wondered if she was offering a prayer to Rhiannon, but she quickly returned to her self-possessed, convivial self.

The guests applauded appreciatively, but I sensed that Madam Izzy had not revealed all that she saw.

"Now, my friends," she announced, "it's time for music, a poetry reading, and best of all, sweets from Rapunzel's own table."

Nancy wheeled in a cart filled with bonbons, candies, and sweetmeats. There were oohs and aahs from the guests as they surrounded the cart, taking the desserts of their liking.

∞

The next morning Madam Izzy set out a hearty breakfast of bacon, eggs, toast, and black pudding, a kind of blood sausage made of pig's blood, oatmeal, and pork fat. I had never been fond of this so-called delicacy and hoped my host wouldn't notice my declining to partake of it.

"It is my tradition to serve black pudding after these soirées," she said. "I need to replenish my energy."

As that was her only reference to the night before, I hesitated to say anything else about my part in it.

She smiled, and I felt as if the sun was shining directly onto me.

"I was at your christening, but you would hardly remember that," Madam Izzy continued as if she was alone in the room. "How your mother hated the ceremony, so out of character with her own beliefs. That night, after your father had fallen into a drunken stupor, your mother and I took you to the attic. Once there, we placed candles in a circle. After placing you in the center, we lit the candles and pledged your spirit to the gods and goddesses. You had screamed during the church christening as if the devil himself was holding you instead of the priest, but when she offered your life force to the gods and goddesses and the natural way of the world, you began to smile and coo.

"I saw it as a way for your mother to find comfort and never thought too much of it. It reminded me of some of the secret ceremonies we had as girls. But after last night... Most of my soirées are for entertainment, but I saw your future with a crystalline clarity that thrilled me. As I said, it promises to be most unusual."

Madam Izzy put aside her plate and took up her coffee cup. "Dylan worked hard and did without to save for your passage. Sadly, he barely had enough for steerage. Your mother and I could not tolerate that thought. Do you recall the gentleman who represented the hunter from Little Red Riding Hood? I introduced you, but you may not remember his name, Captain Angus Blair."

"I do recall. You made a rather cryptic remark about him saving me from a fate worse than death. I was too caught up in the excitement to pay your remark much mind at the time."

Madam Izzy smiled. "You are most perspicacious, my child. His costume and yours were no mere coincidence. As the hunter saved Little Red Riding Hood, so shall Angus keep you safe on your voyage to America." She caught my puzzled look. "You see, Angus is the captain of a packet ship. He will be taking you on his ship to New York. That is the first part of your journey."

"The first part?" I asked. *Was there to be more than one part?* My voice quivered and my lips trembled, signs I was about to burst into tears—a habit leftover from girlhood I wrongly thought I had learned to control.

Madam Izzy's voice softened. "Yes, my dear. It's a long and difficult journey from New York to San Francisco. Your mother and I looked at all the options and discussed them at great length with Captain Blair. You must first travel to New York and from there you will board a ship to San Francisco."

I dabbed my eyes and Madam Izzy was quick to hand me a hanky.

"How I wish your mother could have been here," she sighed. "In some ways, I don't know if I'm suited to care for a young woman. You and I are somewhat alike. We have chosen to follow our hearts and to reject what others seem as proper. There's satisfaction in striking out on your own, but it also comes at a price.

"I will accompany you to the ship and make sure you are settled in your cabin. Angus will see that you are watched over, but there is a set of conditions, put into place by your mother."

"Conditions?" I asked meekly.

"It has been arranged for one of the women traveling in steerage to act as your chaperone. Her name is Olivia; Angus Blair recommended her to your mother. You are to remain in your cabin except for meal times and strolling upon deck as the weather permits, and the captain allows it."

I nodded my agreement.

"I told you how your mam and I would share our stories. We had both suffered the loss of our mothers at a very tender age. Your mam told me of her dream to have a daughter and to be in her life until she was...let me think of how your mother put it...ah, yes, until her teeth fell out and her bones crumbled. We both giggled at the description, but I knew that should she be blessed with a daughter, she would do everything she could to remain in her life.

"At first, when your mam and I put our heads together to hatch these plans for your escape, it was as if we were children once again, planning some adventure at Mrs. Strickland's. But as the days and weeks went on and our plans became a reality, I could see the suffering in your mother's eyes.

"We both knew that once you arrived in America you would be caught up in the whirlwind of a new life. It was during one of her visits that she blurted out her deepest fear: 'How can I send my Bran away, without giving her all that I have to offer?'

"Those were her exact words. I hated to see your mother suffering and after much discussion, she decided to give you a part of herself by writing as much as she could about her life as a woman and as a healer. With a passion, she set about sharing all that she knew about the natural way of healing. It will be your task, during your voyage to New York, to study and absorb all that your mother has to give. Enid asks that you free yourself from all distractions during this time of learning. It is her request that you set aside writing in your journal during this time."

I nodded my agreement to concentrate on what I assumed would be my final gift from Mam.

"I was hoping against hope that I might see Mam one more time before I leave," I said. "I may never see her again."

Madam spoke in a soft kind voice, not unlike Mam's. "Separation is filled with pain, my child. Your mother is doing her best to keep you safe and to always be near you through her writings. You must put your trust in your mam, who loves you so much that she is willing to sacrifice her own life."

"I will do so," I replied. "However, Madam Izzy, I must ask: how long shall the first leg of the voyage be?"

"Angus said that is up to God and the forces of nature. He estimated perhaps forty days. The second part of your journey will be longer and more arduous. Once you reach New York you will board the *Flying*

Cloud clipper ship bound for San Francisco on her maiden voyage. It's a long trip around Cape Horn, and not without its dangers, but it will take you to Dylan."

"And how long shall I be aboard the *Flying Cloud*?"

Madam Izzy spoke so softly I could barely hear her. "Between one hundred and twenty to one hundred and forty days."

I gasped. *Up to six months on board two ships! Will I ever see Dylan?*

"Are you having doubts, Branwyn?"

"Doubts?" I repeated, more angrily than I intended. "At the risk of sounding ungrateful, I fear Dylan will wait and wait for me, not knowing when or if I shall come."

"You forget that Dylan is a man of the sea. There will be points of communication; it has been arranged."

Regaining my composure, I said, "I shall be ready for the coach tomorrow. At what time?"

"We'll leave at five in the morning. We shall see the new day aborning from the ship."

And now, as I await the coach that will take me to Captain Blair's ship, I close my journal, to return I know not when. I wonder about the future, about leaving everything I know behind. I am still troubled over Madam Izzy's predictions from the night of the soirée. She said I would live a long life, but I was certain she had not revealed everything she had seen.

For the present, my dear friend, farewell.

Villia felt the journal sliding from her lap and made a quick move to catch it before it landed on the floor.

"What is it, Emilee? You look so sad."

"Grannie, do you remember when we came here last year for the Fourth of July?"

"Yes, I thought we had a lovely time. Gramps and your father took out the flatbottom boat, we barbecued, and then we sat on the patio and watched the fireworks."

Emilee continued: "That night on the way home, Mother and Father had an argument."

Ethan nodded. "We could hear it...loud and clear. They thought we were sleeping but we just pretended."

"Father was all excited because Gramps had taken him sailing on the flatbottom boat. And Mother got really upset about his going on the boat. We thought she was having—"

"A meltdown," Ethan interjected.

"Yeah. You know how Mother is usually certain and firm about things?"

"Yes, that is one of your mother's traits," said Villia. "Not all bad, by the way."

"This was more like a tsunami," said Emilee. "She kept saying, 'I hate that boat, and I hate hearing about it.'"

Villia sighed. *What do I do with this? Dammit, Oran, where are you when I need your practical wisdom? Wait! What would Dr. Toni Grant advise?*

Villia spoke as if Dr. Grant, a certified psychologist with a popular call-in radio show on KABC whose pragmatic advice was worth listening to, had taken possession of her spirit.

"Sometimes it's difficult to understand our parents and for parents to understand their children. I wish I had a simple answer for you. Hey, I just thought of something! I have April's senior high school yearbook. Would you like to see it? It might give you a glimpse into your mother."

"Cool," said the kids simultaneously.

Dr. Toni would be proud of me. All those years of waiting in school pick-up lines while listening to her radio show have finally paid off. A positive followed by diversion. It's working!

Villia went to the closet and, after shuffling through family artifacts, pulled out April's senior yearbook.

Handing the yearbook to Ethan, she stifled a yawn. "It's getting quite late and I have a few things to tend to. I'll check in later."

∞

Emilee and Ethan huddled together on one of the beds, their mother's yearbook resting between them. They turned each page, their eyes straining for a glimpse of their mother as a young girl.

"I spotted her first!" said Ethan, pointing to the cheerleaders' group photo.

Emilee squinted. "Is that her?"

"Yeah! See the beauty mark on her cheek? The one we said looks like a heart?"

"Look at that hair!" Emilee laughed at the 1980s'do. "It looks like a lion's mane, puffed up and all. Wait! Wow! Mother was voted the most likely to succeed." Emilee flipped quickly through the book. "The prom! Look at her dress!"

Ethan said, "Yuk to the dress. Who would wear all those ruffles? And what are those glassy things?"

"They're rhinestones. It was the style."

"Mother looks so happy in all these pics. What could have happened? Do you think Grannie's hiding some deep, dark secret?"

Emilee said, "Grannie's hiding something all right."

"I think so too."

"You know that old adobe house?"

"Yeah."

"Did you notice how Grannie doesn't want us to go inside?"

"Yeah."

"Well, did you also notice there are four locks?"

"Yeah."

"Why would anyone need four locks unless they have something to hide?"

"Yeah."

Emilee let out a sigh of relief. "I'm glad you agree, 'cause I'm having one of my brilliant ideas."

She moved closer to Ethan and whispered, "After Grannie leaves tomorrow..."

Ethan's eyes widened. "Yeah."

∞

Villia rapped gently on her grandkids' bedroom door.

"Come in," they sang out in unison.

She was struck by the two cherubs sitting on one of the twin beds, holding their mother's yearbook and looking up at her with soulful eyes. *Right out of Raphael's* Sistine Madonna. *All they need are wings to make the likeness complete.*

Villia spoke in a hushed tone, as if she was in a place of worship.

"Tomorrow morning I'll run my errands to the senior center and then to the cleaners. Hopefully, they got the blueberry stains out of your shirts. I better fill up the gas tank as well. Why don't you try to sleep in? There's plenty of food for breakfast, and I shouldn't be gone more than an hour—two max. Can I get you anything special for lunch?"

Before Ethan could get a "no, thank you" out of his mouth, his sister gave him a slight nudge with her elbow.

"That would be wonderful, Grannie. We'd love a coupla subs, wouldn't we, Ethan?"

"Sounds perfect to me. Could we get chips and Cokes too?"

"I think that can be arranged. Okay, then, if I don't see you in the morning, I'll see you when I get back."

She felt chipper, light on her feet. What had she ever done to be blessed with these delightful, caring grandchildren? She made a mental note to tell April what a splendid job she had done in raising her children.

At the same time, she had a strange feeling that behind those cherubic eyes, some mischief was brewing.

CHAPTER 14

Ethan and Emilee were up in time to hear Villia bustling around in the kitchen. The sounds that at first had seemed so peculiar to them, now seemed oddly comforting—words murmured to Pooch, the sound of the tablecloth being placed over the kitchen table, and even the jangle of Grannie's spoon against the earthen cereal bowl.

"I'm hungry," said Ethan.

"Deal with it, Ethan," Emilee shot back. "We'll stay right here until she leaves. I'll keep my ear to the door, you look out the window."

They heard Grannie puttering around the kitchen and muttering about finding her keys, then the sound of the front door opening and closing. Ethan, positioned at the window as instructed, watched as Grannie's car left the driveway and entered the road.

"She's gone," he said. "Now what?"

Emilee said, "She keeps the keys in the kitchen."

"Are you sure we should be doing this?"

Emilee tapped her foot to the cadence of her words. "You're shaking. Look, if you're so scared, stay here. Or come with me. It's up to you."

"I'm not scared, but you know she might have a hidden camera or booby traps."

"Ha! Grannie doesn't even have cable. All we're going to do is look around the adobe, and leave. We won't touch a thing."

"Promise?"

She ran her hand through her hair, making sure that her fingers were crossed.

"Of course."

∞

The hefty door to the adobe made a screeching sound when the dynamic duo pushed it open. Emilee, working hard to appear fearless, put one foot in the room and froze. "Maybe you're right. It does seem kind of weird in here. Look at all the jars."

Ethan said, "This place gives me the creeps. Mother was right: our Grannie is a witch. Let's go!"

"Waitaminute...let's explore a little." Emilee glanced around the room, pointing excitedly to a corner. "Look, this must be Branwyn's trunk from, like, eons ago. I'm going to open it."

"Em, don't. *Please* don't! You don't know what evil spirits might be waiting to pop out. You said you wouldn't touch anything. Oh, God, I think I'm going to throw up."

"Wait outside if you're about to hurl. Leave no DNA—get it?"

"I'm better," said Ethan, making a swift recovery.

"Look, there's no lock on the trunk." She swung the top opened. "It's empty. Just an old empty trunk."

Ethan peered inside. "Check for a false bottom."

"Ethan, you are finally showing your brilliance."

Holding her breath and hoping that her own fear would not overcome her, Emilee tugged at the fingerhole, releasing the false bottom.

"I knew it, I knew it!" she exulted. "A third journal and an envelope. Just as I suspected all along, Grannie was holding back critical information. The wonderful old sneak."

"Now what?"

"We're taking them with us. To read. Tonight, after Grannie goes to bed."

∞

Villia returned carrying takeout bags from her favorite sub shop, Underground Subs. Thrilled with the cooperation from her cherubs, she had added to their order a slice of pie for each of them: chocolate for Ethan and lemon meringue for Emilee. The "cherubs" were not so guilt-stricken over their subterfuge that they for a second considered protesting her thoughtfulness.

"I usually don't believe in a lot of sugar," Villia said, unloading the bags on the kitchen table, "but you two have been most helpful and cooperative. And since tomorrow is our last day, I thought we should have special treats. I can't imagine what your camp food will be like."

Emilie and Ethan exchanged quick glances; neither had the heart to tell their grannie that one of the camp's highlights was gourmet cooking at its finest.

∞

That night, Emilee and Ethan waited for the house to become silent, which of course really couldn't happen. As Grannie had once explained, "Everything in nature is a living entity. Each one has a distinctive voice."

Emilee whispered to Ethan, "This house is sure a lively, living entity."

They both giggled at its creaks and groans. Their giggles stopped when Emilee turned on her camp flashlight and reached under the bed to retrieve the envelope discovered in Branwyn's trunk.

"We've hit the mother lode," she said, spilling the contents onto the bedspread. "Letters, plus a photo and what looks like a handwritten announcement."

"Let's read the letters first," Ethan suggested.

Emilee said, "Okay. The first one is addressed to Madam Latham from Branwyn's mother."

"Well, share it then and don't turn any pages until I'm ready."

"Okay, it's just that I'm a fast reader."

"Yeah, but I'm more observant."

∞

March 26, 1851

Dear Izzy,

I have sent this letter by my trusted friend, Dylan's father, Mawrth.

By the time you hold this in your hands, Bran will be safely on her way to Dylan's side in America.

No words can ever express my heartfelt gratitude.

As you know, I returned home after my birthday visit with Bran. The house was quiet; Lewis was away and my sons are now living in London.

I was never as brave as you, dearest Izzy. While I wish I could have seen my Bran once more, I had to stay and pretend all was well until she was safely on her way to America.

I spent those days in quiet contemplation and gratitude for our friendship. My memories went to the years we spent together at Mrs. Strickland's. What dreams we had, imagining two women on their own, without men deciding our every move, our every thought.

I steeled myself for Lewis's homecoming; I knew I would pay a steep price by giving Bran the freedom she deserved.

When Lewis returned he was boisterous and stank of hard liquor. In one hand he carried a whiskey bottle, half empty, which he clumsily deposited upon a table. "I bring good news!" he shouted.

I must admit I trembled in fear.

He continued: "Where is Bran? Not outside climbing trees, I trust." He smiled broadly at his jest and took my hand.

"The best of news! I met with Lord Bishop. We spoke of how the union of our children will mutually benefit our families. Why, it will place us among the greatest landholders in all of Wales!"

Like a dutiful wife, I managed a wan smile. His bluster continued unabated.

"I brought a gift for you from Lady Bishop: material from London in patterns of the latest styles. You and Branwyn shall have new dresses. No more of this Welsh provinciality."

As he was speaking, he kept hitting his riding crop against his boots. I remained silent.

His tone became serious. "Where is that child? Why is she not here to greet her father and to thank me?"

I looked him in the eye and, with every bit of courage I possessed, said, "By now, I would say she is somewhere in the Atlantic Ocean and safely on her way to America."

"What?" he laughed. "Silly woman, now is not the time for joking. It is time to celebrate."

When I gave no response, he narrowed his eyes at me. Even in his profound drunkenness he ascertained I had made no jest.

"What have you done, woman?" he growled, beating a menacing tattoo upon his boot with his riding crop as he staggered toward me.

"I have placed my daughter out of harm's way." I repeated: "Bran is somewhere in the Atlantic Ocean, on her way to America."

He lifted his riding crop and struck me across my face. The cut ran deep and bled, but I stood my ground and made no move to either acknowledge the pain or to stem the bleeding. I shall have a scar, not a bad one I think, but a reminder nevertheless.

I thought of you and how brave you have been to live as an independent woman. Strangely, I had never felt so angry and, at the same time, at peace.

I spoke from determination and righteousness. "She's free! I could not have her spend her life married to someone she could never love."

His face turned a bright red and his eyes bulged. "Do you have any idea what you have done? The loss of income? The shame you have brought upon me? Upon our family? I curse the day I married you and brought your pagan ways into my home. I should have torn Branwyn from your arms the moment she was born. At least," he snarled, "she is baptized."

I gave vent to derisive laughter. "I did not accept the baptism. During the ceremony I prayed to the gods and goddesses to be stronger than the Church and to surround her with the love of nature. And afterward, late at night, I performed the circle of light ceremony and dedicated her to the gods and goddesses."

Grimacing, he seized the bottle of whiskey on the table and hoisted it to his foul mouth. The fury I had kept bottled up inside for more than twenty years bubbled to the surface. I impulsively picked up the riding crop that had fallen from his grasp and struck him on the back. He lurched forward, sputtering, and dropped the whiskey bottle.

"There! Now you know how it feels. You are a weak excuse for a man."

"You bitch!" he hissed. Before I could elude his grasp I felt his calloused hands around my neck, choking me. Spittle from his mouth sprayed my face as he unleashed a torrent of profanity. I was certain I would die, but suddenly his arms fell to his sides. I collapsed against the wall, massaging my throat and gasping for breath. What force—pity, shame or an unseen deity—stayed his hand, I shall never know.

I saw his lips moving, searching, I guessed, for the most hateful invective they could conjure. At length he smiled evilly and said, "You and your witch of a daughter are dead to this family."

I could not stop myself from screaming, "You, sir, are cursed from this moment on! You will know no peace!"

"Empty words. I desire never again to behold your homely visage. Be gone from this house by morning."

And with that, he picked up his bottle of whiskey and climbed the stairs.

My dear Izzy, my momentary bravado has been replaced with abject fear. I will take nothing but my clothing and healing properties.

May I come to you? Is it too late for us to awaken our dream from so long ago?

Enid

∞

"Boy, I hate Bran's dad," said Ethan.

"Me too," said Emilee.

"What do you think happened?"

"Hold on, there's more inside the envelope. A note from Madam Latham."

∞

March 26, 1851

My dear Enid,

It is never too late.

Come to me posthaste. Let Mawrth know there is a place for him as well.

I await you at 5 West Morley Street.

Izzy

∞

Emilee picked up the remaining documents and photo.

"Look, it's an invitation to a soirée." She read aloud: "'Madams Izobelle and Enid invite you to an evening of exploration and healing.' Check out the pic—got to be Izzy and Enid. They look happy. The one on the right must be Bran's mother. See the thin line on her face? It's the scar."

"Shall I read from the journal?" asked Ethan.

"Yes, you can be Grannie's stand-in."

Ethan made a makeshift megaphone with his hands. He deepened his voice and announced: "This is Ethan Preston, with a reading from Branwyn's journal about her journey to America."

Sighing, Emilee decided not to make any comment about her brother's childish behavior, and instead settled back on a pillow to enjoy story time.

∞

May 29, 1851. My dear journal, my friend, we are nearing the end of our voyage from Cardiff to New York. I think Mam would forgive me for not waiting any longer to continue my entries. After a long ocean voyage, I hold you once again in my hands. I hope I have not forgotten how to write. We are nearing our destination, and I have spent most of this trip absorbed in Mam's teachings. At first, I was disturbed at having to put you aside and actually shed a few tears as I placed you in the trunk. I must admit, I was terribly upset, as you have become such an important part of my life. But I get ahead of myself.

Madam Izzy accompanied me on the carriage ride from her home to Cardiff Harbor. Once here, she made sure my luggage was placed in the cabin that would be my home for the next several months.

She stayed until we heard a sharp knocking on the cabin door. It was a young lad, no more than twelve I would think, who reminded me of Dylan at that age.

He tried to speak as a man, but his voice went abruptly from a deep octave to a high one. "Captain's orders. All visitors must disembark. Preparing to weigh anchor."

I had never heard that term before; sensing my confusion, Madam Izzy hugged me. "They're getting ready to lift the anchor and sail away," she explained. "I must leave or I'll be on this voyage with you." She smiled. "After I go, look inside the trunk. There is a bundle for you to open. Actually two. One from your mother and a small token from me. Go with a light heart; I will watch over your mam."

The concern that had been plaguing me eased and I thanked her again for all that she had done.

She whispered her parting words: "Remember, your talent lies within a forest."

I opened the trunk and removed the bundles that were sitting on top. The first was from Madam Izzy. Inside was a journal, with a brief note, which read: "For your future writings. With deep affection, Izzy." I was now the proud owner of three journals.

Next, I opened the package from Mam in a hasty manner and discovered two books. The first was filled with detailed information about illnesses and cures. The second appeared to be Mam's own journal, filled with her thoughts and poetry. I held that book to my heart and felt as if my mam was right next to me.

I had so much to learn that I immediately set about taking in all that I could. I now realized that my writing could become a distraction from the world I was destined to enter. I vowed not to disappoint Mam and pledged that for the length of this voyage I would be engrossed in her teachings.

As I would soon discover, the length of the voyage depended not only upon the captain's seamanship, but upon the forces of nature. The high winds and rough seas were followed by a sudden stillness in which our ship barely moved.

There were times, before the stillness, when I was ill from seasickness, but others fared much worse. The ship's benighted doctor knew no balms beyond laudanum and bleeding.

I continued to focus my energies upon the wealth of knowledge gifted to me by Mam. Her instructions were not completely foreign, as I had followed her as she picked herbs from our land and showed me how to harvest and dry them for future needs. She called me her little shadow. How much I have missed my mam!

As Izzy Latham has explained, I had my own shadow in the form of Olivia, a Swedish woman only a few years my senior, but already a mother with two children. She was going to meet her husband, who had immigrated to America a few years before. He had never met their youngest, a boy, as she was pregnant when he left; Nils was now three.

Olivia was housed in steerage, whose conditions she described as appallingly filthy, and was delighted to have a place to go outside of her usual limits. Sometimes she would bring her two babes, and I would save something from my meals to share with them.

Time went by, and not as slowly as I had once feared.

About halfway through our voyage there was an outbreak of dysentery within steerage. Captain Blair sternly refused my offer to render aid and ordered me to stay in my cabin and let the doctor tend to the passengers. One man died and they buried him at sea. I could not stand idly by any longer. Flouting Captain Blair's orders, I put on a camphor mask and took the ladder that went below the deck into steerage.

It was another world and the foulest of scenes. Drawing upon the passengers' description of their symptoms and my own observations, I was able to use my mother's teachings to create a remedy. After I administered aid, I went to Captain Blair and spoke my concerns with great conviction.

"The ailment will continue to spread; it will go beyond steerage and sweep throughout the ship. Their disease is caused by stifling, fetid air and general uncleanliness. We must take drastic measures to stop it from taking any more lives. The passengers need to have clean water and soap to wash their bodies and clothing. Their living and sleeping areas must be scrubbed clean before they return."

"I gave you an order to stay out of steerage and you disobeyed," he said angrily. "That sets a bad tone with the crew and other passengers."

I stammered, "I-I was trying to help."

"I cannot have you running around the ship as if you were Joan of Arc. Look around you...I don't always get gentlemen for the crew. You put your life at risk and upset the balance of power that keeps this ship afloat. I will make apologies to the ship's doctor for your interference and try to smooth things over."

His face softened. "If you were my daughter, I would be proud of you. I will see that your suggestions are put into place but don't ever disobey my orders again. Do you understand?"

I was quite shaken and unable to speak. I nodded my understanding and managed to croak out a thank you.

It was quite a sight to see the steerage compartment emptied out and its tenants on deck. Clothes and bodies were washed. The beds, which were merely hard wooden planks with straw mattresses sans linens, were scrubbed down, as were the floor and walls.

I thought about my home, my room at Mrs. Strickland's, and my cabin with a soft bed. The differences between the classes had never been so clear to me. I had never known hunger or wanted for anything, except my freedom.

Oh, how I wish I could thank Mam once again for all the things both large and small that she did for me. Who was by her side when she had to face my father's rage? No one. Realizing this, I felt a twinge of guilt and sucked back my tears.

That night I had a dream. The goddess Rhiannon visited me. She was bathed in golden shimmers and smiled down upon me as she spoke.

"Do not fear for your mother. All that is good in this world will be hers."

I woke with a start, but the worries that had filled my heart were gone. And once again, my thoughts turned to Dylan and our future together.

∞

Emilee reached for a tissue and wiped her eyes. "I wish I had known her. She was so brave."

"Em, do you think we're spoiled?" asked Ethan.

Emilee thought about her walk-in closet overflowing with clothes. *When I get home, I'm giving away half of what I have.* "Yeah, I guess we are."

Ethan nodded rather shamefully. "What do you think they ate in steerage?"

"I don't know, but it couldn't have been gourmet grub, like we'll get in camp."

"I wonder why Mother never talks about her childhood?"

Emilee shook her head. "It's a mystery and I want to solve it! My turn to read," she said, reaching for the journal. "Perhaps as we go along we'll find some clues."

∞

May 31, 1851. We arrived today at the port of New York. Captain Blair dropped anchor this afternoon and I will set foot on American soil tomorrow morning!

Captain Blair called for a celebration. For a few hours the differences between the classes was set aside and all passengers reveled together. By now, the passengers and crew alike knew about the purpose of my trip, partly from my own shy remarks, but mostly from Olivia's garrulousness. I was surrounded and given enough blessings to last a lifetime.

The women from steerage had made a quilt for me and Dylan. I blushed, as they called it a wedding bed quilt. I knew I could never have a richer gift.

I said my goodbyes that evening to Olivia and gave her one of my dresses as a gift.

The next morning, as soon as the sun rose, the gangplank was lowered. Captain Blair asked me to wait until the other passengers had disembarked. He then had my belongings gathered and I prepared to leave the ship.

"My orders," he said, "are to deliver you safe and sound to Mrs. Creesy. I envy you the opportunity to be on the *Flying Cloud* for her maiden voyage. What an opportunity! What an adventure!" He spoke so excitedly. "The *Flying Cloud* just sailed from Boston to New York Harbor. Come, we'll find Eleanor."

Captain Blair held out his arm for me to take and walked me down the gangplank like a doting father. In spite of being on firm ground, I felt the rocking of the ship and nearly lost my balance.

A petite woman, with eyes as round and luminous as an owl's, approached us and, smiling, put her hand on my arm to steady me.

"Perfectly common," she said. I looked at her, wondering about a stranger reaching out like that, but Captain Blair returned her smile. "Just like you, Eleanor, always ready to help. This, my dear friend, is your charge, Branwyn Rees. Branwyn, meet Eleanor Creesy. Navigator and curer of all shipboard ailments."

"You flatter me," Eleanor replied.

I could not help but say, "Navigator?"

She replied, "Among many other tasks aboard the ship, yes. Quite a surprise, is it not? I'm used to raised eyebrows and gasps. If you learn nothing else from this voyage, never underestimate the capabilities of a woman."

It had never occurred to me that a woman could rise to such an important rank on a ship.

"I've reserved a room for you at the New Yorker Inn," she remarked. "Another day's delay and you would have missed the *Flying Cloud*."

Captain Blair said, "We ran into some unexpected doldrums, but here we are."

"Good enough! Now, Branwyn, do you have a nickname?"

"My friends call me Bran."

"And mine call me Ellie. How does a real bath sound?"

It was my turn to smile at the thought of a real bath in a real tub. I had become skilled at sponge bathing with saltwater; a far cry from Madam Izzy's luxurious bathroom, so dear to my memory.

Captain Blair took my hands, slipping an envelope into them. "From the passengers and crew. Blessings to you and Dylan."

I was overwhelmed at this display of generosity and only managed to murmur a few inadequate words of thanks.

With a tip of his cap, the Captain turned sharply on his heels and returned to his ship.

I walked to the inn with Ellie, who assisted in toting my meager luggage. Once I was settled in my room, she said, "I must return to the *Flying Cloud*. We are beginning to load provisions. This is not the best time of year to be taking this voyage and any delay could have serious consequences. The innkeeper will see to your meals. Will you be all right on your own?"

I barely got a yes out when Ellie said, "Tomorrow you shall meet the other passengers and if all goes well, on Monday we will set off on our journey. I should be around by two in the afternoon." And with that, she left my room.

The next afternoon she appeared exactly as the courthouse clock chimed two. There was a cart waiting to carry my luggage. The cart was drawn by a horse that looked quite old and ill. My heart went out to the poor nag. I reached inside my pocket for the apple I had not eaten at lunchtime. I whispered, "Soon, my friend, you will get the rest you deserve." I knew the horse did not have long in this world; I hoped he would find peace in the next life.

Mrs. Creesy took my hand. "That was a kind gesture. News travels fast here at the harbor. I heard that you acted as a doctor for the steerage passengers."

"Yes. I got into trouble with Captain Blair for disobeying orders."

"So I heard." She laughed heartily. "I'm the nurse by number on board the ship."

"By number?" I asked.

"I have numbered bottles and powders. Then there's a sheet that matches the numbers with symptoms."

"Does it work?"

"Yes and no. About half the time, I'd say. I would like you to show me some of your healing ways. No harm in expanding my repertoire." She stopped. "Here she is, the *Flying Cloud*."

As a devout landlubber I gazed open-mouthed upon the magnificent clipper with its three soaring masts. The sleek ship was a beehive of activity as sailors swabbed the deck and tended to the rigging. I thought of Dylan, the budding shipwright, and how he would have given anything to be on this voyage aboard such an impressive vessel.

"She's beautiful," I remarked breathlessly.

"Yes, she's a real lady."

Ellie took my hand and we boarded the ship. I had no idea of what might be waiting for me and the other eleven passengers on this trip.

Ellie showed me to my cabin. "This is the best we could do and I do apologize. The rest of the staterooms were all reserved."

"It is more than adequate, Ellie," I remarked politely—and a trifle doubtfully.

The spartan room, with its single bunk, was no greater than six feet in either direction. My trunk had already been carried to the cabin and fastened to the wall with fittings to hold it in place. A few shelves and drawers completed the tiny space that I would call home for the next few months.

Ellie pointed to a few books on one of the shelves. "Angus—that is, Captain Blair—told me you are quite well-read, Bran. I had a few books I thought you might enjoy, and perhaps during free moments we can discuss them."

"I would like that."

At that moment I heard sounds that reminded me of our farm.

Ellie said, "That's part of the provisions, everything from chickens to pigs to lambs. Fresh vegetables too, and blocks of ice to keep them as fresh as possible. I think you will find the food on board to be quite satisfactory. I do take great pride in providing our passengers with freshly cooked victuals."

I asked her about the straps that were part of the bunk.

"There will be times," she said ominously, "when you will be grateful to be tied into your bunk."

And with that, she turned and left to assume her duties as navigator, nurse, and procurer for the *Flying Cloud*.

CHAPTER 15

"It's nearly midnight," said Ethan, yawning prodigiously. "How much longer are we going to read?"

"What's the matter, is it past your beddy-bye time, little baby?" Emilee teased.

"I can stay up as late as you anytime...even later!" said Ethan. He snatched the journal from his sister's hands. "Now it's my turn to read."

"I just hope the flashlight batteries hold out," said Emilee.

August 31, 1851. Each passenger had his or her own reason for being on the *Flying Cloud*—adventure, love, or business. All I know is that I survived, and if I live to be one hundred, I doubt I could ever have an adventure to match this one!

The *Flying Cloud* made the journey from New York to San Francisco in a record-breaking eighty-nine days and twenty-one hours. Ellie was right; there were times when I was grateful to be strapped into my bunk. There were other times when the heat was so stifling and sticky I thought I would die; I am ashamed to admit I welcomed the thought of death. I gazed forlornly upon my journals, unable to pick up a pencil to enter the day's happenings. There were other occasions when I reverted to infancy and cried into my bunk for my Mam.

From time to time Ellie and I would discuss a poem we had both read—Edgar Allan Poe's "The Raven" was a mutual favorite—and I shared with her some of Mam's ways and cures. I saw mankind at its best and at its worse. For instance, men working together, risking life and limb to triumph over nature. Then there were others who shirked their duties, putting both ship and lives at risk. I realized that I was more of an innocent child than I dared to admit.

At last, we approached the Pacific Ocean and sailed toward San Francisco. I stood on deck with the other passengers as a pilot schooner guided the *Flying Cloud* into her berth.

Ellie came over to me. "You will start life now with Dylan," she said. "I can only hope he is like my Josiah, a man who, while captain of the ship, sees a woman as his equal. I am to get word to your mother of your safe arrival. Godspeed!" And with a quick hug and some tears on both our parts, Ellie turned away, and I combed the crowd to find Dylan.

I do admit I feared Dylan might not be waiting for me, or that I might not recognize him. He would have grown from a lad to a man during our long years of separation. Then, I saw him. He was taller, his skin tanned by the sun, and his hair lighter. It was his eyes and his smile—unchanged, still as dazzling as ever!—that told me it was my Dylan. All at once I knew I had made the right decision. It was as if I was a puzzle with a missing piece, and as soon as Dylan reached out his arms and drew me close, that piece fell into place.

As we ran into each other's arms, he whispered, "Bran, my Bran."

He did not need to speak any more than that; I knew I had come home.

I can barely remember that first week. I collapsed and could not leave the bed. Dylan fed me weak broth and put cold cloths on my forehead. I slept for three days straight, or so I was told, and had nightmares about ferocious storms and, even worse, the doldrums common to the equatorial region of the Atlantic Ocean.

On the fourth day, I opened my eyes, unsure of where I was. Dylan had found a living space below the first floor of an apartment house. At first, I thought I was in steerage, for it was so bare and dank. I saw Dylan sitting beside me looking frightened.

"I thought I was going to lose you," he sobbed.

I took his hand. "I'm here," was all I could say before falling back into a peaceful sleep.

We never knew what caused my collapse. Perhaps it was just the strain from the last few months. I suppose one of the greatest gifts of youth is being able to recover quickly. As each day passed, I became stronger and stronger. One morning I woke up and stood on my own. Dylan had gone to work and I set about putting in order what would be our home for a while.

The next few weeks passed by quickly. It was like the winds sweeping down from the mountains, causing a flurry of leaves and needles to fall from the trees.

One day on the third week, Dylan said, "I have two surprises for you. That is, if you feel strong enough to venture out."

I put down the kettle I was readying for morning tea and turned toward Dylan. "Well, my love," I said, "don't keep me in suspense any longer!"

He took my hands and raised them to his lips. "The first surprise is, I've been building a boat."

I was so taken aback at his announcement that I blurted out, "Where did you get the money?"

He kissed the top of my head. "It will please you to know it cost me nothing."

He saw the look of disbelief on my face and said, "Bran, we can't get ahead of ourselves or the surprise won't be a surprise. All I will say for now is, I've done nothing dishonest. Do you feel up to walking to the shipyard? It's not too far."

"I've been walking the neighborhood while you were at work. Yes, as long as you are there to catch me should I stumble."

"Get dressed then, and prepare yourself to be impressed!"

There are hills in Wales and hills in San Francisco, but that is where the similarity ends. The hills in Wales are covered in a green; no eyes have beheld any greener. Sheep graze lazily and sometimes the shepherds rest under the trees while the sheepdogs are working. The hills in San Francisco go straight up; they are crisscrossed with dusty roads and lined with buildings sometimes three stories high! It was a Sunday morning and everywhere we walked we heard church bells, yet neither of us felt the desire or need to attend. And the throngs of people! So many men, women, and children that I wondered where they all might be going—and why they weren't in church!

I became overwhelmed by the buildings and masses of people but Dylan held my hand and guided me. I was like a lamb being shepherded to an unknown destination.

Our first stop was at a deserted shipyard. A sign hung on the fence:

MASON AND SONS SHIPYARD. CLOSED ON SUNDAYS

Dylan took out a key and unlocked the gate. I knew then that Dylan must have won Mr. Mason's trust and had earned a place of importance.

Dylan spoke softly, which is his way. "Come see where I work." He took me on a tour, pointing out boats under construction and others undergoing repair. We stopped at a building toward the back of the property. Dylan took out another key and swung the door wide open.

In the center of the room, with the sunlight shining right upon it, was a flatbottom boat.

"This is ours," said Dylan. "I work six days a week from first light until dark building boats for others. On Sabbath days—and the Lord will forgive me my transgression—I built this boat for us."

He set a gangplank against the boat and, taking my hand, walked me onto the deck.

"Run your hands over the wood," he said, taking my hands and putting them upon the starboard rail. "Not a splinter in sight."

I could see how proud he was. "What wood is this?" I asked, noticing that it looked different from anything I had ever seen.

Although we were quite alone, Dylan came closer and whispered, "About two hundred years ago there was a cold spell that besieged this area. No one could understand how or why, but it did something to the oak trees. They grew slower, and it took longer for them to be ready to harvest.

One day, Mr. Mason asked if I would work on a Sunday and I said I would. He told me he needed an old warehouse cleared out." Dylan lowered his voice to sound old and gruff. "'I leased that building to another boat builder who decided not to pay his rent and left,' he told me. 'Anything you find there of value is yours.'"

"I didn't mind coming in on a Sunday; it was quiet and I could dream of the time when I would hold you in my arms. It was a musty old building holding nothing I considered of value. I started to clear out the trash—broken tools, scraps of wood, that kind of thing. I worked for most of the morning and stopped to have a noon meal. Afterwards, I continued my labors and went to the rearmost section of the building. My eyes opened in amazement. There, against one wall, was a neatly stacked pile of oak timbers. A beam of light was shining through the window, right onto the center of the room. Just as it is right now—filled with angel dust. I followed the light, and I was amazed to see the beginnings of a flatbottom boat. I knew I had found a treasure; the next day I spoke to Mr. Mason about finishing the boat."

Dylan again lowered his voice to a comical timbre. I wanted to laugh, but I kept it inside lest Dylan think I was making fun of him.

"'Give me your word that you'll work here for two years and the building is yours to use, rent free,' he said. 'Borrow any tools you need.'"

"We shook hands on it. I think the wood might be the same wood Noah used for his Ark," he said most seriously.

Again, I had the urge to laugh. This time it was not at his change of voice, which I found so amusing, but at his childish beliefs in the Bible stories that we had learned in Sunday school. But then I thought, others might think the same about my stories of gods and goddesses.

"She's beautiful," I said, and that was my true self speaking.

Dylan beamed. "I changed her a bit to make her seaworthy. I added a mast like one would see on a trow. Remember how we would see the boats lowering their masts to go under a bridge? And I have added a keel—a wood log strapped with chains—just like the trows have. And for your...*our* comfort, a cabin."

While the cabin was small it had a door, an area for washing or fixing food, and a mattress that leaned against the wall.

"I did spend money on the mattress. Stuffed with cotton, not hay," he said quite shyly.

"So, is she a trow or a flatbottom?" I teased.

He smiled. "Once a flatbottom, always a flatbottom. She'll take us where we want to go, river or sea."

"And where might we be going?"

"That's surprise number two. We have a chance to buy some land in California, but I didn't want to decide without you. I know it's a lot for you to think about, but I'd like you to meet Phineas P. Poswell, attorney at law and justice of the peace."

I planted my hands on my hips and said waggishly, "And why would we be needing an attorney *and* a justice of the peace?"

"The attorney to make sure the land is legal." He blushed. "And, uh...well, the floor is getting mighty hard, you see."

"And?" I continued to tease.

"And it's time we share our bed!"

I reached out and touched his arm. He kissed me then, the first real kiss we had exchanged since my coming to America. He held me close until I thought I would never catch another breath.

My heart smiled as we left to meet with Phineas P. Poswell.

"Wow, this is getting pretty hot," said Ethan.

"Yeah, it's real Lifetime Channel stuff," said Emilee. "Gimme the journal. My turn to read again."

"With pleasure. My tongue's getting tired."

Dylan told me many people were coming to California to make their fortune in gold and San Francisco was a jumping-off point. Then he whispered before we entered the attorney's office, "Our gold will be in the land we own and the children we will have."

A rather rotund gentleman greeted us and held out his hand. "Phineas P. Poswell," he said, giving my hand a solid shake. "Welcome to our fine city. Please sit," he said, pulling out a chair for me. "I understand this visit is twofold. Which would you like first: the wedding ceremony or a discussion of the property?"

Dylan, with a turn of his head, deferred to me.

"Property first." I replied, knowing after my wedding I wanted nothing other than to be alone with Dylan, my wonderful husband.

Mr. Poswell took us to a table that held a large surveyor's map.

"This is the parcel I'm recommending," he said, using a short wooden pointer. "And a choice bit of land it is. One hundred and sixty acres, most of it suitable for livestock or farming. It has a natural harbor and there is a structure ready to be used as your home."

He stroked his scraggly beard. "I'm an honest man—as honest as the day is long, I've been told. So I'm obliged to point out one caveat. This plot of land is isolated from the other settlers, so you will be pretty much on your own. The owner's selling it dirt cheap for two reasons. Number one: your nearest neighbor is an Injun. A heathen. No one else wants to come near the place. Afraid of getting scalped. Now, if you ain't afraid I can get you a great price."

I bit my lip to keep from laughing. *With me and my ways, I would be lucky not to be called a witch. Perhaps the "heathen Injun" and I would become fast friends.*

Dylan was looking at the map and poked his finger at one area.

"What about this forest backing up against the fields?"

"Not included." Phineas P. Poswell couldn't hide a shiver. "That's another reason the land is so cheap. The story goes that the forest is haunted. It's said a curse will fall upon anyone who enters, and the poor fool who tempts fate is never seen again. It's a shame, because it's got the best timber in the region, ripe for harvesting."

I noticed a large wall map of California and asked Mr. Poswell if he could show me where the property was located.

The portly attorney pointed to San Francisco. "This here is where we are now." His finger moved downward. "And this here is where you'll be going. South about four hundred miles overland. I have connections with the railroad. They can take you partway, then I have a wagon service that will take you directly to your land."

Dylan announced, "We'll be traveling by sea."

"By sea? You might want to think that over. There can be some rough seas now and then."

"I own a boat."

"Do you, now? What kind of boat do you have?"

"I'm finishing her now. She's a flatbottom, or as some folks like to say, a flatbottomer."

"Kind of risky to take a flatbottom on the open sea, ain't it?"

"She's been modified to be seaworthy. I've been sailing and building them since I was ten."

"That makes this property even more valuable for you. Here," Mr. Poswell said, pointing at an area on the survey, "you'll see part of your land goes down to the Pacific Ocean, to a cove actually...a natural harbor."

Mr. Poswell smiled. "You won't find anything like this for what you can afford to pay. Look, California is now part of the United States of America, and at this price it's a steal. Plus, the owner will let you pay it off over ten years. Can't beat that."

He sat back in his chair, took a fat cigar from the humidor on the bookcase behind him, and lit it with a matchstick he struck against a clay Scottish terrier figurine on his desk.

"It's legal and it's yours," he said, exhaling billows of bitter smoke that made our eyes water.

"Why so cheap, if the land's so desirable?" said Dylan, coughing a mite. "I mean, who would be scared about a forest?"

"I can see you are a bright young man. The landowner is land rich and cash poor. He needs to raise funds for cattle."

Another person walked into the outer office.

"It's yours now, but if you wait..." Mr. Poswell stood up. "I'll give you time to think, while I greet this new customer."

Dylan looked at me and said, "I have a good feeling about the property. Instead of frightening me, the idea of a haunted forest and a heathen for a neighbor suits me just fine."

"I do agree."

Mr. Poswell returned and sat back down at his desk.

"We'll take it," said Dylan.

"A wise decision. Now, let's fill out the transfer of deed and then we'll continue with the wedding. Your full name?"

"Dylan, son of Mawrth."

"Hmm...that won't work. I need to have a proper last name to go right here." He tapped the signature line in his record book.

He leaned back in his chair, his more than ample stomach filling his colorfully embroidered waistcoat.

"I'll tell you what, you being a man of the sea and sailing a flatbottom boat beyond the rivers, it seems only right that your last name from this day forward should be Flatbottom." And without waiting for an answer, he wrote our name in the book.

"Now, do you want a civil marriage ceremony, or I can use my license as a preacher and give you a real nice religious ceremony?" He lowered his voice. "No extra charge."

Dylan looked at me. "Civil, please," I said.

Phineas P. Poswell spoke a few words about the sanctity of marriage, then stopped rather suddenly and asked Dylan if he had a ring. Dylan reached into his pocket and slipped the ring he had made from the antler of a white stag on my finger.

With great pomp and circumstance, Mr. Poswell uttered the most beautiful words I had ever heard: "I now pronounce you Mr. and Mrs. Dylan Flatbottom."

And so, on this blessed wedding day, we acquired a parcel of land next to a bewitched forest, a heathen as a neighbor, and a proper American name.

"Oh, I just love a good romance!" said Emilee. "Don't you, Ethan? Ethan!"

Her little brother was nodding off. She nudged him hard with her elbow; his eyes flew open wide.

"Huh? What?" he mumbled groggily.

Emilee smiled. "We'd better hit the sack. Morning comes early around here. Besides, the flashlight's just about to give up the ghost." She tucked the journal and other documents back in the envelope and slipped it under the bed. "G'night, baby bro."

Ethan was already fast asleep.

The next morning Villia had a difficult time rousing Emilee and Ethan for breakfast. When they finally did stumble out of bed, they shambled under the table for their Cream of Wheat like two adorable zombies. Villia didn't press them on their uncharacteristic lethargy, figuring they'd stayed up later pursuing some childish activity. *Best to let sleepy zombies lie.*

Villia was washing her own breakfast dishes when the phone rang. Zombified as they were, Emilee and Ethan perked up their ears to listen to one half of the conversation.

"Yes, this is she. ...Why, yes, at the bus stop tomorrow. ... WHAT! ... I'm calm. WHAT! A WEEK! ... Do you really think I care about a refund or a credit for next year? ...Yes, yes." Her voice softened. "I understand, and I'm sorry I yelled. I can't imagine having to call all the parents. ...You're welcome. One week from today, then. They'll be there. Goodbye."

Grannie turned to the kids and said, "The road is still washed out. I guess you're stuck with me for another week."

That grand announcement brought the zombified youngsters back to vibrant life. Emilee and Ethan scrambled out from under the table, grabbed each other's hands, and began to dance the hora.

"Don't tell me—you learned that in another class?" asked Villia.

They nodded as they flew in a circle of two. "It's called Dances Across the World," Emilee shouted, as they suddenly switched to a Bollywood number.

"While you two are dancing, I must make a quick visit to the adobe—and no, you can't come with me. Eat your breakfast, clean up, and we'll talk when I get back."

Grabbing the keys, she walked out the back door, went down the steps, and trotted toward the adobe. She unlocked the bookcase and removed the same jar she had previously used to contact Rhiannon. Once the lid was unscrewed, the lilac-scented vapor appeared. When it had cleared, an eagle appeared on top of the Mountain of Dreams, flapping its wings, readying itself to fly.

"Rhiannon, is that you?"

"I got bored hanging out at my castle and thought I would try something a little different."

"Could you change back?"

"Like this?"

Villia sighed. "Grace Kelly, as I live and breathe! Exactly how you looked when we first met."

"Don't get stuck in the past," countered Rhiannon.

"I've got a problem."

"Have you forgotten I am all-knowing and all-seeing? I would say you have more than one."

"You mean besides the babysitting issue?"

"Yep. 'What do I do with the kids?' is one issue. The other is, Emilee and Ethan snuck in and took the third journal from the trunk."

Villia hit her forehead with the palm of her hand.

"I haven't seen you do that since you were ten."

"That long ago?"

"It was Christmas Eve, as I recall. Your sibs had been teasing you. Remember?"

Villia sniggered. "I replaced the chocolate in their stockings with Ex-Lax. Did Mam know?"

"Of course! We had many laughs over that one, and many conversations—not unlike the one we're having right now."

"What do I do about the ceremony? I have no one to watch Emilee and Ethan, and if I take them April will kill me and I'll never see them again."

The Ancient One began to fade. "Villia, everything will work out in the end. Life is preordained—you know that. I must go, it's time for my class in Dances Across the World. If you decide to take Emilee and Ethan, remember: one teaspoon of Elixir for kids and one tablespoon for adults."

"What about the journal?"

"Figure that one out on your own." Rhiannon paused. "I've known you for all your lives. You've been blessed and cursed, as all humans are. Your blessing is compassion and your curse is fearing to make a mistake. Take risks, my child. That is the lesson you must learn in this lifetime. Have more faith in yourself; you'll know what's right."

Villia fed the feral cats before returning to the house. Her anger at Emilee and Ethan had waned, at least below the boiling point. Before taking the stairs back to the house, she sat beneath the weeping willow trees, remembering how they had started as two apparently lifeless twigs.

She had watered and fed them and even prayed.

If she had not watered them, would they have given birth to their first leaves?

If she had not fed them, would they have flourished?

If she had not prayed to the gods and goddesses for their well-being, would they have survived?

Ethan and Emilee were two twigs that needed to be nourished with love and understanding. Had the journal become so important to them that they would break into a forbidden place? Were they also searching, as she was? Was there an answer within the journal for them...for herself...for the island?

She took the stairs with a renewed sense of purpose. Having finished washing their breakfast dishes, Ethan and Emilee stood at the counter, sobbing.

"We know you know," said Emilee. "We only wanted to know the truth."

She nodded. She took the wooden spoon from the drawer, the one that her mam had used, more than once, on the backside of an unruly child.

She remembered all those nights as a child when she would huddle beneath her covers, a flashlight in her hands, bent on finding answers to her questions about life within a book. *King Arthur and His Knights of the Roundtable* to understand her life's quest, and *The Count of Monte Cristo* when she wanted to get revenge on her siblings.

"If you want to continue reading the journal, you must kneel."

Ethan's eyes flew wide in alarm. "Are we going to get spanked?"

"You must trust me if I am to trust you."

She took the spoon and tapped them on their shoulders.

"With all the powers from the gods and goddesses and the Flatbottom blood that flows through your veins, from this moment forward you shall be known as the Seekers of Truth.

"Now rise! We will set aside the past, stay in the present, and look forward to the future with all its adventures."

CHAPTER 16

As the trio sat in their usual places in the living room, Villia picked up the third journal. "Well, how far did you get?"

"We know how the Flatbottom name came about," said Emilee. "And how Dylan and Branwyn married and bought this very land." Her eyes brimmed with tears. "Grannie, I'm sorry. It was my idea."

Ethan murmured, "But I went along with it."

"I shouldn't have pushed you, Ethan."

"Don't think for one minute I approve of what you did," said Villia. "But I do approve of your feeling remorse. I'll read from the journal and let the two of you think and feel what it must have been like for Dylan and Branwyn starting out on their own. In today's world we would consider them barely young adults, yet they left their families to venture to places they had never been and without knowing a soul. Perhaps we will all become enlightened."

September, 29 1851. The next few weeks were filled with love, work, and preparations for the voyage to our new life. I had never felt happier. I had recovered physically, and any fears I had of this unknown adventure were assuaged by having Dylan by my side, my best friend...my husband.

181

Together, we went through Mam's wedding trunk and gave many blessings to my beloved mother, for she had filled it with things needed to start our home. There were blankets, dishes, and clothing, as well as packets of herb and vegetable seeds for our garden, and a special treat for Dylan: the toffee he loved so much. At the very bottom were some baby clothes wrapped in a baby blanket. A note from Mam told me that I had worn those very garments.

Dylan held an infant gown close and whispered, "One day soon, I pray."

The day arrived when Dylan and his mates tested our flatbottom boat. From sunrise to sunset they sailed in and out of the harbor and into the sea. Dylan came back kissed by the sun, but with a grin as wide as San Francisco Bay itself.

"She's perfect," he said. "But not as perfect as you," he added hastily. Then he kissed me as a man kisses the woman he loves.

We spent the next few days loading the boat with supplies. Dylan's mates were as excited as we were. They had prepared charts showing all the harbors along our journey. Dylan said, "We'll take our time. If it looks like bad weather we'll drop anchor at one of the harbors and stay put." He patted the boat as if she was alive, and for a moment I felt a pang of jealousy that she might become my rival for his love.

We did hit a bit of a snag, when Dylan feared we might not have room for Mam's trunk. But I said, "I'll sleep standing up if I must." But it worked out after all.

And so it was on a sunny Saturday that we set sail for Rancho de los Palos Verdes and our new life.

As soon as we left the harbor a pod of dolphins surrounded our boat. I don't know which gods and goddesses were looking after us, but I am convinced they had sent their blessings. The dolphins stayed by our side for many hours, but as the sun began to dip they left us at the entrance to Monterey harbor.

The next morning, as we left the harbor, the dolphins joined us once again, and so it went for six days until we reached Rancho de los Palos Verdes.

Standing upon our harbor dock was a man unlike any I had ever seen.

Short of stature, his hair was black as pitch and his skin was coffee colored. Dylan whispered, "This must be the savages we were warned about."

I felt myself getting angry and said, "We have known savagery from my own father and others with the palest of skin. I don't believe any person is more or less a savage than any other."

It was our first falling out, and I surprised myself at the sharpness of my words.

Dylan cast his eyes downward and said, "You're right."

The man gestured toward us to throw the dock line, whereupon he caught it effortlessly and tied it to a post. With the gangplank in place we went ashore to meet the person who would turn out to be our new neighbor and dearest friend.

Dylan held out his hand. "Dylan Flatbottom. This is my wife, Branwyn."

"Luke Aguilar. I've been waiting for you for the last few days."

"How did you know when to expect us?"

"I received word from Poswell but had no idea of when you might arrive. The dolphin is my spirit animal, and yesterday when I spotted a single dolphin scouting about, I knew you were on your way. Come, I will take you to your home and land."

I was surprised that the stranger's English was as good or even better than mine. I thought back to Dylan's earlier comment when I became angry and realized that I, too, had my own set notions. I knew I would have to talk to Dylan and apologize for my harsh words. I remembered Mam saying to me more than once, "A great sin can enter through a small door. Best to right a wrong whilst it is small."

The path to our land was rather steep but leveled off when we got to the top of the cliff. We walked for perhaps a quarter of a mile, with Luke indicating the boundaries of our land.

Luke stopped abruptly in front of a large stand of trees.

"Is this the forest?" I asked.

He nodded. "This is the north boundary of your land."

Dylan turned to face our fields, then knelt to scoop up a handful of soil. "It's rich," he declared, smiling up at me with the black dirt sifting through his fingers. "We shall grow the best of crops."

Luke said, "It has lain fallow for more than a year. The Fosters, the people who owned this property before you, were warned about the forest but didn't take heed."

"Do you believe it to be bewitched?" I asked.

Luke spoke thoughtfully. "This forest has been bewitched since the earth was young, long before it became part of the United States, before the land belonged to Mexico and eons before the Spaniards came. We Tongva people have always known about the haunted forest." Luke gestured toward the sea. "Our islands were a day's trip away by canoe. We had lived there since the earth was formed, but at times we would take our canoes to this land to hunt. We only took what we needed, but even during times of scarcity, we never went near the forest.

"Hundreds of years ago, we were taken from our island home and brought here by Spanish soldiers to build the missions. They laughed at first about our warnings of forest demons. From time to time, acting on a devil-may-care impulse, or perhaps as the result of a dare or too much wine, a man would tempt fate and enter the forest. He was never seen again.

"The Tongva knew there was a spirit deep within the forest who protected the animals that lived within its borders. If you hear strange sounds, ignore them. Don't be tempted to cut down a tree, no matter how much you need the wood. Respect the forest and all who dwell within and you will be respected. Taunt them, or provoke their wrath, and suffer the consequences."

We continued our walk in silence until we reached a small shelter. I had never seen anything like it, as it appeared to be made of mud bricks.

"This is your home," said Luke. He opened the door and we walked inside. I gasped at the sight of the chipped walls and chairs and tables battered to pieces. It was as if a malignant spirit had entered and attempted to destroy everything. I looked at the bare earthen floor and thought about my home in Wales, with my mam making sure that meals were prepared, our clothing sown and our needs taken care of. But that was another lifetime ago, and my curiosity vanquished my momentary fears.

"What happened?" I asked Luke.

"As I said, the Fosters didn't listen to my words of warning. They laughed them off as if I was nothing more than an ignorant heathen. I am no heathen. I was baptized and attended the church school. I can read and write and have mathematical skills, as well. Pardon my defensiveness. Too often I have been the victim of people judging a book by its cover, as it were."

Luke smiled most charmingly, and I found myself liking him all the more. I knew Dylan felt the same.

"I wish I were half as well-spoken as you, Luke," said Dylan. "Now, tell us what happened and hold nothing back."

"The Fosters came not by sea, as you did, but overland. I picked them up from the train station and showed them their land and the house, which was quite nice at the outset. The furniture had been built at the mission and had more comforts than some of the other homes hereabouts. The man, whose name was Edward, laughed at my warnings and called them superstitions from a heathen. He put his hand on a Bible and said, 'This will protect me!' Even though I myself have been baptized, I knew the forest demons were stronger than any book.

"I worked with Edward to ready his fields for planting. His eyes were more on the forest than on his crops. Winter came...an unusually cold winter. After a while, he kept talking about how he could use one of the trees for firewood. I arrived one morning and, to my dismay, saw him cutting down a tree on the forest's edge. He demanded I help him but I turned my back to him. He offered me some of the wood but I refused to take it. A few days later he cut down a second tree. He smirked and said, 'You see? Nothing to fear, just ignorant superstition.'

"I saw him change. Little ways at first, like stopping his work to ask me if I heard singing. Then, he began to drink; he neglected his appearance, got scruffy-like. The music that only he could hear was driving him crazy until one day, as we were working in the fields, he stopped, sudden like. He turned and asked me again if I could hear the singing. I said no, but I knew their source. Other sounds followed, more than just forest creatures or the wind blowing through the trees.

The sounds continued, sometimes humming, sometimes whispering, that only he could hear. He said the forest was calling to him. One day, he said to me, 'I'm going in.' He did, and he never came out."

Dylan returned my uneasy glance. "Maybe Edward just upped and left," he suggested.

"No," said Luke, "He was a man possessed. I saw it with my own eyes."

"But what happened that the furniture should be broken?"

"His wife said he had been going slowly"—he tapped a coppery fingertip against his temple—"loco. Drinking too. And having what she said were fits of rage, breaking furniture one piece at a time until there was nothing left. After he disappeared, Mrs. Foster stayed for a while until the neighbors collected enough money for her and their children to return to her family in Utah."

"That's quite a story," Dylan said. He turned to me. "Don't worry, Bran, we'll stay on the boat and in a week, I'll have this place shining."

Luke acted as if he hadn't heard our words and continued with his tour of the house.

"This is how we build our houses here. The walls are strong and the roof won't leak. You have two rooms, Mrs. Flatbottom, and unlike some local homes, your cooking can be done inside. I can bring helpers and, in a few days, the furniture will be repaired and your walls whitewashed."

Dylan said, "I have little to pay them with."

"They'll help you and you'll help them. It's how we do things here."

Luke then looked directly at me with a gleam in his eyes. "Don't worry, Mrs. Flatbottom. You will meet my wife, Maria, and she'll help you with the birthing. By the time the baby comes your home will shine and your fields will be planted."

Luke said goodbye and disappeared almost as quickly as the forest ghosts we feared.

Dylan said, "Baby?"

"Perhaps," I said, feeling the comfort of his arms around me, but I knew in my heart that Luke's shrewd conjecture was correct.

∞

"Grannie, the adobe we broke into, is it the same one?" asked Emilee.

"It's been repaired many times and we've made some alterations, but yes."

"And the bewitched forest, is it still here?" Ethan asked, shivering.

"To discover that we'll have to continue with Bran's journal."

"Grannie," asked Ethan, "so you believe in ghosts and stuff? I get awfully scared at night."

Dare I even tell the children what I believe in?

Villia alone heard Rhiannon's soft voice say: "Tread softly; what needs to be revealed will show itself in due time."

"Ethan, perhaps your questions will be answered as we continue reading. Shall we?"

The kids said as one: "Yes, please, Grannie."

∞

October 1, 1851. We spent that night on our boat and upon rising, walked from the boat to our new home. We passed the forest, which seemed unusually still. As we approached our house, we heard the voices of workers coming from inside. A table had been repaired and placed beneath an arbor of trees. Several women brought food and were busy cooking on an outside grill while chatting in Spanish. They stopped when they saw us. One woman stepped away from the group and approached me.

"I am Maria, Luke's wife," she said. "And these monkeys"—she pointed to three boys climbing a nearby tree¬—"are our sons."

After Dylan and I introduced ourselves, I noticed some herbs growing next to the house. Taking a pinch, I raised it to my nose and sniffed. "Good for healing bruises," I said, motioning to the boys, who were now swinging from the tree and about ready to let go.

Maria smiled and took my hand. She went to another plant and said, "Poison." She pulled it up by its roots and threw it into the fire that had been started for roasting corn. She smiled at me, saying, "We have much to learn from each other."

I knew at that moment I had met my teacher in this new world.

And in this way of newly discovered friends our life in Rancho de los Palos Verdes began—surrounded not by landed gentry, but by the people of the earth.

Phineas P. Poswell had warned us about the heathen and a haunted forest. But I soon learned that these were people who had been forced to give up their beliefs and enter into what became near slavery.

Two nights later, Dylan and I slept in our own bed, in our own house. I wept, perhaps because of the new life I was carrying, or perhaps it was the realization that while we had left the servitude of my father's world, this new world was not without its own bondage.

We followed Luke's advice and lived in harmony with the forest. Dylan wasn't bothered by voices or sounds except the occasional chirping of a bird or the rustling of leaves.

Our days passed, one after another, in work and friendship. Dylan rose before the sun to care for our fields. The life within me grew until I felt a flutter, as if butterflies were kissing me on a warm summer day. I wrote to Mam to tell her the good news and prayed we would see each other again.

∞

It was a few months after we had set up housekeeping at Rancho de los Palos Verdes when I met evil itself. It was my habit to bring Dylan and his helpers lunch. I had stepped outside with my lunch basket in hand when I saw a man riding a wild black stallion of such gigantic size that I thought the devil himself had come to pay me a visit. The rider, dressed in all black, stopped next to me but did not dismount.

"I'm looking for Dylan Flatbottom," he barked. "You be his wife?"

I nodded. "Who might you be?" I asked, trying not to show my fear.

He dismounted and stood towering over me. I could see the whites of the horse's eyes as it pawed the ground and snorted.

"I am the person who sold you your property. I came to introduce myself: Dawley King, at your service."

Villia stopped reading; she felt her heart fluttering and her hands trembling.

"Is something wrong?" asked Emilee.

"No, I just need a moment."

She went into the kitchen and leaned against the counter.

How long had it been since she had read the journals? She was young. Before Bruce and Ebrill were born. Before she had married Oran. She had forgotten; how could she have forgotten? What had it been¬—forty, fifty years? The Kings wouldn't have meant anything to her at the time, but now she could barely abide the name.

She returned to the den and picked up the journal.

"Let's pick up where we left off," she said to the kids. "Bran has just met the man who rode up on the black steed."

∞

"I am the person who sold you your property. I came to introduce myself: Dawley King, at your service."

He inched closer until his protruding belly nearly touched mine. "It has come to my attention that you have become friendly with some of the heathens. They are believers in dark magic, even though they have all been baptized. It is best if you stay with your own kind."

"They are my own kind," I said, hoping my voice was not as shaky as I felt.

He shrugged. "You don't want your husband to go the way of the last man who tried to tame this property." He spat out his words as he mounted his horse and left.

I ran to the fields where I found Dylan, Luke, and two other men hard at work. Luke and the helpers came over, took their lunches, and walked away, giving Dylan and me our privacy.

"Bran, you're all out of breath. What is it?" asked Dylan. He placed his hand on my belly. "Is the little one up to mischief?"

I shook my head, but I couldn't stop the tears from coming. I described my disturbing meeting with Dawley King. "He's evil, Dylan. Don't ask me how I know, I just know."

"We've dealt with evil before."

"Not like this. Remember in Sunday school when we learned about heaven and hell?"

"I thought you didn't believe in that."

"I didn't until now."

Villia closed the journal.

"What is it, Grannie?" asked Ethan. "You look like you've seen a ghost."

"Nothing. The day seems to have flown by and I'm unusually tired."

"Why don't you relax and we'll take care of ourselves." said Emilee.

"And, we promise no more shinanigans," added Ethan.

Villia smiled. "I'll turn in then and we can continue reading tomorrow."

Villia got into bed and pulled the covers over her head as she had done as a child. The Kings had plagued the Flatbottom clan from the beginning, and remained a thorn in her side after more than 150 years.

Had she crossed a line by reading the journal to the children? What else was in it?

April would kill me if she found out, and I couldn't blame her.

CHAPTER 17

Villia tossed and turned that night, causing Pooch to leave her bed and roam the house. He stopped in front of the children's room, saw through the crack in the door that Ethan and Emilee were also tossing and turning, and decided to sleep in the kitchen. He crept under the table, lay down with his head between his legs, and with a sigh bespeaking his concern for his humans, fell asleep.

Ethan was dreaming of being chased by a scary man riding a giant black horse that breathed fire. He woke Emilee. "Sissy, I'm scared," he whispered.

"You must be—you haven't called me Sissy since you were four." Emilee pulled her covers back and patted the mattress. Ethan crept in and snuggled close to his sister.

"I had a bad dream about the mean man and the giant horse. I don't want the devil to get Dylan and Branwyn."

She spoke soothingly. "It has to turn out okay, otherwise we wouldn't be here." But in her own way, she was as distraught as her brother and stayed up the rest of the night trying to understand the last few days at Grannie's house.

∞

A pall hung over the people living in the house that stood on rickety stilts.

Emilee and Ethan stood at the kitchen window, their noses pressed against the glass. Dark clouds covered the sky. Rain fell in buckets. Thunder crackled in the distance.

Villia took out the ancient cast iron waffle iron.

"What's that?" asked Ethan.

"This is a waffle iron," she replied. "It was my mother's."

"Oh, I've never seen one like that."

The batter sizzled as she ladled it into the mold. She closed the lid; presently a heavenly aroma filled the kitchen. About five minutes later, the first batch was ready. Ethan and Emilee fairly inhaled the waffles, slathered with maple syrup, with gusto.

Villia was pleased. "I take it they're to your liking?"

"The best, Grannie," Ethan enthused.

Emilee said, "Ethan had a bad dream last night, and I was up most of the night wondering about what happens next."

"I didn't sleep too well myself," Villia admitted. "I haven't read the journals for many years and had forgotten there's some scary places in them."

Ethan said, "It was the gigantic black horse that scared me. Grannie, do you think there really is a devil?"

Villia looked out the window. *Most unusual to have this kind of rain in June. It won't be stopping any time soon.*

"Not the way Bran thinks of one. Perhaps we should put the journal back where it belongs—in the trunk."

"Not fair," protested Emilee. "You can't take us this far and then not finish the journal."

"What about you, Ethan? Do you want to stop?"

"Yes and no. Yes, because I'm scared, and no, because I think Bran was scared too. And if she could keep going, so can I!"

Emilee looked at her brother, grinned, and applauded.

Villia said, "Okay, here's the deal. Rain or shine, I've got to feed the cats. You two clean the kitchen, brush your teeth, and make your beds. Deal?"

"Deal!"

Chapter 18

B y the time Villia trudged up the steps and into the house, Emilee and Ethan were ensconced in the den, sitting quietly on the couch—waiting.

"I've got to dry off," she said, as much to herself as to her waiting grandchildren. She shook her head, and the kids laughed at the way drops of water flew about the room.

"Oh, Grannie, you look just like Pooch when I squirted him with the hose!" said Ethan. "Oops. I probably shouldn't have said that." He immediately became pensive again.

"You two are acting awfully suspicious," said Villia. "What's up? Or should I say, what have you been up to?"

Emilee and Ethan exchanged knowing looks.

"Nothing, Grannie," Emilee said. "We were just talking while you were gone. We want to say thank you."

"For what?"

"Well, for everything. For the waffles and the beach, but most of all for listening to us and letting us finish the journal."

"I'll always treasure the time we've spent together." *And once your mother finds out, I may never get to see you again.* "Back in five," she said, rushing out before she was overcome by tears.

No time for a bath or even a shower. She reached for a towel, dried in a flash, and slipped into her terry cloth pants and zippered long-sleeved top.

Emilee and Ethan had solemn expressions and looked as if they hadn't moved since she left the room.

There's no going back now. I suppose April will have to double their sessions with Dr. Meyer.

With a sigh, Villia opened the journal.

"This entry is written by Dylan. I don't remember reading this part, so I suppose we shall all be in for a surprise."

April 15, 1858. My name is Dylan Flatbottom and I am writing this story for anyone who, many years from now, reads Bran's journal. I asked Bran to enter my story in her journal, but she shook her head no. I asked her why not. She came over to me and hugged me tight. "You are as much a part of my life as anyone can be. This part of the story is yours to tell."

What I am about to relate is the gospel truth. Future generations need to know that things exist in this world that can only be seen by true believers.

I am a farmer and fisherman living in Rancho de los Palos Verdes, California, in the United States of America. My wife Branwyn and I settled here seven years ago and we have three beloved children.

I was working in the field that borders a forest, known to be haunted. Lest you scoff, wait until you have heard all that I have to say.

Winters in this area are generally mild and we had some days when the children could run outside in summer clothes. But, the weather had been unusually cold and wood to keep our house warm was dear. It was early in the morning; I had left the house just as daylight was breaking. My eyes went first to my field that had been planted in root vegetables. I would harvest the beets and turnips to sell at the open market and to store in the small cellar I had built only last year. I looked at the forest; it was quiet, as it usually was. I bowed as I did every morning and wished all who lived there a blessed day. Thereupon, my eyes fixed on a fallen tree lying by the edge of the forest. I stared at it; there were no marks to show it had been cut down and I thought it must have fallen, since the roots were still moist and caked with earth. Tempted though I was, I remembered the stories about those who dared to steal from the forest and let it lie.

Luke, my friend and helper, along with some other workers, came to help with the harvest. Luke and I had planned to leave the others to do the harvesting while we took my boat out to sea with the hope of catching enough fish to sell or trade for firewood.

Luke caught me staring longingly at the fallen tree. He looked at me and said, as if reading my mind: "The forest can be filled with trickery to lure you into the woods, never to be seen again."

The next morning the tree had somehow moved closer to my field. I looked at it for a long time and thought of how my children had shivered in the cold that morning. I turned away from temptation, thinking the tree's movement must be the trickery of forest demons.

It rained for the next two days and I could see our supply of logs, once stacked to the roof line, was now barely as high as my knees.

After the rain ended, I passed by my field on the way to the harbor where my boat was safely moored. Perhaps today would give us enough fish to sell or trade for firewood. I stopped. There lay the tree, now resting well inside my field. There were no drag marks or footprints in the soft soil. No human could have moved the tree; I shivered, believing supernatural forces were afoot.

I looked at the tree longingly, thinking again of how the wood could bring warmth not only to my home, but also to my neighbors'.

The fish were few, but I caught enough to purchase firewood for the night.

I returned home to a house bursting with the energy of our three children. Huw, the eldest, was six. Gavan was five, and our youngest, Caron, was still a babe of less than eighteen months. That night after the children were fast asleep, I told Bran about the mystery.

"I think the forest fairies want me to have it. I feel no trickery. They are not luring me toward the forest; instead, they are trying to make me feel safe."

Bran looked at me and there was a look in her eyes I had not seen before.

"Bran, tell me."

She looked down at the floor, at first shaking her head. When she looked up her eyes were filled with a wisdom greater than I had seen before.

"Years ago, I was forewarned of my connection to a forest," she revealed. "There is something being put into motion that is beyond our human understanding."

"What shall we do, dearest?"

"What does your heart tell you?"

I thought for a while. "To let the forest beings lead us to our destiny."

Bran smiled. "What can I say, my love? Follow your heart."

The next morning Luke and I began to saw the tree into logs. The word spread quickly and our neighbors came to help. That night each family had enough wood to warm their houses and feed their cooking fires.

All was quiet for the next few weeks. There was a stillness in the forest; not a chirp from the birds or any sound of movement from the forest creatures. Then one morning another tree appeared well into my field. And so it went for the entire winter, the forest spirits leaving offerings of warmth and life. It wasn't only fallen trees that magically appeared. There were gifts of fruit, the likes of which we had never seen, and herbs to heal the sick.

Our neighbors were of the Tongva tribe and while they had been taken from their families as children and raised in mission schools, their beliefs in the spirit world had never left them. With those beliefs came respect and gratitude for otherworldly beings. No one person took more than their share of wood and all gave thanks to the forest and those who lived within.

In this way, the winter season passed and spring came to take its place. I had begun to ready the fields for planting when I looked up to see a growing fierceness in the sky. It was not unheard of for winter to put up a final fight with spring and give us one last storm, but I had never seen angrier clouds, with claps of thunder rarely heard in this region and bolts of lightning striking and spreading out to sea. With every thunderclap, the storm moved closer and closer to my fields.

The wind from the ocean sent a shiver up my spine; I had never felt anything as chilling, not even in the coldest of winters in Wales. I was picking up my tools and thinking about my wife and children safely sheltered inside a warm house, when I saw something stirring within the brambles that marked the forest boundary. I blinked my eyes several times, unsure of what I was seeing, and fearing bewitchment, I stood frozen as a naked child wobbled toward me out of the forest.

I could not lift my feet, not to run away or to move forward. I had no choice but to wait, for I knew the forest was an entity to be respected.

The child continued to stumble toward me; was this a lost child or a forest demon? I could now see it was a girl-child. She looked up at me, a slight tremor passing through her body. Her eyes were not filled with evil as I had imagined, but with confusion and fear. Tears trickled down her face, leaving a thin trail upon her mud-caked cheeks. My heart went out to this poor one who looked about the same age as my youngest, Caron.

Large drops of rain began to fall. I took off my shirt, and motioned for her to come closer.

"You'll come home with me," I said, as I wrapped my shirt snugly around her shaking body and picked her up. I then gathered my woolen cape around us and told her she would not be harmed. I wasn't sure if she understood my words, but she settled cozily against my chest, which gave me to know she felt safe. Our hearts, pressed together in this fashion, seemed to beat as one.

I headed for home through muddied fields and paths. In my imagination I could see Branwyn cooking while a warm pot of water waited for washing. Our children would be helping Bran or doing their school lessons.

Opening the door, I was greeted by the fragrance of vegetables roasting on the fireplace grill and the sound of a pot of porridge bubbling away.

Bran asked me, "What are you carrying?"

"A surprise from the forest. It came to me through the brambles."

"A bunny?" asked Caron, who already showed a love and respect for all creatures.

I smiled. I had once brought home a wounded rabbit for Bran to heal and ever since then, all Caron could think of was bunnies.

I replied, "Another gift, yes, but not a bunny." I opened my cape to reveal the child, fast asleep against my chest.

I saw a look in Bran's eyes, not of surprise but of knowing.

"Come, give me the child and dry yourself before you become ill."

My Bran took the child into her arms. The girl stirred and made a sound not unlike that of a mewing kitten.

"We have a new sister," announced Huw, the eldest of our children. "Sent to us by the gods and goddesses."

And with that, the children welcomed their new sister.

Bran, as always, knew what to do. "Gavin, put on a clean cauldron of water and fetch the shears. This child's hair is more tangled than the brambles she walked through."

I watched as Bran bathed the child and cut her hair. After diapering and swaddling her, she put her to her breast; as the babe suckled, she reached her hand upward and stroked Bran's cheek. The sounds that came from her, in-between suckling, were not human. When you live as close to nature as I, you learn to recognize the sounds of all creatures. These sounds were akin to the soft hooting of an infant owl, or the chirping of a young squirrel.

Bran looked into the child's eyes, now wide open, and mimicked the sounds that were so familiar to her. She leaned over, and while her voice was soft, I could hear what she was saying: "I know who you are. You were sent here to be cared for by us."

"What shall we call her, Mam?" asked Huw.

"Her name shall be Rhianwen, but you may call her Wen."

I was surprised by how quickly Bran had chosen the child's name.

That night as we lay in our bed with the sleeping child between us, Bran spoke in a soft, lyrical tone and told me, in great detail, of that night at Madam Latham's soirée.

"Many years ago, before we were wed, it was predicted that I should have a child not from me but of me. Last night the moon goddess, Rhiannon, came to me in a dream. She told me that evil has come to the forest. Evil sent from the underworld, so powerful that she will not be able to protect the forest and all who dwell within. She told me the fallen trees were our first test and we will be tested many times and in many ways. She said she was sending us a special gift, beyond wood to burn, or fruit to eat, or herbs to cure."

I asked, "How did the babe's name come to you so quickly?"

"I was told her name, all those years ago. It has never left my mind." Bran kissed the head of the sleeping child. "Where this will lead I know not. We must now put our future into the hands of the goddess Rhiannon."

And with that, we let sleep overtake us.

Villia set the journal aside and looked wistfully out the window. "The rain has stopped, and I could use a break."

Emilee asked, "Grannie, are you okay?"

"I told you we'd wear her out," whispered Ethan.

Villia smiled, despite the ache in her heart. "No, it's not you. You have been wonderful company and I've enjoyed every minute we have shared. I have a difficult decision to make and I need some alone time."

Emilee said, "Grannie, a timeout sounds good, and I promise our breaking and entering days have ended."

Villia's mam had once told her the story of her first bath. "I put you in the water and your eyes grew wide, and the biggest smile crossed your face. Then you became focused and began to kick your legs with excitement. I called in your tad and we both laughed at how solemn you were, as if this was your job. I could hardly get you out of the tub. I knew then you would be a water baby."

For as long as Villia could remember, whenever she was sad or upset she would find her way to a body of water. She no longer challenged the sea by diving beneath its waves; that was replaced with walks along the beach while the sea kissed her toes. And then there were the long baths; almost a nightly ritual, or in cases of extreme angst, taken during the day.

These were dire times, she thought, and headed directly for the bathroom and the waiting bathtub.

When Mam and Tad retired and Villia became the Keeper, the Ancient One had handed her a gift wrapped in palm leaves and tied with hemp twine. She opened the package and gazed at three tiny glass bottles, each one the color of one of the lakes. Bewildered, she looked to the Ancient One.

Rhiannon said, "The time may come when you need the island but cannot be here. Three of four drops into your bathwater and the lake will come to you."

She knew this bath would be like no other. She had only done it once, years ago, when she felt overwhelmed by the weight of the world on her shoulders. Oran was gone more than he was with her, and Bruce and April were both teens. She tried not to burden him with her daily worries and turned to the Lake of Wisdom for guidance.

She reached beneath the sink and removed the package holding the three bottles, labeled in a delicate script by Corey, the kori bustard. The large African bird had won the contest to be Rhiannon's secretary. He strutted around the island in a constant state of puffiness usually reserved for mating season. The females giggled at how foolish he looked, preferring less vainglorious males.

Villia held the bottles in her hand. They were small, holding no more than an ounce each. *Just a few drops in your bath water and the lake of your choice will come to you.*

But which lake, she now wondered? Certainly not the Lake of Sorrows. Wisdom, perhaps? From experience she knew that wisdom didn't always come easily, not even if she had soaked in the lake for hours. What about the Lake of Dreams? She remembered once, when she was still quite young, she had entered the Lake of Dreams thinking she could wish for something and it would come true. She had wished for Bobby Wilson to ask her to the school festival. When she saw him walking toward her at school she was certain that her dream was being granted. Instead, he continued walking past her and asked Joanne

White out instead. She had sobbed into her pillow that night, her heart broken.

Rhiannon had appeared. "I usually don't make house calls."

"It's not fair!" she had shouted. "What good is a Lake of Dreams if you never get your dream?"

Rhiannon smiled benevolently. "Once I went into the Lake of Dreams and, like you, asked for someone to fulfill my dreams, to ease my loneliness. Then when someone entered my life, I thought it was because my dream had been granted. But remember, nightmares are also dreams."

"What do you mean?"

"Bobby Wilson may not be who he seems." And with that, Rhiannon vanished.

Years later, Villia ran into Joanne White, now JoJo Wilson, at the local farmer's market.

They chitchatted, catching up the past twenty years in a few minutes.

At one point JoJo said, a mite sheepishly, "Remember when we had that school festival and Bobby asked me instead of you?"

Villia smiled. "Yes, of course."

"Kid stuff, huh? I sometimes wonder what my life would have been like if Bobby had asked you instead of me. I lied before...Bobby doesn't own an auto repair shop. He does auto repair but it's in prison."

Villia began to say how sorry she was, but JoJo had scurried away.

Villia's tad had a favorite phrase and used it whenever there was a large problem brewing: "You got yourself into a fine kettle of fish. Now you gotta get yourself out."

Villia returned the vials to their spot under the sink. The lakes weren't meant to be used selfishly. It's one thing when you're a child. It's another when you're an adult. She knew what Oran would say: "Show those grandbabies of ours how to stand up and deal with adversity."

She knew what she had to do.

She returned to the den. "Tomorrow's going to be a busy day. What say we finish the journal? The next entry is from Dylan. Who wants a turn at reading?"

"I'll take it," said Ethan.

∞

July 22, 1861. Bran and I have now been married for ten years. The United States is in a terrible war, the South against the North. Here in California, we have had our own disagreements; some have wanted California to leave the Union and join the Confederacy. I devoutly oppose this proposal, as I cannot tolerate the thought of one man owning another.

In spite of the political differences surrounding us, our family has flourished. Our land next to the forest has grown crops greener and taller than anywhere else on Rancho de los Palos Verdes.

I continued to plant close to the forest but always left enough space to show my respect.

Things changed though. More and more people started making their home here. Instead of building the houses out of adobe, they wanted them to look like the houses they left behind, and that meant lumber was in high demand.

I didn't like what I was seeing. Rancho de los Palos Verdes, once a hidden jewel, had attracted the attention of opportunists and thrill seekers, as they called themselves. There were rumors of treasure buried deep within the forest. There were gambling bets to see if anyone could enter the forest and survive. The reports of missing people grew until not even Dawley King, who everyone knew lusted after the trees, dared to face up to the forest.

One day a stranger came up to me while I was plowing the fields.

"Mr. Flatbottom?" he asked respectfully, holding out his hand. "I'm Mr. King's new foreman, Joshua Hunter. I'm here to inform you that the forest is coming down. In a month's time, there will be a trainload of loggers coming in. We are going to start at the outside and work our way inward."

I wiped my brow with a kerchief. "You know about the curse?"

The man threw his head back and laughed. "No curse is invincible. There is always a chink in the armor; you only must be clever enough to discover it. You'll see...no one will disappear or die."

I went home feeling confused. This man seemed so sure of himself.

The children greeted me as they always did. I opened my arms and Wen and Caron jumped in.

Wen had become one of the family, blood of our blood. If she remembered anything about her previous life she never spoke of it.

Huw and Gavin were getting too big for childish play and soon would be helping me with farming and fishing. Gavin was a born farmer, but Huw was taken with cures and learned all he could from his mam.

The next day would be Sunday and while we didn't go to church, we didn't work unless you counted riding herd on four climbing, running, chattering, laughing children as a chore. Bran and I didn't; the children were a blessing we thanked the gods and goddesses for every day.

Sunday morning after breakfast Bran and I sent the children outside to play. After a few minutes Wen came back in and tugged at Bran's skirt. "Mam, I had a dream last night," she announced, her eyes gleaming.

Bran loved to hear the children tell their dreams and with four, it was a regular dream factory. Bran opened her arms, sat Wen on her lap, and drew her close. "Tell us about it."

"I was visited by a goddess, wearing a golden, flowing gown. She told me I came from her body and she blessed you both for caring for me. She said the animals that live in the forest are no longer safe. She asks that you and Tad come to the forest when the moon is at its highest point in the sky."

Wen knew of how she came to us and now began to weep. "Mam, Tad, will I have to leave you?"

"I don't know," said Bran. "You have been the sun that shines through our window and warms our hearts. Tad and I must follow your dream and go to the forest."

I picked up my daughter. I had feared this day might come. Wen was now three and had grown so, her legs dangled close to the ground.

"You've gotten so big, I can hardly pick you up. Try not to worry, Wen. In three days the moon will be at its highest point and then we will know more. For now, I think your sister and brothers would like to have you play with them." I lowered my voice to a whisper. "And if you check the chicken coop, you'll find some eggs."

Wen ran outside, her disquiet replaced by the thought of gathering fresh eggs.

Bran said, "What could a goddess possibly want from us? You a farmer and a fisherman, and I a mother with four children."

I could see the worry in Bran's face. "You forget you are also a healer and a teacher," I reminded her. I motioned to the bookcase I had built, overflowing with books. "Look, we have quite the library. Our children are thriving and learning. People come to you for cures. We don't know what is wanted from us, but we must follow Wen's dream."

A few nights later, the moon was at its highest point. Bran and I put on our warmest clothing and left the house. I carried a lantern, even though the moon shed its light upon the path. We stood at the perimeter of the forest and waited.

"It might have been only a dream," whispered Bran. "A child's need to know about her mother."

"We'll soon see."

We waited patiently at first, then became restless. I said, "We'll wait a bit longer. If nothing happens, we'll return home."

Scarcely a minute had passed when Bran cried "Look! They are parting!" She pointed her finger toward the brambles that surrounded the forest.

A woman walked out of the forest, and she was just as Wen had described.

"It's warmer in the forest," she said. "Please enter my world."

We followed her through a path that avoided the prickly undergrowth. The forest was quiet except for the occasional hooting of an owl. The trees formed a tight canopy and the moon, even though at its brightest, cast only a dim light.

The woman stopped when we came to a small clearing. "I am the goddess Rhiannon. I have been watching you since you came to this land, and even before. The animals are shy and wary; you are the first humans that have been welcomed here. We have inhabited this forest since before time, as you know it, began. There was a fierce storm, not from a flood as your Noah story tells it, but from man's need to conquer and enslave the animals. They were being driven to extinction, and that I could not allow to occur.

"I went to the other gods and goddesses and begged them to help me. After much deliberation we created this enchanted forest where the animals could live in safety and peace. A curse was put around the perimeter so that any human who went beyond the brambles would face death.

"We lived in peace and harmony for many thousands of years, but I became lonely and longed for the companionship of a man. A few years ago, a man entered the forest. I looked at him and fell under the spell of love. Surely, I reasoned, he has been sent by the gods and goddesses as an answer to my prayers."

Rhiannon breathed a heavy sigh and wiped away her tears.

"Ah, he was like no other human I had ever seen. Tall, handsome, with hair as black as a witch's familiar and teeth as white as the snow atop Mount Olympus. Joshua Hunter, he told me, was his name. I fell under his spell, and he stayed for three days and three nights, becoming my lover. During that time, he asked me many questions about the forest; blinded by my love for him, I divulged its secret.

"When he left I could not bear the separation, and as I can change form at will, I followed him as a hummingbird. As he walked he cheerfully whistled a melody, seemingly of love. I almost turned away, but something told me to continue along with him. Soon he came to a large estate that belonged to an enemy of the forest: Dawley King.

"It was a large hacienda with a barricaded gate guarded by fierce-looking men with guns.

To follow him into the house I had to change form once again, this time as a flea sitting motionless on the back of his neck.

"Dawley King greeted him as if they were the best of friends. He offered Joshua a cigar and a glass of whiskey. It was then that his betrayal became known. Joshua related that he had discovered the way to cut down the trees without inviting peril. For a generous fee he would reveal the secret and destroy the forest and all that lived within. It was then I realized Joshua had seduced me for his own ill-gotten gains.

"Dawley King grinned; it was the most malignant grin and even as a flea, I shuddered. Joshua felt it and took a swipe. I barely avoided death. Imagine, death as a flea and not as a goddess!"

In spite of her pained expression she smiled briefly, then continued with her story.

"I left vowing I would not allow this to happen, but not before I bit him on the back of his neck. Luckily, I jumped off before he could squash me. I'm sure you are curious regarding the secret of the forest."

"It has crossed my mind," said I.

"Mine as well," added Bran.

"During the time of a blue moon, the protection of the gods and goddesses is lifted. As long as no human knew our secret, we felt safe. We would intensify our most frightening sounds during the cycle of the blue moon. It has been enough, all these millennia, to keep humans at bay. According to Joshua's plan, men would descend upon the forest during the time of the next blue moon to cut down the trees and kill the animals.

"When I discovered this treachery, I went to the gods and goddesses and confessed. I begged for help and forgiveness; it was my fault for having fallen under the spell of passion. They were furious! I had broken the most important rule and had betrayed all who lived within the forest.

You should know that gods and goddesses can make things very difficult. They wanted to teach me a lesson, and I do admit I was a bit puffed up by my responsibility of overseeing all the animals ever created." She sighed. "Ah, but forgiveness from the gods and goddesses is hard won.

"Ultimately, I was given a chance to redeem myself, but it came with a condition. The gods and goddesses would create an island where animals representing all the species upon earth would reside in harmony, safe from man's barbarism. This island would be invisible to all humans except for one. And that person must agree to be the Keeper of the Island of the Blue Moon. That is why I called upon you." She gestured toward Bran.

I stared. "Branwyn?"

"Yes, with you as her knight, so to speak. I have watched you both since you came here. I saw your love blossom and I watched as you overcame injustices and temptations. I saw how you were with the Tongva, your kindness toward them and your acceptance of their customs. I sent you my daughter; that was the ultimate test. Dylan, you put her next to your heart to keep her alive, and Bran, you fed her from your breast as if she was your own.

"Rhianwen, or Wen as she is called by your family, has learned from the kindness that can come from humans, but now I must take her back, as I have much to teach her."

Bran began to cry. "I'll miss her so, as will our children."

"They, too, will be able to visit the island, as will your descendants," Rhiannon assured us. "For as long as there is a Flatbottom alive who remains kind of heart, the island and all its inhabitants shall survive."

I asked, "When does this take place, and how will you move the animals to the island?"

"We have a few weeks before the Blue Moon appears. As for the animals' transportation, I am still a goddess, possessed of many powers. Come with me deeper into the forest, where a clearing lies. There are a few friends who wish to greet you. Then you shall decide."

After walking a short distance the trees began to thin and we entered a clearing fully illuminated by the stars and moonlight.

Gathered there were the animals who inhabited the forest. Many were thought to be long extinct, known only to mankind through books and stories. They whispered among themselves. "I can understand them," said Bran. She smiled beatifically as if she had known all along all the earth's creatures shared the same language.

Rhiannon held up her hand to quiet the animals. As one they knelt and cast their eyes downward in respect. For a moment Bran stood frozen; I wondered what her decision would be. Then, just as the animals had fallen to their knees, so did my Bran. She was sobbing, as if the world had finally come full circle.

"I knew you were the one," whispered Rhiannon.

I knelt next to Branwyn. "If you will be the Keeper, I will assist you in every way."

Rhiannon said, "Be in your boat in one week's time and you will be guided to the island. And yes, Bran, you may bring the children."

Bran looked up in astonishment.

Rhiannon smiled. "I can hear your thoughts. I have much to teach you, and we shall become the dearest of friends."

We walked out of the forest and stood at its edge, looking toward our fields. "It will be a good crop," I said.

"Everything grows from your hands and your heart," Bran said.

"The children won't believe what they will see."

"I'm not sure I will either."

I kissed her ever so sweetly on the cheek, as I had when we were but children.

"My Branwyn," I said proudly, "the Keeper of the Island of the Blue Moon."

CHAPTER 19

Villa paused and smiled at her grandkids' blissful expressions. Emilee and Ethan looked like they were floating on a cloud.

"Wow, Grannie," Ethan gushed, "that was better than *The Lord of the Rings* and *The Lion King* and *Harry Potter* all put together!"

"There is a brief final entry made by Branwyn," said Villia. "Emilee, why don't you read it?"

"With pleasure, Grannie."

∞

October 1,1863. My dearest journal, I was but a child when first we met and now I am a woman with children and the responsibilities of the world resting on my shoulders. It is time to say goodbye.

What a journey we have had! Thank you for being by my side.

I am a mother with three—dare I say three and one-half children? I, and the rest of my family, could not bear to be separated from Wen. Yet, it is her task to learn of her mother's world. I think it might be difficult for her to have human and goddess parts swirling around inside her, and I'm quite certain at times they will be at great odds. Rhiannon and I agreed that Wen will need all of us.

I don't know what the future holds for me or the Island of the Blue Moon. Will there always be a Flatbottom to act as the Keeper? I will say to all who read this journal, all we can do is our best. Perhaps as we utter our individual and communal prayers the world will learn that all it takes is kindness.

So it is written in The Book of Truths, and so it shall be.

Branwyn Flatbottom

∞

Emilee closed the journal upon her lap. "Grannie, is it true?" she asked breathlessly. "Does the island exist?"

"In my eyes it does. But as I was told by Rhiannon, the Ancient One, everyone sees the island through their own eyes and heart."

Ethan asked, "Are you the Keeper?"

"I am. And now I must share my struggle. First, I want you both to understand that my initial reaction on the phone about camp was not about you. Even though I explained it as best I could, I could see where my startled response could be seen in a negative way."

"We thought it was about us," Emilee confessed. "I'm not a very nice person. I planned the break-in. I'll probably end up in jail."

Ethan added, "And I stole some snacks late at night."

Oh, God, how I love these kids!

"Emilee, what you did doesn't deserve a medal, but it also doesn't mean the loss of my love. You are young and impulsive, but you are also caring and curious. If you work at controlling your impulses and cultivate your caring and curiosity, there will no stopping you.

"And you, Ethan. You should never feel ashamed about your body. You are thoughtful and have a kind heart. Be proud of who you are.

"My outburst on the phone was over my need to be on the island for an annual ceremony. It is written that the island will disappear If I don't attend and pledge to be the Keeper for another year."

"Can't we go with you?" pleaded Ethan.

"Your mother would never forgive me, and I won't lie to her."

"What if Father went with us? He does love to sail," said Emilee.

"He would have to delay or cancel his Paris trip. Perhaps the answer will come to us, but first thing tomorrow, I want to go to the boathouse and check the sailboat. Any helpers available?"

They both grinned and nodded.

"One last thing: are there any other secrets you haven't told me? This is the time to come clean."

Ethan went to his bed, reached underneath, and pulled out a bag. Returning to the den, he waved it in the air. "Last year's Halloween candy collection. I've been hiding it for camp."

Villia looked puzzled. "Why?"

"To bribe any bullies. It's not easy being the chubby kid on the block."

Emilee went to her bed and reached between the mattress and the box spring. Upon her return she held the object in the air for Villia's inspection. "My cell phone. Mother gave it to me before she left in case of an emergency."

"I see," said Villia. *No doubt along with a warning about her crazy mother.* "That's it, then? No dead bodies?"

The kid's eyes opened wide.

"Not one? Then let's call it a day."

CHAPTER 20

The recent outing to the beach had been filled with excitement. Now, the three took the steps leading to the boathouse somberly and with a cloud of uncertainty hanging over their heads.

Before reaching the dock, Villia stopped suddenly. Tied to the dock was an electric boat with HINKELBERRY PRIVATE PATROL emblazoned upon the starboard in bright red letters.

Decked out in an 1800s naval petty officer's uniform—white pants and double-breasted jacket with gold buttons, topped off with a straw hat—was the proud business owner, Steven Hinkelberry.

"Hi, Mrs. Flatbottom," he said, waving. "Remember me?"

She gazed hard at him. "Steven? Steven Hinkelberry?"

"None other."

"Of course, I remember you! You and Bruce were grand school chums."

"Yes, ma'am. I was on my way to knock on your door. Got a problem here."

He pointed to the sullen youth standing next to him, whose hands had been restrained behind his back with plastic handcuffs.

Villia squinted. "The sun's in my eyes. Is that who I think it is?"

"If you're thinking Dawley King—"

The youth interrupted, proclaiming haughtily: "I am Dawley King the seventh."

"Okay," said Steven, "Seventh it is. Seventh broke into your boathouse and did some real damage. You best come with me, Mrs. Flatbottom."

∞

Villia observed the daggers being shot between Dawley VII and her warrior grandchildren. They came to an abrupt halt at the boathouse doors.

"The locks are untouched," said Villia. "How did he get in?"

"Tried the windows first, but they were too small," said Steven. "He climbed on the roof, smashed the skylight, and lowered himself with a rope."

"The sailboat...?"

"Yes, ma'am. Some major damage. Caught him before he got to the flatbottom boat."

Villia unlocked the doors and looked around. "My God," she muttered.

Seventh had used the tools that had created the flatbottom boat to damage the sailboat.

How will I get to the island? She turned to Seventh. "Why would you do such a thing?"

Seventh snarled, "You're an enemy of the Kings."

Steven said, "Mrs. Flatbottom, you can press charges, but most folks around here just send a bill to the King Company."

She looked at her grandchildren's disbelieving expressions. *I've got to show them that brats born with silver spoons in their mouths can't get off scot-free for their mischief.*

"Well, Steven, I guess I'm not most folks. I have been taught to show compassion even in the sight of evil. But I also believe that we must pay for our actions."

Seventh growled, "How much, lady? Name your price. My great-grandpa will pay."

Villia indulged herself in a rare smirk. "Not that kind of payment. Steven, I want to press charges, and I will attend Seventh's hearing."

"Hearing, my ass!" spat the brat. "You stupid old witch! Don't you know who owns this town?"

Villia ignored the comments.

"I'll take care of it, Mrs. Flatbottom." Responded Steven.

Seventh sneered. "Flatbottom! What a dumb name!"

"And what do you think of the name Hinkelberry, Seventh?" Steven inquired.

"Hah! Maybe even dumber."

Steven guided Seventh to the dock. "Let's go kid and careful you don't trip getting into the boat...*whoops!*"

Villia and the kids didn't bother to restrain their laughter as Seventh took a header into the drink. When Steven fished the brat out, he was madder than a wet hen.

"You tripped me on purpose!" he spluttered, shivering and dripping on the dock.

Steven shook his head. "No, you tripped over an uneven board. Isn't that right, Mrs. Flatbottom?" He winked at her discreetly.

"Yes, Mr. Hinkelberry," said Villia, winking back, "that's exactly what happened."

Villia leaned against the sailboat. *Are all the gods and goddesses against me?* she wondered.

"What about the flatbottom boat, Grannie?" asked Emilee.

"It's more than I can handle on my own."

"You've got us."

"That's right, I do! Let's go on deck."

Villia rubbed her hands over the wood rails. *You're still perfect, old girl.*

"Emilee, does your cell phone work out here?"

Emilee pulled it out. "Yep! Four bars strong."

"Call your father for me."

Emilee scrolled to "Father" in her contacts list and pressed call. "Hello, Father, this is Emilee. Grannie wants to talk to you." She handed the phone to Villia. "Grannie, it's going to be Paris or the island. And if what you tell us is true, I don't think you have a choice."

Ethan chanted to himself. "Say goodbye to camp and hello to an invisible island. Move over, Harry Potter. Ethan is on his way!"

"Michael, it's Villia. I—*we* need your help. ...Yes, now! ...No, the kids are fine. You should be proud of them. But there are things you need to know. ... Paris. I know. Just get here as soon as possible."

Michael sat in traffic, silently cursing the parking lot known as the 405 freeway. It would be a two-hour drive from Los Angeles to Palos Verdes, and on this weekday evening, a helluva lot longer. There was no sense in calling April until he had all the facts sorted out. He never could fully understand the intensity of her anger toward her parents, particularly Villia. He liked her; a bit off-center but with a heart of gold. And she always showed an interest in his volunteer work. He spent one month every year teaching and performing heart surgery in Sri Lanka.

He recalled the Fourth of July when they had sat on their deck and watched the fireworks. April and the kids had gone into the house to get some snacks and Oran had taken Pooch inside, away from the noise. They were alone; the ocean breeze had chilled them, and they sat next to each other huddled under blankets.

Villia had asked him, during that brief break, how his month in Sri Lanka went.

He set down his drink. "Every time I hold those tiny hearts in my hands, I know I have found God. Any differences in religion or politics falls away when we are in the operating room."

He fell into a meditative state. Was it the hush between the fireworks, or the sound of the ocean, or something coming from Villia that allowed him to open his own heart?

"Have you ever felt that you're on the wrong path? We have all that we need, even more. After the joy I see in those who have so few possessions, I must believe we're missing something, something intangible."

At that moment the door opened and April and the kids came outside, loaded down with drinks and bowls of fresh fruit.

"Did I interrupt something?" asked April.

Before Villia could say anything, Michael responded, "Just kibitzing." He stuffed his feelings back down and, until Villia's call, had not allowed them to surface.

Now, as he crept along the road to Palos Verdes with night darkening all around, he couldn't stop thinking about his life and lost opportunities.

He had returned from Sri Lanka a changed man. Something about seeing the look in the parents' eyes when he first gave them a glimmer of hope, and then when he came out of the operating room, smiling and flushed with success. It wasn't any different at the University of California at Los Angeles (UCLA), except the patients' parents knew that, in both emergency and non-emergencies, there were many competent surgeons on hand, and the fear that their child would die before aid could be rendered was not nearly so pronounced. He trained five physicians while he was in Sri Lanka. They were eager to learn and raptly attended his every word and action.

He returned to UCLA, his staff, and his busy routine. Operating rooms with modern surgical equipment, bright, idealistic residents eager to prove themselves—it was all that he should need...or was it?

He saw a flyer on the bulletin board. FOR SALE: 1980 VW CAMPER. IN NEED OF TLC. JUSTINE.

April looked at him curiously when he told her he wanted to buy the camper.

"You've met Justine. She works in Pediatric ICU."

"Yes, I remember her."

"She's selling her camper. I'd like to restore it. We've got the extra garage."

April had glowered at him, as if to say, "You know my distaste for anything that comes close to camping."

"It's a project," he had reassured her. "I used to work on cars with my dad when I was a teen. It'll be fun."

She had looked relieved. "Oh, a hobby. I think it's a great idea."

Yes, a hobby. And a dream.

The 1980 VW camper sat in the garage pleading to be taken on the open road. During a rare free evening or on a Sunday, he went to the garage, put on music from the eighties, and tinkered. He thought about completing the restoration by repainting her, but there was history in the paint's patina. He spent hours detailing her, fantasizing about the four of them taking a vacation. The kids in the back, playing old-fashioned board games, soaking up the scenery...and no electronic devices allowed. April would be sitting next to him—laughing, not wearing makeup, not caring if her hair was out of place. They would park by a stream and work together to set up camp. He would buy a tent for the kids in case they wanted that sleeping outdoors experience. They would sit around the fire, roasting hot dogs and toasting marshmallows. No one would worry about allergies or gaining a pound or two; hikes would take care of any extra calories. They would fall asleep listening to the sounds of the stream, the birds, and animals. And the memories....no photos necessary, they would be stored forever in their hearts.

He had turned down the opportunity to return to Sri Lanka to spend time with April in Paris. He knew the signs of a marriage falling apart. He had witnessed them with his parents, and now he saw it in his own relationship.

He was yanked back to reality by a sudden break in traffic. He set aside his disappointments and fantasies and took the exit to the Flatbottom home. It only took a few seconds for his knock to be answered by Emilee and Ethan.

Squealing, they flung themselves upon their dad, hugging him so tight he found it hard to breathe.

"Whoa, whoa," he said lightheartedly. *Were these his children?* He had never seen them so happy and spontaneous. He sniffed the air. "What smells so good?"

"We cooked dinner with Grannie," said Emilee. "Plus, we made a blueberry pie for dessert and homemade ice cream."

"Look, Father," said Ethan, flexing his budding biceps. "I've grown almost a foot, too!"

"You're both amazing," he said, feeling the words that came from his heart, not the latest book on how to increase your child's self-esteem.

The kids grabbed Michael's arms and pulled him into the house. Villia emerged from the kitchen wiping her hands on her apron.

"Set the table, children," she said.

They disappeared into the kitchen.

Michael was duly impressed. "'Set the table, children' and no arguments or whining? You must have worked magic."

You have no idea, but you are about to find out.

"Thank you, Michael, for coming on such short notice," said Villia, managing a feeble smile. "You'll never know how much this means to me. Have you talked to April?"

"Not yet. I thought I should find out exactly what's going on."

"We'll have dinner first. The kids have worked really hard on this meal."

Michael smiled, leaned down to Villia's ear, and whispered, "Wow, the kitchen looks like a cyclone hit it."

"Two, actually. But they're on the cleanup squad."

"A scrumptious feast," said Michael.

"You haven't had dessert yet," said Emilee.

She exchanged a look with Ethan, and they said in unison: "One to eat and the other to learn by."

Michael grinned. "You both look very smug, or as my grandmother used to say, like the cat that swallowed the canary. Is this where we pause and I find out about the mysterious and urgent problem?"

Villia replied, "It's as good a time as any. Let's go into the den."

Michael heard the kids—in-between bursts of laughter—singing the lyric "to let the punishment fit the crime" from Gilbert and Sullivan's *The Mikado*.

"They know the words to 'A More Humane Mikado'? How'd you pull that one off?"

"I do have my ways," she said.

"I'm still in the dark. Although I must say it was well worth the trip just to be served by those gourmet cooks."

Michael took off his shoes and flopped down on the couch. "I haven't been this full or relaxed in a long time. Is it true? Did you cast a spell on the kids, and will it last?"

He sat up. "What is it, Villia?" he asked, seeing the tears rolling down her cheeks. "Are you ill, or has something happened to Oran?"

"No, but I do have a story to tell you and something to ask of you. I know you might think I'm truly insane, but hear me out."

"Okay ... shoot."

She stood up, and taking the three journals from the bookcase, placed them on the side table next to Michael.

"These were written by the first Flatbottoms. For the most part by Branwyn, but a couple of entries are by her husband, Dylan. I would like you to read them. Then and only then will I be able to tell you the rest of the story."

Looking a bit dumbfounded, Michael picked up the first one. "I could use a cup of coffee."

"I'll be right back. Let me know when you're done."

Villia cherished those moments of silence. The kids had gone to bed and Michael was still in the den. But silence wasn't always golden, of course. In the past, when Oran was gone and she was alone for weeks at a time, she would sometimes scream, just to hear the sound of a human voice—even from someone admittedly a little batty.

She heard the den door open. Michael stepped out, holding the three journals.

"These belong in a museum," he said with reverence. "I don't know what to say or what to think. Have the kids read them?"

"Yes, and before you judge me—"

"I don't."

"My reading the journals to the kids started out as a story about a girl around their age who had lived many years ago. It snowballed and I do admit, at times, things got out of control."

"Hmm, I'll bet Emilee led the pack on that one. If it's true, and if such an island does exist... You may not have known it, but April still has nightmares about visiting an island. This island, is it where all the forest creatures went?"

"Yes, and it does exist."

"How can I help?"

"The kids are sleeping. Come down to the boathouse with me, please."

It was a dark night with clouds blocking any hint of light from the moon and stars. With flashlights in hand, Villia and Michael took the steps down to the boathouse.

She hesitated before opening the door, remarking, "The boathouse was broken into and the sailboat vandalized." She flicked on the lights and walked to the sailboat with Michael.

"Did you catch them?" he asked.

"The private patrol did. He's in juvey hall right now. I'm pressing charges."

Michael walked around the boat, surveying the damage. "Damn, he sure did a number on it."

"Can it be repaired?"

"Anything can be repaired, but it'll take moving her to a shipyard. A couple of weeks at least."

"I have to sail to the island in two days, and I can't manage the flatbottom on my own."

Michael walked over to the flatbottom boat. "She's a real beauty. Still seaworthy after all these years. I'd have to cancel my Paris trip." His eyes met Villia's. "I'm not sure our marriage can survive that kind of disappointment."

"I guessed you and April were having some trouble." She smiled weakly. "The kids want to go to the island."

He laughed. "Oh, what an adventure that will be."

"There's one other thing."

"Which is?"

"Because you don't carry the Flatbottom name, you'll have to take a tablespoon of Elixir."

"Elixir?"

"Yes, sent by the Goddess Rhiannon."

"Let me guess: brought here by carrier pigeon?"

"I know you're teasing me, but no. It was brought by two crows, Edgar and Annabelle...that talk."

This is getting better and better, Michael thought. "And the kids? They'll have to take the Elixir as well?"

"Yes, but only a teaspoon. Only then will the island become visible."

He stared at Villia. *April's told me how crazy she is, but* is *she, really? Maybe this insanity has been passed down through the generations, or maybe this "fantasy island" thing is really true. I may not be able to take the family camping, but I'm not missing this one. We're going!*

"I'll have to go home. My vacation started today, but there are a few things I have to take care of, and I must call April. I can't keep this from her. You understand, don't you?"

"I would think less of you if you weren't honest. Michael, if you change your mind, I'll manage...somehow, I will get to the island."

Michael squeezed her shoulder fondly. "Don't worry, Villia. I'm not about to let you down."

∞

It was 10:30 p.m. before Michael left the rickety house built on stilts—a good time for freeway driving in the Los Angeles area. It would be 7:30 a.m. in Paris. The distance between Michael and April was measured not only in miles and time, but also by April's lingering memory of a visit to a bug-infested desert island.

After spending time with Villia and reading the journals, he had to find out for himself if the story about the island was true. He would wait another hour before calling, as April liked to sleep in when she could.

∞

April and Michael had met fifteen years ago at a real estate open house. It was New Year's Day and Michael had recently completed his surgical residency at UCLA. He was saddled with student loans, but after years of living in dorm rooms and fusty apartments, he was bent on owning a home...anything that he could call his own. The banks were more than willing to back a loan based on his current and future earnings. He hoped he could find something near the hospital.

Being single and loaded with student loans, bribery worked on him every time. Two tickets to *The Phantom of the Opera* at the Pantages Theater in Hollywood in exchange for taking Sharon's New Year's Eve shift. How could he refuse? He didn't have anyone to take, but what the heck.

Emergency was stacked up with victims of DUI accidents and casualties of celebratory gunfire—three innocent bystanders that learned the hard way that what goes up, must come down, and one drunken fool who managed to shoot himself in the leg. He worked sixteen hours straight before walking out of the hospital and into his barebones apartment, where he sat at the kitchen table eating a sub sandwich and tackling a week's worth of mail. *Who else is so pathetic they do this on New Year's Day?* he wondered. One by one he set aside the bills and tossed the advertisements in the trash.

One particular ad caught his eye. It was a slick mailer with photos of apartments recently converted into condominiums.

OPEN FOR VIEWING, RESERVATIONS, AND PURCHASE.
IN WESTWOOD AND ADJACENT TO UCLA
OPEN NEW YEAR'S DAY 9:00 A.M. – 3:00 P.M.
THE LATEST AMENITIES INCLUDING POOL AND TENNIS COURTS.

He took his first taste of the latte from a Starbucks wannabee—the only open coffee shop he could find on New Year's. *No worries, Starbucks. It doesn't begin to measure up.*

He flipped the mailer over, idly glancing at photos of the apartments' interiors. *Whoa, waitaminnit.* His gaze fell on a photo of the realtor. *What a knockout! Probably a model, or at least Photoshopped.* He saw her name: April Davis, ABR, ALC, CRS, GRI, and PSA. *Damn, she has more designations after her name than I do.*

He didn't know or care what they meant, but there was a *look* about her. It was her eyes: deep blue, mysterious, yet slightly overcast with sadness. He hadn't felt that kind of attraction since his break-up five years ago.

He put down his coffee, stood up, and reached for his keys. He stopped. *What are you thinking?* He hadn't been home in more than two days. He felt his stubble and sniffed his armpits. He put his keys down and headed for the shower.

∞

The building was near the center of Westwood and close enough to jog or walk to the hospital. A sign—OPEN HOUSE, 10TH FLOOR— pointed to the elevator. In a few moments, he was whisked up to the penthouse suite.

And there she was, walking toward him, a little smile playing across her face, her eyes sparkling. After making small talk for a few minutes, she said, "I think I have just what you're looking for—this unit."

Michael chuckled. "A penthouse with three bedrooms? Sorry, I don't have Hugh Hefner's dough—or that many girlfriends."

She smiled at his self-deprecation. "Consider it an investment. Most of the units are already sold. Truth is, this one was also sold. But the buyer's loan fell through at the last minute."

He followed her from room to room, only half hearing her description of the luxury features and benefits that came with penthouse living.

I'm going to marry this woman, he thought, *as they stood on the private veranda.*

She pointed to the hot tub. "So much better than having to share with neighbors."

"I'll take it under one condition."

"I'm listening."

"I have two tickets to *The Phantom of the Opera*. Will you go with me?"

She smiled. "I'd like that."

The penthouse would become their first home.

The ride back to Sherman Oaks was trouble-free and there was nothing to distract Michael from his overwhelming feelings of loneliness. In his mind, he compiled a CliffsNotes version of his and April's relationship. They had slowly drifted apart; while they had tried to talk about their disconnection, nothing changed. They became two parents with hectic schedules that created a need for others to pick up the slack. At first it was a three-day-a-week housekeeper and a cook. Then, when Emilee was born, a baby nanny; later, an au pair to help with the kids' busy after-school schedules; more recently, an internet food service to take care of meals.

They sold the condo after Emilee was born. April was right: it had turned out to be a brilliant investment.

"I found us a house," she had said one night. "A little further to drive, but you can go over Coldwater Canyon. I hope you don't mind but I put a deposit on it today. It was too good to pass up."

He looked up, surprised. Had they really become so separate that decisions were made singly?

She was right about the house. He didn't mind the extra miles to UCLA; the kids were happy, and it did have three oversized garages. Enough for six cars. Two so far, and when the kids started driving another one or two. That would leave space for a dream of his.

They'd planned the trip to Paris to see if they couldn't rediscover their dreams. He dreaded making that phone call to April. *She'll be up by now,* he thought. He pushed the call button and waited for the voice without a name to tell him what to do. *Please tell me how to get out of this mess,* he begged the disembodied voice. She began her routine questions that would connect him to his wife.

He could have sworn he heard her say, "No advice allowed." He started, and then realized she was saying: "Call by number or by name?"

"Name."

"Name, please."

"April."

"On home, work, or cell phone?"

"Cell phone."

"Dialing."

He heard the phone ring.

"Hello?"

"Hello, April."

"Michael, I'm so glad you called! I've made dinner reservations for tomorrow at this most romantic spot."

CHAPTER 21

The phone remained in April's hand as she paced up and down the hotel suite. She spoke into it as if Michael was still on the other end.

"Damn you, Michael. I warned you about my mother."

Married for fourteen years, following our plan. Didn't we do well, Michael? Our kids, our careers...us?

"I thought...I thought you were the one to take me away from this pain. The way you held me in your arms... For the first time I felt safe...comforted. I can't let this happen. You have no idea, Michael. I must protect the children—and us—from this homegrown insanity."

For a moment she gazed at the phone, as if it was her only lifeline; an entity that held all the answers.

She dialed. "Air France? Yes, I need a flight to Los Angeles; it's a family emergency."

CHAPTER 22

Villia tilted the jar ever so gently until the contents swirled around, rainbow colors of confetti mixing, then settling. She repeated to herself: "One teaspoon for kids."

"I wasn't sure of what to pack," said Emilee. "I'm taking my bathing suit. Will I need a sweater?"

"Only if you climb a mountain."

"Oh, I'll just take everything."

"Open wide," Grannie said. Her hands trembled. *I really don't know what this will do.*

Ethan said trepidatiously, "Grannie, you're sure we won't turn into frogs or something, right?"

Emilee giggled. "This is right out of a *Harry Potter* story. Have you read those books, Grannie?"

"No, I've lived them. Ethan, if you turn into a frog, I'll put you in my pocket and you won't miss the trip at all."

"Where's Father?" asked Emilee, before opening her mouth and swallowing the Elixir.

"He and some of Gramp's buddies are getting the flatbottom ready."

"They don't know about where we're going, do they?"

"No one knows except for us."

"And me." The back door banged against the wall as April angrily strode inside.

"April—you're back, I see," said Villia nonchalantly.

"And doesn't that just ruin your plans."

"Not really. I think it adds to them."

Ethan jumped up and down. "Mother, Mother, we're going off on an adventure!"

April ignored him. "The kids aren't going, Mother. If you and Michael want to be insane, go right ahead. Kids, get your things, we're going home."

"No, they're not," said Michael. "I was right behind you on the steps. The boat's ready. Come with us, April," he pleaded.

"So, it's everyone against me. Why am I not surprised?"

Michael put his arms around his wife. "It's everyone *for* you. Look, if there's no island then we'll know it's a figment of you mother's imagination. And maybe your earlier experiences hooked into that. We read Branwyn's journals and it's part of our children's history, you know? Whether it's the truth of just a creative young girl's fantasies, to be able to read something written by a relative over 150 years ago...that in itself is quite a gift. Let them...us...have this experience."

Villia held up the canning jar. "One tablespoon for adults and one teaspoon for kids," she repeated.

"Oh, great," April moaned, "now we have to take something that's probably a hallucinogenic."

"I took mine hours ago and I don't feel or see anything differently," replied Michael.

"Why do I have to take it, Mother? I remember your story about direct descendants being able to see the island. We certainly didn't have to take anything when I went there before."

"That's true. But, when you changed your last name to Davis..."

"This gets crazier and crazier by the minute. Okay, if that's what it will take to bring some sanity back to this family, I'll take your witch's potion."

"Wait, Mother," said Ethan. "We have to say this. Ready, Emilee?"

"Ready, Ethan."

The two of them recited the verse they'd written just for the occasion:

"Over the lips
Under the gums
Watch out island
Here we come."

It was a solemn group that took the steps from the house to the dock where the flatbottom boat was moored. They went single file, except for Emilee and Ethan, who walked abreast holding hands. They weren't out very far when a pod of dolphins began circling the boat and continued to swim alongside as they put out to sea.

They had been out an hour before they left their secluded spots on the flatbottom boat and gathered at its bow to watch the dolphins and enjoy a picture-perfect day. Michael was focused on navigational charts that showed no indication of an island.

Villia joined him. "You won't find the island on those charts. Here, Michael." She handed him a small wooden case with a blackened latch. Opening the case, he removed a chart marked with Oran's scribble: Island of the Blue Moon. He set the course and gazed at the open sea. He was on course for either the greatest adventure, or the greatest letdown, of a lifetime.

Michael asked, "Villia, can you take the wheel while I tend to the sail?"

"Of course. I've done this many times." She thought fondly about how Oran would call out "Island ahoy!" when he first caught sight of land.

Villia spotted the mist hanging over the island. "We're almost there!" she shouted. Emilee and Ethan rushed to join her.

"The mist covers the island, but watch as we get closer. Michael, April—come join us!"

They were now a family of five, straining their eyes and their hearts. April looked down, angry that her mother had once again taken them on a misadventure. Angry that her children would be as disappointed as she had been.

Villia shouted, "There she is! Island ahoy!

"Kids, tell me what you see."

"Fog, Grannie," said Ethan.

"Yeah," Emilee echoed. "Tons of it."

April muttered under her breath, "See what I told you, Michael? Just another disappointment."

Emilee and Ethan began to jump up and down.

"I see it, I see it!" Ethan yelled.

Emilee's voice was dreamy. "Oh, Grannie there really *is* an island, and it's beautiful!"

"Look, Mother, look!" Ethan urged.

April continued to look down. Michael came over to her. "April, maybe what you saw as a child isn't what you might see now," he said. "Maybe you just weren't ready. Take a chance on it, on us. Everyone deserves a second chance, don't you think?"

She looked up at Michael as if she was seeing him for the first time. Her Michael, so pure of heart. Then she gazed out to sea. At first her view of the island was obscured by her mother and children. She moved forward to be closer to them.

"I see it," she said tearfully. "Oh, Mam, it's beautiful!"

Villia closed her eyes and said under her breath, "Thank you, Rhiannon, and all the gods and goddesses for looking after my baby." She turned to the kids. "Look, children, look at the dock. What do you see?"

Ethan: "A dragon!"

Emilee: "A unicorn!"

April sobbed. "I see Rhiannon. Exactly the way you described her to me when I was young, Mam. I remember so much now—eating breakfast under the table, some of the stories you told me. All to prepare me for this."

"And you, Michael?" Asked Villia.

"I see where I...*we* belong."

CHAPTER 23

Rhiannon and Villia walked the same path they had taken when Villia had first come to the island as a child.

Rhiannon took Villia's hand. "It's been more than fifty years. Do you remember your first day on the island?"

"I've never forgotten it."

"There was something I wanted to tell you but feared you were too young and would be overwhelmed. Come, let's sit by the Lake of Dreams and put our feet in the water."

"Am I old enough to know?" Villia asked playfully.

"Perhaps. You have lived many lives, and have many more to live, but your first life was from me."

"From you? I don't understand."

"You were my child from Joshua Hunter. I broke a solemn oath and the gods punished me over and over again. I had to send you away as a final punishment, and in order to test Branwyn and Dylan of their worthiness. My heart broke every day and every night while you were gone. I fear the pain from that separation has followed you throughout your many lives. I wanted to tell you, to set you free, but I had to wait for you read all of Branwyn's journal."

When, after a long moment of reflection, Villia made no response, Rhiannon gently stroked her cheek.

"I suppose this comes as a bit of a...what is the human word? Oh, yes: a *bombshell* to you."

Villia smiled. "That is the understatement to end all understatements. But everything makes sense now. Tad would tell me a story about how I got my name. He told me I was named after a song about a witch of the woods who met a hunter."

"Ah yes, that was from the operetta *The Merry Widow* by Franz Lehar, an acquaintance of mine. I inspired him when he was at a low point in his life. The music came from my desire to have my child brought back to me. Finally, the gods felt I had been punished enough and allowed Dylan and Bran to return you to my arms."

"If my first life was with you as a goddess, does that mean I'm only part human?"

"No, it means you are all human, but with the soul of having once been a goddess's daughter.

It's why you feel so deeply and suffer for the pains of others. You have carried a heavy weight since you were a child. You were what the island needed, and your mam trained you well."

"Why is it I feel there is something else you want to tell me?"

"Because you are an empath." Rhiannon smiled. "Villia, there is one more thing."

Michael, Emilee, and Ethan had gone to explore the island. Their guide was a Ceffyl Dŵr, a water horse known for its shapeshifting ability and power of flight.

"It's been a long time since we have had young'uns on the island," he said in a deep, gravelly voice. "I gave your grannie a ride when she first visited as a child. So, hop aboard and off we'll go to the top of the mountain, where you can take a tour of Rhiannon's castle. Ever been in a goddess's castle before?"

"Nope, it's a first for us," said Ethan. "What about getting down? Will you whisk us back?"

"Well, I've thought this out. I can fly you back, or if you sit in the river you will float back down to the lake."

"You mean like a water slide?"

"Exactly."

Emilee asked, "What's behind the mountain range? It looks like a valley."

"That is where no one goes."

"What do you mean, no one? Not even us? After all, we are the heirs to the, shall I say, throne."

"It's a valley where only sadness lives. It's off limits."

"Off limits?"

"Yes. I really think the Ancient One should be explaining this to you. I'm only an auxiliary guide."

"No problem," said Emily. "I'll talk to her, all right. I've been making a list of my duties, obligations...and benefits."

"Good luck with that one," the water horse chortled.

"What is the valley called?" asked Ethan.

"I can tell you that much. It's called the Valley of Trepidation."

∞

April scanned the hut made of bamboo, straw, and mud. The only furnishings were a small table and sleeping mats. The mats were beginning to look increasingly desirable. *So simple,* she thought, yet she felt a peacefulness and wholeness unknown to her since she was a young child.

Lost memories of her mam and tad had been flooding her senses since she stepped upon the island. Feeling exhausted, she lay down on one of the mats and fell asleep.

When she awoke, she was alone but didn't feel lonely. Michael and the kids had gone off with a flying horse. A deep belly laugh came from out of nowhere and surprised her; it had been years since she had laughed this way.

She slept again and woke some hours later, stretched, and yawned loudly.

"Those are my favorite yawns," said Rhiannon.

Startled at first, April said, "I thought I was alone."

"I hope you don't mind; I've only been here for a few minutes."

"I'm completely disoriented. What time is it?"

"Time has no meaning for us, but in human terms, it is not quite dinner time. I thought we might take a walk around the island. It is a tradition that I act as a tour guide for the Flatbottom family."

"I'm so thirsty."

Rhiannon handed her a glass of water.

April drank thirstily. "I've never tasted water like this. Is it alkaline?"

Rhiannon laughed. "You have much to learn and I have much to teach. Come, take my hand."

CHAPTER 24

It was the evening of their second day on the Island and time for the Ceremony.

The animals began to gather, one by one and then in growing numbers until the clearing was filled. They came from the highest mountains, their desert lairs, and the rivers and lakes.

There was a rumbling and the earth began to shake. Emilee and Ethan's eyes grew wide.

"Is it an earthquake?" asked Ethan.

Rhiannon said, "It's Hairy Ella-Phante. She is a wooly mammoth and quite large, you know. Hairy was elected to represent the animals thought to be extinct and will have a special place of honor."

This would be a solemn ceremony: the renewing of the vows by a Flatbottom. Clad in the island's traditional linen robes, the Flatbottom clan joined Rhiannon on the stone and wood dais. Rhiannon stood between Villia and Ebrill, and behind them stood Michael, Emilee, and Ethan.

"Do you think this robe makes me look fat?" Ethan whispered to Emilee.

Villia turned her head and shot him the most intimidating side-eye he'd ever seen. He hushed.

Rhiannon spoke: "Once again, we are given another opportunity to survive and live in harmony. Many years ago, I stood in this very place and waited for the first Flatbottoms to arrive: Branwyn, Dylan, and their children. They came in the flatbottom boat, unsure of what would transpire, but filled with hope not only for the safety of the animals, but also for peace and kindness throughout the world.

"As you know, Villia Flatbottom has been the Keeper of the Island for many years. As is our custom, we shall bow to the Keeper of the Island and ask her to renew her vows for another year."

The animals bowed their heads. Villia stood and addressed the wondrous assemblage: "Oran, who has been my greatest ally and friend, wishes he could have been here. I have known you since I was a child, but I grow weary. It is time for me to pass the mantle of Keeper of the Island to the next Flatbottom in line: my daughter, Ebrill Flatbottom."

Emilee and Ethan's jaws dropped to the ground.

Emilee whispered, "Well, that was one helluva surprise."

"Don't swear!" Ethan whispered back. "Does this make us a prince and princess? Like, next in line for the throne?"

"We could share."

"Fifty-fifty?"

"I'm the oldest; I was thinking sixty-forty."

"No way! It's fifty-fifty or nothin'. I know I'll get teased about my new name: Ethan Flatbottom."

"Actually, it has a nice ring to it. And so does Emilee Flatbottom. Correction: *Princess* Emilee Flatbottom."

Rhiannon hushed the whispering youngsters. She turned to address Ebrill. "Ebrill, do you promise to keep the name of Flatbottom and be next Keeper of the Island?"

"I do."

Villia removed the chaplet she wore and placed it upon her daughter's brow. The two looked into each other's eyes for a long moment and then embraced. Michael, Emilee, and Ethan were moved to tears. And all the animals that could cry, did so; the others displayed emotion in their own unique ways.

"Your mam will have much to teach you during this year of transition," Rhiannon remarked.

She turned again to the assembly. "I have had many concerns that Villia would be the last Keeper and that which we have worked so hard to maintain would disappear. With Ebrill accepting the role of Keeper of the Island, we have been granted another year."

The cheers were deafening.

She held up her hands.

"Time, like life, is finite and precious. Let us celebrate tonight and return to our duties in the morning."

"Duties?" asked Emilee.

Rhiannon stood next to Emilee and Ethan.

"Did you think it was all fun and games?"

"Excuse me, Your Goddess," said Ethan, bowing. "But yeah, that's pretty much what we thought."

Rhiannon smiled. "You have much to learn. Before you leave tomorrow, we shall take a stroll."

She looked to see Ebrill and Michael sitting close together, their hands intertwined.

"From the looks of your parents, I don't think they'll mind."

CHAPTER 25

Villia stirred her Cream of Wheat. She glanced at the clock: 8:30 a.m. *Oran should be driving up about now*; she hoped she had timed everything right. She glanced at the two cereal bowls waiting to be filled.

Oran's email from last night said, "I have a few stories to tell you. Are you sitting down? There were pirates! But we fought them off. What a way to end my days in the Merchant Marines."

He had attached a JPEG of the entire crew dressed as pirates. Oran, she thought, looked sexy with an eye patch.

The email continued: "Can't wait to get home to some peace and quiet. I hope you weren't terribly bored while I was gone. Your email about the ceremony was sketchy. Hmm...anything more you need to tell me? I've been thinking about a vacation, but not to any island. Perhaps touring Italy?"

The kitchen door opened. Oran stood there, beard gone and freshly shaved.

She handed him his bowl of Cream of Wheat and they scooted under the table.

"So, things went smoothly, did they? No island pirates or anything like that?" he asked.

"No dear. Nothing quite like that."

CHAPTER 26

Villia had requested that Judge Sinker preside over the hearing in her case against Dawley VII.

She and Oran, along with four generations of Kings, sat in the courtroom awaiting Judge Sinker. She entered. Those who were able to stand, did so. Dawley King IV, who was wheelchair-bound, sat and glowered. To Villia, he looked just as mean and nasty as Mr. Potter in *It's a Wonderful Life*.

Judge Sinker motioned for them to sit.

"Well, well, well, if it isn't my favorite people, the Flatbottoms and the Kings," she said wryly. "I haven't seen you since 1969 or thereabouts. You know, you were my first case and now…it's nearing time for me to put my robe in mothballs and retire. You will be my last official case. Rather ironic, yes? But don't worry, I've offered my services to the court as a consultant. Now, down to business. Dawley King VII, you do understand that you could be tried as an adult?"

He nodded.

"Cat got your tongue? Stand and address the court! Do you understand you could be tried as an adult?"

"Yes."

"Yes, what?"

His attorney whispered in his ear.

"Yes, Your Honor."

Judge Sinker picked up a sheath of papers. Flipping through, she remarked, "You have quite a history of vandalism, theft, and bullying. Looks like you were bailed out every time."

"I object!" said Dawley King IV, leaning forward in his gold-gilded wheelchair. "Just a child feeling his oats."

Judge Sinker banged her gavel. "I'll have order in this court! *I* object to you interrupting the court. You will speak when spoken to. One more outburst and I'll hold you in contempt." The judge turned once again to Dawley VII. "I'm going to give you a choice, which is more than you gave Arthur when you stole his lunches every day at school. Or Lucie, when you tormented her about having different-colored eyes."

Dawley VII smirked and made a snorting sound. His attorney again whispered a warning.

Judge Sinker sighed. "Still don't appreciate the gravity of the situation, eh? Let's pretend this is a game show. Will you pick Door A or Door B? If you pick Door A, you will be committed to the California Department of Corrections, Division of Juvenile Facilities, for rehabilitation until you are twenty-one. You might—*might,* I emphasize—be released earlier, if it is determined you can demonstrate you're ready to be a contributing member of society. As to Door B, I think Mr. and Mrs. Flatbottom can explain this second option."

Oran and Villia stood.

"Thank you, Your Honor," said Oran. "I was at sea for two months when the vandalism occurred. Regrettably, dealing with this situation fell on my wife's shoulders. After a great deal of discussion and soul-searching, Mrs. Flatbottom came up with a novel idea for young Master King to pay restitution to us, which I wholeheartedly endorse."

Judge Sinker nodded. "Mrs. Flatbottom, if you'll explain."

"Yes, Your Honor. We propose that Dawley King VII become our temporary ward, until he reaches the age of eighteen. We have outlined the parameters."

"Never!" shouted Dawley IV. "My great-grandson being influenced by a Flatbottom...it's an abomination!"

Judge Sinker banged her gavel. "You're in contempt! Bailiff, remove him from the courtroom."

The bailiff wheeled Dawley IV, muttering and spewing profanity and epithets, through the courtroom's double doors.

"Any other Kings care to spend twenty-four hours in the hoose-gow?" The courtroom was as silent as a tomb. "I thought not. I will now read the conditions under which Dawley King VII will avoid Door A. Seventh will live with Oran and Villia Flatbottom until the age of eighteen with no possibility of early parole, as it were. During that time, he will have no contact with any of his family or friends without permission and supervision by a Flatbottom. He will abide by their directions, including performing chores and volunteer work."

The judge turned to Villia. "Mrs. Flatbottom, for the court's enlightenment, would you describe the nature of these activities."

"Yes, Your Honor. Chores in our family include gardening, caring for animals, cleaning the house, and taking care of the boats. I have arranged for Dawley to work at the animal shelter one day a week. He will also volunteer at the homeless shelter, working right alongside me."

"Very good," said Judge Sinker. "Do you have anything you wish to add, Mrs. Flatbottom?"

"Thank you, Your Honor, as a matter of fact I do. I want Dawley to be aware of some of the rules of the Flatbottom house. We own a TV, but we do not have cable. Dawley will have to be content watching what *we* watch, which is mainly classic series from the fifties and sixties. Oran has a cell phone, but that will *not* be available to Dawley VII, nor will he be permitted to have his own phone. Our diet is primarily fruits and vegetables, and nearly every day for breakfast, we have Cream of Wheat cereal. That is our tradition."

Judge Sinker looked at Villia and said, "I love Cream of Wheat."

Then she observed Seventh making a nauseated face. "Don't like Cream of Wheat, young man? Tough! Better get used to it. Now, as to the damages you caused to the sailboat, the money for repairs, which Mr. Flatbottom will supervise, will come out of your own pocket, earned from the part-time job I am ordering you to get. Under no circumstances will you go to your family for these funds, unless you want to spend your life up to the age of twenty-one *under* the jail. Do I make myself clear?"

"Yes, Your Honor."

"Good. Seventh, rise and face the bench." Her voice softened. "This is your moment of truth. Many of the kids that you bullied had no second chance given to them. Which door do you choose?"

Seventh turned to look at his family, apparently seeking some tacit sign; then he spoke briefly with his attorney. "I pick Door B, Your Honor."

"Good choice," said Judge Sinker. "I don't imagine that, at this time, you have any remorse for your destruction of property and tormenting others that you perceive are weaker than you. I believe that your only regret is that you were caught red-handed. I am hoping that under the careful tutelage of the Flatbottoms, you will develop true remorse. Are you willing to abide by their terms?"

"Yes, Your Honor."

"I'm taking a personal interest in this arrangement and will be meeting with you on a weekly basis. One slip-up—and I do mean *one*—and you're off to Door A." She banged her gavel. "Court is adjourned!"

∞

Villia and Oran Flatbottom walked out of the courtroom with Dawley VII safely ensconced between them.

Oran put his arm around Dawley's shoulder. "Well, son, you certainly have shown an interest in boats. Misguided, I must say, but still an interest."

Dawley hung his head.

"Every boat, like every person, has a history—a story to tell."

Dawley looked up. "A story?"

"Why, yes. And Mrs. Flatbottom is quite the storyteller."

"You flatter me, dear," said Villia. "I do have some fascinating stories about one boat and the people who built and cared for her. We'll sit down and have a little chat." She ignored Dawley's eye roll and added, "I think tomorrow at breakfast would be perfect."

Acknowledgments

A book—either fiction or nonfiction—cannot come to life without those who support the author.

I feel fortunate to have Kevin Cook and Pamela Cangioli (Proofed to Perfection) as my editors. Thank you, Kevin and Pamela, for your guidance and encouragement to reach higher and deeper levels of writing. (www.proofedtoperfection.com)

Jeannine Henning took my fantasy of the perfect book cover and created a work of art. I am so very pleased! (www.Jeaninehenning.com)

As always, Maureen Cutajar provided insightful changes through her formatting and interior design. (www.gopublished.com)

A special thanks to Jessica Chase, who was kind enough to review my use (and misuse) of nautical terms and to offer her insightful corrections. Thank you, Jesse. You are an inspiration.

To my cast of characters, thank you for entering my life and trusting me with your story. I have laughed with you and cried with you. There were times when I felt my heart shatter, but most of all, I have learned to never give up on love or the goodness of humankind.

ABOUT THE AUTHOR

Sunny Alexander lives in Southern California, near the beaches and the Santa Monica Mountain hiking trails.

Though she once struggled at school, she returned to college after raising her children, became a Licensed Marriage and Family Therapist, and established a private practice in 1988. Compelled by her fascination with dreams and seeing the power of deeper work, she continued her education and received her doctorate in psychoanalysis.

The use of therapeutic storytelling has been an important part of her private practice. In a similar way, she believes that novels in themselves can be therapeutic and assist the reader to grow, resolve issues, and make changes.

Now retired from her practice, she has brought this philosophy to her novels under the banner of her publishing company, The Storyteller and the Healer.

In her leisure time, Sunny enjoys walking and flying kites along the California beaches near her home and spending time with her family.